Never Tied Down

Anie Michaels

Never Tied Down

© Copyright Anie Michaels 2015

Prologue

The loud buzzer from the oven startled me, sending my pencil point carelessly across the page.

"Shoot," I mumbled as I tried to erase it. Math wasn't my friend and I was already confused, now I would add to it by erasing parts of the equations I'd managed to complete so far. I threw my pencil down on the table and went into the kitchen.

I turned off the blaring timer, then put oven mitts on and opened up the oven door. The scent of baking chocolate wafted over me and I couldn't help but take a big sniff.

"Yum," I said, putting the cake on the counter to cool. Then I picked up the wooden spoon and stirred the stew I had cooking on the stovetop. Stew was one of the meals I'd mastered in the last two years. It was pretty easy, but it always tasted like it was really difficult to make. Mom always loved when I made stew.

I returned to the kitchen table and tried to finish my math homework.

An hour later, Mom finally came home from work.

"Sorry I'm late, baby. Carla didn't show for her shift so I had to stay until they found someone to cover her tables." She ran past me, kissing me on the head before she went back to her bedroom to change. It was her ritual. She always stripped off her waitressing uniform as soon as she walked in the house because it smelled like grill. Like greasy, burned, fatty food. If she left her uniform on, the whole room she was in would begin to smell, so I never got in the way of her dash to her bedroom.

When she emerged from the back of our mobile home, I could see the bags under her eyes and knew she was tired.

She left early in the mornings and worked in the bakery at a big box grocery store, then after she was done there, she was a waitress at a truck stop. Every once in a while she had a day off from one of the jobs, but it was usually a weekday, so I didn't really get to see her. Besides, when she had time off, I tried to let her sleep. She'd been exhausted for two years, maybe even longer.

"Happy birthday, baby," she said, placing a small box wrapped in paper with colorful balloons all over it and a big red bow in the corner on the table.

"Mom, you didn't have to get me anything." I was already feeling guilt wash over me.

"Nonsense, Kalli. It's your birthday." She kissed the top of my head again and walked into the kitchen. "You baked your own birthday cake." Her words fell somewhere between a statement and a question, and I knew from the tone of her voice the cake was upsetting to her. "I was going to make you a cake."

"It's okay, Mom. I knew you wouldn't want to come home from working two jobs and make *another* cake. It was just one of those dollar store boxes."

"You made yourself a dollar store birthday cake?"

Crap. I could tell she was getting upset, and that was the last thing I wanted. I'd been trying to make things easier for her.

"Mom, how about we have dinner, then ice the cake together, and we can eat it while we watch *Full House*."

"You made dinner too?" Now she sounded slightly panicked. "I thought you were turning nine, not twenty-nine."

"It's not a big deal, Mom. It's only stew. I threw it all in a pot and turned on the stove." I watched as my mom walked back to the table, sat in the chair across from me, and put her head in her hands. I stood up, went to her, and wiggled my way onto her lap. "I'm sorry I made you sad." Her arms squeezed around me.

"You didn't make me sad, baby. You're such a good girl. I just wish I could have given you a better birthday. Made your cake at least, or thrown you a party."

"I don't want any more birthday parties," I said quickly. The last time I'd had a birthday party my family had fallen apart. I didn't have any extra family to lose.

"Come on," she said, patting my back. "Time to open your present."

I hopped up from her lap and went back to my chair, pushing my homework aside. I lifted up the colorful gift and shook it back and forth. It didn't make any sounds that gave away what was inside, so I flipped it over and started tearing at the paper. When I could finally see what my mom had given me, I stilled.

"Mom, no." I shook my head, and put the box down on the table, pushing it toward her.

"What's wrong? Is it the wrong color? There were a few choices, but I thought red was the color you'd like best. We can take it back and exchange it if you want the blue one."

"Mom, we can't afford that." My eyes darted down to the brand new Game Boy Color I'd seen in the store the week before. They'd had a display set up and I'd spent a half hour standing there playing it. I'd seen the price tag. There's no way my mom could afford to buy me such an extravagant gift.

Her eyes softened when she heard my words, but she didn't agree. "Don't worry about what we can afford. It's your birthday, and I know you want it."

"Mom...." I didn't want to argue with her, or seem ungrateful, but how could I play on a new game system and eat cake I'd bought at the dollar store? Or play on that game system when, in a few weeks, I'd hear Mom cry because she didn't know how she was going to pay the electric bill? The gift, although I wanted it very badly, would haunt me every time I knew things were tight.

"Listen, last week a few of the girls at work donated their tips. So, I didn't buy it all on my own."

I could hear in her voice it hurt to admit that and I thought, in that moment, it was probably pretty hard for my mom to accept money from her coworkers. I didn't want to make her feel any worse.

"That's awesome, Mom. Thank you." I went to her and gave her a long and tight hug. When I pulled away I kissed her cheek. "You're the best."

"No, nine years ago I gave birth to the best. I'm so lucky to be your mom."

I hugged her again, feeling like I was the lucky one.

We ate dinner, iced and ate my cake, and my mom sang me an extremely out-of-tune rendition of "Happy Birthday." Then we sat in the living room and watched *Full House*. Well, *Full House* was on the TV, but I was busy playing on my new Game Boy.

That night, as my mom pulled the covers up to my chin, I asked the question I'd been thinking all evening but hadn't found the courage to ask. Perhaps being in the darkness of my room gave me strength.

"Did you check the mail today, Mom?"

I saw her shoulders slump in the light sweeping in from the hallway. I also heard the sigh that escaped her. Both of those things told me the answer to my question before she said the words.

"I did, baby. There was nothing there for you." She leaned down and pressed a kiss against my forehead, lingering there. The longer she kissed me, the harder it became to hold back the tears welling in my eyes, and ignore the stinging in my throat. "You are the best thing that ever happened to me, Kalli. Just because your daddy isn't here, it doesn't mean he doesn't love you."

I wanted to argue with her, wanted to shout that was exactly what it meant, but the words were trapped below the lump that had formed in my throat. If I opened my mouth, the only sounds that would come out would be sobs.

"Somewhere, he's thinking about you and he wishes he could be here with you. But he can't, baby."

I knew it wasn't true. I knew she was only saying the words she thought would make me feel better. I couldn't fault her for that, for trying to comfort me on my birthday, but I didn't have to believe her.

I never brought it up again, but every year on my birthday I silently hoped to hear from my father.

I was disappointed every single time.

Chapter One

Made of Glass

Kalli

I heard the sounds of Ella moving throughout the house, heard her sweet voice floating up the stairs as she spoke to her adorable little girl, Mattie. She was a master at the "mom voice." You know, that voice women use when they're talking to babies? It's almost the same tone you use when talking to a puppy, but not as shrill and just slightly more singsong. Ella was saying something to Mattie about their day, telling her that her daddy would be home later that evening, and then I heard a smacking kissy noise and I could picture Ella's lips mushed up against her daughter's chubby cheek.

I lay in bed, staring out my window, until I heard the front door close, then slowly climbed out of bed and walked up to the window to watch Ella's car disappear down the extensive driveway of her Salem home. It was early October and the trees lining her property were turning beautiful shades of orange and red, and the sun breaking through the leaves as it rose made for quite a breathtaking view.

Much like anything beautiful or worthwhile I'd witnessed in the last six months, it only accentuated the pain that was still lodged inside me, making no effort to dissipate. It was just another wonderful sunrise Marcus would never see, that I would witness alone.

I groaned at my own depressing thoughts and decided to make a conscious effort to not be completely morose for the entire day. I'd always been a big subscriber to the idea that one was in control of their own outlook on life. I'd managed, for years, to live through some of the worst circumstances imaginable and still lead a pretty happy life. All those notions were challenged when Marcus died.

Sure, I took the obligatory time to grieve, lived through his funeral and the wake, floating on some sort of removed cloud of distant engagement. Then I landed firmly on the other side of the whole ordeal, putting myself squarely in a dark existence. For weeks I was inconsolable, but I still felt as if that was normal, still felt as though I was owed a period of sadness. I was angry, too. Unimaginably angry. I was also dealing with guilt so heavy it kept me in bed most days.

For weeks I survived simply by the good graces of Nancy and my friends, who'd made sure I never went more than a day without eating, forced me to get up and at least shower, always telling me I was entitled to grieve however I needed to, but still insisting on making sure I wasn't doing myself harm.

After a few weeks passed, I eventually started feeling better. I was still sad, angry, and full of guilt, but it wasn't as overwhelming as it had been. It was manageable. That was to say, I was able to pretend for short periods of time I wasn't completely broken, even though I absolutely was.

Two months after he passed away, I decided I couldn't be in my house anymore. Nancy had already left, coming to the same conclusion I had, finding it too difficult to be in the house where she'd cared for and loved on Marcus as if he were her own. She told me gently one morning that since I was feeling better, she was moving in with Bob. I nodded, accepting her words, finding them to be just as painful as if she'd hurled something solid directly at my face. I couldn't expect her to stick around forever, there was absolutely no reason for her to do so, but it was just another loss I'd have to endure and was ultimately responsible for.

It took just one day of being alone in the house for me to realize I couldn't be there by myself. It was entirely too hard. So I packed a few suitcases, turned off the power to the house, and drove to Portland with absolutely no plan. Luckily, when I landed on Megan's doorstep she'd welcomed me with open arms, and I'd been drifting ever since. It took a few weeks to find work again, but I picked myself up and pretended to dust myself off.

When I was on set, working, I was professional and efficient, and actually preferred to be there because with each job came new coworkers. Usually I could meet new people and pretend as though I hadn't lived through the worst months of my life. It wasn't like my brother's death was big news, but once a few people from the business found out, it had spread and I'd received condolences from many people I'd worked with in the past. So, finding new people, who didn't know me or hadn't heard of my tragedies, was refreshing. It allowed me to pretend to be happy and unaffected for a day, to put my grief to the side and ignore it.

And although I loved my friends dearly, to be around them was to be constantly reminded I was fragile because that was how they treated me, as if I were made of glass.

So, much like this morning, I tried sometimes to keep my distance from them in order to spare everyone's feelings. I would be eternally grateful to Ella and Megan for allowing me to stay with them when I needed a place to crash between jobs, but I definitely tried to give myself space. They didn't need constant reminders I was crashing in their guest room, anyway.

After I'd showered and dressed, I was downstairs utilizing the fancy coffeemaker in the Masters' kitchen when the front door opened and Porter appeared.

"Kalli, good morning," he said, as he made his way through the open floor plan of his house. "I just forgot some blueprints I needed for a job in town this afternoon." He paused as he came to a stop at the island in the middle of the kitchen, his eyes on me, fingers drumming on the countertop. I could tell by the look in his eyes he wanted to ask me how I was doing, to check up on me, but he resisted. "How much longer do you have at the shoot you're working on?"

"Just a few days, then I'll be out of your hair," I said with a polite smile.

"You know that's not why I'm asking," he replied, his voice tinged with just a little regret, which in turn made me feel like an ass. Porter had never made me feel like I was unwanted or a burden, and treated me with respect and kindness while I stayed with him and Ella.

"I'm sorry, that was rude. I just can't imagine you enjoy having me around all the time."

He was silent for a moment, but then said, "Your being here makes Ella happy and that, in turn, makes me happy. Listen," he said, running a hand through his hair, "it's not like you're couch surfing because you were irresponsible and lost your job. You're here because you need to be surrounded by people who care about you. And we do. There's no pressure for you to leave until you feel like you're ready."

"Well, thank you. I appreciate that. But still, I'll be gone soon."

"And you're welcome back at any point," he said, without hesitation. He smiled the pitying smile I had gotten used to, then continued through the house, heading to his office to get the plans he'd forgotten, I assumed. I took the opportunity to head back upstairs to my room to get my purse and shoes, more than ready to leave the house for the day.

I'd been working nonstop for a few weeks, lucky enough to find jobs that lined up perfectly, leaving little time between them. I was trying to keep myself occupied, to distract myself. When I was idle, my mind wandered and my heart hurt.

That week I was working on an odd job, but it was beautiful, nonetheless. The Oregon Ballet Company was shooting their winter promo and I got to watch ballerinas dance around all day. Obviously, the ballet company had their own costumes made especially for their show, so I didn't have to figure any of that out, but I was hired to make sure the continuity was good and that everything looked great. Jobs like these could get tricky because the actual costume designer for the company was there, looking over her precious costumes, and sometimes could cause drama.

It wasn't unusual for a production company to hire a costume manager on top of a costume designer; there were things I took into consideration that she probably wouldn't. Like how the production crew's lights were harsher against the costumes than her house lighting, so we had the house add some blue to try to tamp that down. I also noticed, halfway through the shoot, the prima ballerina's headpiece was switched with another dancer's, which during the actual ballet wouldn't have been such a big deal, but in a thirty-second commercial, someone would notice.

"How often do you think those guys have to defend themselves against ignorant assholes?"

I turned to see Logan standing directly to my right, looking at the dancers on the stage as they performed the same minute-long routine for the millionth time.

"What do you mean?" Logan was a grip and local, like me. I saw him a few times a year if I was working in Portland. He was a nice guy. I figured he was a few years older than me, but he'd always been friendly.

"I mean, they're male ballerinas. I would assume, every once in a while, some assholes would give them a hard time."

I shrugged. "They look pretty built, what with all the lifting of the women," I said, gesturing as, sure enough, one of the men lifted a girl over his head. "Plus," I said, turning to face Logan, "I don't think the kind of ignorant assholes who would torment male ballerinas actually come to the ballet."

"You're probably right. I guess I just remember all the shit the male cheerleaders went through when I went to high school."

I cringed. "High school was the worst."

"Agreed. Although," he said, as his eyes turned to me, becoming softer as a smile spread across his face, "I can't imagine you had much of a hard time."

My hackles immediately went up, noting the flirtatious tone of his voice. I turned my face away from him, not wanting him to see my panic. "I did all right. I mainly flew under everyone's radar."

"You probably had boys knocking on your door every weekend."

His words weren't unkind, creepy, or out of line. He was being sweet and obviously trying to flatter me, but I couldn't ignore the way my heart raced with anxiety. It took everything in me to remain unfazed as I said to him, "I'm sorry, Logan. There's something I forgot to take care of in the dressing rooms. If you'll excuse me." I didn't wait for him to respond before I took off to head backstage.

When I made it into the lush dressing rooms of the ballet company, I walked straight to the large vanity counter and rested my weight against it, arms stretched out in front of me, head dipped between my shoulders, and breathed deeply.

I feared this was how the rest of my life would go. Any time a man showed any interest I'd lose my composure and panic. It had only happened a few times. I'd sheltered myself so much in the last months, no man really had a chance to get close, but every now and again, someone would say something complimentary or ask me if I was free for a date, and I would close up. Snap shut. Completely lock down. Then I'd spend the next minutes, hours, or sometimes even days trying to block out thoughts of Riot.

I'd been so clear in my desire for him to go away, I made every effort to turn off any residual feelings I had toward him. All of which were unsuccessful. And even though he'd left and gone away, he was still all around me. Sometimes I was convinced I was crazy, and truly I felt that way. If I wasn't thinking about Marcus then I was thinking about Riot, and it was enough to make me scream. I didn't *want* to think about Riot. I wanted the idea of him to be wiped from my memory altogether. I wasn't angry with him anymore and in truth, I had deep regret for ever being angry with him at all. But there was no way I'd ever be able to be with him.

Chapter Two

Celebrities and Hangers-on

Riot

"Riot, good to see you." I looked up at the sound of her voice, a polite smile crossing my face. "Thanks for meeting me on such short notice."

I stood up as Maryanne pulled out the chair across from me, and we both sat down.

"You know I'll always make time for you."

"Well, you've obviously not been in this business long enough if you're still willing to drop everything for your agent." She put her giant bag down on the floor next to her feet and then looked at me, giving a big sigh, as if she were already exhausted by her day, even though it was only 9:00 a.m. "Okay, so, how's the show going?"

"It's going great. We've shot a few episodes of the new season and I've got a really good story line. So far everyone's been incredible."

A waitress came and took our coffee orders, and when she left I turned my attention back to Maryanne. "So, I assume there's a reason you wanted to see me."

"Yes. I received a phone call and you've been invited to a movie premiere."

"Oh. All right. Sounds fun."

"Yes, and the most fun part is that you've been invited to be Lexi Black's date."

"Lexi Black? Isn't she dating George Lebowitz?"

"It's irrelevant who she's dating, she wants to go with you to the movie premiere."

My eyebrows were drawn to the bridge of my nose and I tried to connect the dots Maryanne was obviously laying out for me. "I'm confused. Why would she want to go with me?"

"It's a Hollywood thing. She doesn't want to *date* you, she just wants to be seen with you, and honestly, I think it could do a lot of good for your career as well."

"But I haven't seen her since I did her music video almost a year ago." I forced my mind to stay in the present, to focus on Maryanne and our conversation, even though I could feel the images of Kalli surfacing, pulling me down. I ran the back of my hand under my chin as a distraction, probably looking as if I were unsure about going to the premiere with Lexi when, in reality, I was trying to keep thoughts of Kalli from taking over.

"That is still her most successful music video, and her people and I agree it would be beneficial for you both to be seen together in public." She paused, then added, "It's not a big deal, Riot. You don't have to sleep with her or anything."

"I think you guys might be overestimating my level of fame. It can't do her any good to be seen with me — she's crazy famous."

"Riot, you're the hot young cop on the highest-rated prime-time drama. You've got movie deals in the works, and the two of you have been together on film simulating sex. Her fans know exactly who you are and vice versa."

I groaned and dropped my head into my hands. I was torn. Lexi had given me a huge opportunity and I didn't want to seem ungrateful, but at the same time I didn't want to use her or be used by her. I was still fairly new to the "Hollywood" game. There were always decisions to be made, and I feared making the wrong one. Finally, I looked up at Maryanne with a defeated expression on my face. "When is this movie premiere?"

"It's tonight. Five o'clock. Dolby Theatre."

"Tonight? Dolby Theatre? Shit, Maryanne, this is a big movie, isn't it?"

She shrugged. "You'll be fine. A limo will pick you up at four and Lexi will be in it waiting for you, so don't be late."

"What am I supposed to wear to something like this? I don't have anything except jeans and t-shirts."

"Don't worry," she said, picking up her bag and standing. "I'll have an appropriate ensemble sent to your house in time. And Riot?"

"Yeah?" I asked, wondering what the hell else she could want from me.

"Don't shave." She smiled, dropped a twenty on the table, and walked away, leaving just seconds before her drink arrived.

I stood in my tiny bathroom, staring at a sight in the mirror I'd never seen before. I was in a fancy gray suit with a white button-up shirt. I'd buttoned the shirt all the way up to the neck, but then I'd felt like I was going to pass out from lack of oxygen, so I unbuttoned a few at the top and decided Lexi would have to deal with my lack of tie because there was no way.

My mind thought back to the first time I'd met Lexi, standing on that sound stage in Portland. Lexi was nice, professional even, but not memorable. She wasn't who stood out to me during those few days. From the moment she entered the room, Kalli had been the one to draw my attention. She'd been breathtakingly beautiful, but unaware of her beauty. She'd been sassy and shy all at the same time, and I'd been a goner from the very beginning.

Never had I lived through a more mortifying experience than trying to act as if I were into Lexi while Kalli stood by and watched. It was awkward as all hell, but it'd been a job and everyone had been professional about it, even Kalli. Perhaps even especially Kalli.

My eyes closed and I pictured Kalli on her knees in front of me as she took my measurements that day, blushing and trying not to let her attraction show. From that instant I knew eventually she'd be mine, that I'd do anything to be with her, to see her kneeling before me with nothing covering her beautiful body. Even as I'd made the declaration in my mind, nothing could have prepared me for how it would feel to really be with her.

I shook my head, trying to rid my mind of the images torturing me, but they never fully went away. I was never completely without her, or the memory of us together.

When there was a knock at my door, I took a deep breath and made my way to the front of my small apartment. There wasn't a single time I walked through my living room and I didn't think about Marcus asleep on my couch. Not one time had I walked through there and not thought of him, missed him, and prayed that he was someplace better.

I opened the door, expecting to see Lexi, but instead I was met by an extremely tall, very large, and robust black man. When he spoke, I nearly startled at how low and deep his voice was, but managed to keep my reaction undetectable.

"Hey, man," he said, sounding way too much like Barry White. "I'm Tank, one of Ms. Black's bodyguards. She's waiting for you downstairs in the limo."

"Great," I mumbled, still thrown off by Tank's sheer size and presence. I left my apartment and headed toward the parking lot, where a black stretch limo was waiting. As I approached, a man jumped out of the front passenger door and reached to open the back door before I could. I slowly climbed inside, a little intimidated, never really having been in a car that nice.

My eyes landed on Lexi, sitting on the seat at the other end of the limo. Next to her was another large man, a bodyguard I presumed. I slid onto the seat closest to me, trying to take in everything I was seeing. Rope lights framed the ceiling of the limo. There was a bottle of champagne sitting in a bucket of ice, and multiple bottles of liquor were available as well. My eyes met Lexi's and she smiled at me.

"Riot, it's so good to see you again. I'd totally get up and hug you, but with these shoes and this skirt, I'd never be able to get back down again," she said with a friendly smile. My gaze traveled down to said skirt and shoes, and I had to agree—the skirt was too short to be moving around much, and the heels looked dangerous. I never understood why women liked to risk their lives in heels that were unusually high and spiky.

"Good to see you, too. Although, I'll admit, I was a little surprised with this whole setup."

She waved a hand at me, as if to say, "No big deal."

"It's just a movie premiere," she replied, her voice light and carefree. "I thought it would be a fun opportunity for us both."

"Now, Ronny," Lexi said to the large man next to her, "don't crowd us too much when we get out of the limo, I want the photographers to be able to see us together. And make sure you let Riot help me out."

"You got it," he said in agreement, then continued to stare out the window, checking his watch every minute or so. It was a long and quiet ride, and it was also a little uncomfortable. I had nothing to really say to Lexi, and tried to keep my eyes off her because, due to her skirt, my eyes naturally wandered to the point where her crossed thighs met. I didn't want her to catch me checking out her legs, especially since I wasn't checking them out, per se; I was just being a normal guy. Any twenty-six-year-old man would be mesmerized by all the skin she was showing.

Instead, I pulled out my phone and tried to occupy myself with it. Eventually, I noticed we were pulling up to a long line of limos. We inched our way forward and Lexi touched up her makeup, smiling at me every couple minutes. It seemed like we'd finally made it to our destination when I felt the limo stop and change gears into park. Ronny moved to get out of the limo first and when the door opened all I saw were people and cameras. The people didn't even have heads, it seemed. They just had necks with cameras. And there were so many of them.

"Don't be nervous, Riot. Just be yourself and smile, and make sure you stick with me, it's easy to get separated."

I nodded, unsure of what to say in response. I moved to exit the limo and was blinded by all the flashing bulbs, deafened by all the yelling. I turned back, not forgetting my duty to help Lexi from the limo. I saw her come out of the darkness and reached out to her. When she took my hand, it was as if the cameras went even crazier and the energy surrounding us started buzzing in such a way I could physically feel it in the air.

Lexi didn't let go of me, even after she was out of the limo completely; instead, she laced her fingers through mine and curled into me, clutching my bicep with her other hand. She was smiling still, her red lips surrounding sparkling white teeth, and I couldn't find any words, so I just led her through the crowd, following close behind Ronny and Tank, who seemed to be parting the bodies with camera heads for us.

We made our way slowly down the red carpet and were stopped in front of a backdrop and suddenly the camera heads knew my name.

"Riot! Look this way!"

"Riot! Are you and Lexi dating?"

"Lexi! Does George know you're seeing someone else?"

"Lexi! Give Riot a kiss!"

At the command, Lexi leaned farther into my side and pressed her lips to my cheek. I stilled, panicking a little. I didn't want to be rude to her, but I definitely didn't want to be photographed as she kissed my cheek. I didn't want anyone kissing my cheek. Well, that wasn't true. I'd let Kalli kiss me anywhere. But I definitely wasn't comfortable with what was happening.

Lexi leaned away from me, smiling, then brought her thumb up to where her lips had just been, laughing. "You've got red lipstick all over you," she justified as she tried to brush it away, all the while the flash bulbs blinded and people yelled.

I brought my mouth closer to her ear so she could hear me when I asked, "What the hell, Lexi?" As I said the words, I felt her hand come up to cradle my cheek and she giggled. I pulled away, confused by what she could be laughing about. Then it dawned on me. She was putting on a show.

She was using me.

She didn't just want to go to this event with me, she wanted to *be seen* with me, to make people believe we were together. I pulled away, prepared to drop her hand and find my way back through the camera heads, but before I could say anything, she pressed her lips against mine.

It had been so long since I felt a woman's mouth on mine that for just one moment, I let her linger, caught up in remembering someone else. Letting my heart pretend, for the tiniest moment, that Kalli was here with me instead of Lexi. But then my brain remembered who she was, realized where we were, what was happening, and I pulled away, furious. I put my hand on the back of her neck, trying to keep her close enough to hear me.

"What are you doing?"

She put on her fake smile and replied without moving her lips much, "Just play along, Riot. It'll all be okay."

I searched her eyes, then let her go, stepping back. She laced her fingers through mine again and turned back to the cameras.

"Lexi! How long have you been together?"

"Riot! Has this been going on ever since you shot her music video?"

"Lexi! Is he *the one*?"

"When are you going to put a ring on it, Riot?"

Lexi giggled but didn't answer any questions and I stood there, thoroughly pissed off and pretty sure my mood was evident on my face. I didn't care if I ruined their precious photos, I wasn't happy so I wasn't going to smile.

Finally, Lexi led me into the building and once we were out of sight of the photographers, she dropped my hand.

"What the fuck was that?" I growled, feeling my face turn red with the rage building from my gut.

"Calm down, Riot. It's no big deal. They'll print some stories about us being together, our names will be hot for a few weeks, and then it'll all die down." She looked past me and waved at someone, obviously not caring how I felt about the matter.

"You could have warned me about what you were going to do. I definitely wouldn't have come if I thought you were going to *kiss* me in front of all those reporters."

She smiled at me, a genuine smile that showed me she didn't mean me any harm, and said, "Why did you think I invited you, silly? This is what the business is all about."

"What about George? Won't he be upset?"

For the first time that evening I saw an emotion other than happiness cross her face. She looked hurt and sad, and I immediately felt like shit for bringing him up.

"He doesn't care what I do," she whispered, looking down at her hands, which she was wringing between us.

"Lexi, I'm sorry. I didn't know."

"It's okay. It's not a big deal. Listen, I'm sorry if I offended you. I guess I assumed you would know what tonight was about and how it would play out. It never occurred to me you wouldn't be ok with it. You're still new to the business, I guess. So, I apologize." She paused, looking me in the eyes again, only this time the happiness was gone altogether. "But you need to understand I did you a favor back there. You might not think so right now, but you'll see."

She turned and walked away from me, leaving me speechless. She was right, I was new to the game, but I wasn't dumb. It wasn't that I couldn't understand why she did what she did, I just didn't like the way it made me feel. Used, and a little fake. I never wanted to be anything but myself. I was an honest person. And this was far from honest.

I exhaled loudly, realizing there was absolutely nothing I could do about it at that moment. The damage was done. In fact, there were most likely already posts on social media speculating about our relationship status. I wanted to leave, to bail on this whole evening, but I didn't know how to get out of the building without walking right back down the red carpet, and I didn't have a way home anyway. So I decided to ride the evening out. I took a deep breath, exhaled slowly, and went to find Lexi in the sea of celebrities and hangers-on.

Chapter Three

He's Not Hard On The Eyes

Kalli

It was a Saturday morning, and the first Saturday in weeks I didn't have to work. I enjoyed sleeping in, but woke up hungry, so I padded down the stairs toward the kitchen. As I neared the first floor I could hear Ella talking to the baby and smiled when I came into the great room and saw Mattie happily sitting in her bouncy chair while Ella spooned something into her mouth. The TV was on in the background and Ella watched it as she fed her daughter.

"Morning, Kal," she said cheerily, looking over her shoulder as I came into the room. "I didn't think you were here."

"I got a Saturday off. It's a miracle," I answered, my voice still a little raspy from sleep.

"Really?" she asked excitedly, turning to face me. "I was going to drive to Portland to see Megan and have lunch and go shopping. Wanna come with me?"

"You aren't spending the day with Porter?" That surprised me. Generally on the weekends they were together all the time.

"He has to work in Lincoln City today and then is having dinner with his mom. It's a girls' day!" she exclaimed, turning back to Mattie, using her mom voice again.

"You know what? That sounds like a lot of fun. I think I will go with you." I grabbed a banana, then moved to sit on the couch facing Ella, who was parked on the floor.

"Really? That's great. We've really missed hanging out with you," she stated. She wasn't looking at me as she said the words, but I could hear the underlying meaning. I'd closed myself off from them for a while. Not because they did anything wrong, but because I wasn't emotionally ready to let myself feel anything but sadness and loss. I was staying with them, living in their houses, but I wasn't the same person I used to be. A small smile crossed my face and I decided it was as good a day as any to try to enjoy myself with my friends.

"I've missed me, too," I replied honestly. "And thank you for not giving up on me. I'm trying, every day, to get back to normal. I'm just not sure what normal is anymore."

"Oh, sweetie, you're doing fine. And we'll be here to help you as long as you need."

I smiled at her, grateful for my friend in that moment, but my attention was pulled to the television as I heard a woman speak a name I'd tried for months to avoid hearing.

"Riot Bentley made quite the appearance last night at the Hollywood premiere of *Midnight Ride* when he showed up on the arm of none other than pop superstar, Lexi Black."

My breath snagged in my lungs and my heart skidded to an immediate halt at the mention of Riot, and my traitorous head turned toward the television, where my eyes landed on his image. It was the first time I'd seen him in months, thanks to avoiding the Internet all together. My first thought? He looked amazing. Handsome and delicious in a suit with no tie, top buttons of his shirt undone. It wasn't jeans and a t-shirt, but it was a look he wore well.

"Oh, shit," I heard Ella mumble, then from the corner of my eye I saw her scrambling for the remote control. She speed-crawled across the floor to the coffee table and grabbed the remote. Just as she lifted it to change the channel, I stopped her.

"No, wait, I want to watch this." Obviously, I was into pain.

"Lexi Black, who'd been rumored to be dating famed director George Lebowitz, showed no shyness as she planted a kiss on her leading man right on the red carpet." I sucked in a sharp breath as they showed a slow-motion replay of Lexi leaning in and planting her red, luscious lips right on Riot's. "Fans might remember Bentley as the hot hunk in her most popular music video to date, which was, coincidentally, directed by Lebowitz. Bentley, the current heartthrob on the hit show *Shield to Shield*, looked slightly uncomfortable in front of the cameras, but this was his first red carpet event so we'll give him a pass."

The woman on the television gave a slimy wink and I felt as though I was going to throw up right then and there.

"We'll all be watching to see how this new and exciting relationship develops. It might even be Hollywood's hottest love triangle."

Another "reporter" came on screen and started commenting on something trivial, and all I could do was remind myself to breathe. My teeth were clenched and I could feel the muscles in my jaw start to ache, and my face was definitely heating up. My mind raced as every thought and emotion made itself apparent all at once. That was not the way I wanted to see Riot for the first time in months. Silly as it might seem, I hadn't imagined him moving on. Hadn't even considered the fact that he would be dating someone new. I guess, on some subconscious level, I assumed he was just as wrecked as I was and still nursing his wounds.

Silly me.

Then I was angry at the pair of them. The nerve they had, parading their romance around, practically rubbing my nose in it. Well, I guess not really. They had no way to know I would see a news report about their little date night, but still. My mind flashed back to the music video shoot and the way they'd looked as Riot had lain on top of her, kissing her, running his hand along her body. Had they been seeing each other the entire time I was with him? Suddenly, I felt like a complete idiot.

"Are you all right?" Ella asked hesitantly.

"Not even a little bit," I instantly replied.

"Oh, Kalli. I'm sorry." She reached forward with the remote and switched off the television. Mattie squawked and Ella went back to sitting on the floor in front of the bouncy chair to continue feeding her. "That Lexi girl looked horrible."

I turned to look at Ella. "She looked amazing. But, thanks," I said, mustering a tiny smile. Lexi really had looked great. She was thin, young, and had an amazing body. Plus, she had a team of people to make her beautiful every day. I couldn't compete with that. Not that I was in competition with her. I sighed.

"Have you talked to him at all since…." Her voice trailed off and I could tell she didn't want to speak the words.

"No," I squeaked, shaking my head and looking down at my hands in my lap.

"Maybe," she offered slowly and gently, "you should call him or something. You never really got any closure with him, Kal. There was just so much going on and too much for you to deal with." She paused, perhaps waiting for me to say something, but when I didn't, she continued.

"Perhaps if you spoke with him, talked about things, you'd start to feel better."

"Talking to Riot won't bring Marcus back," I whispered.

"No, it won't. But sweetie, nothing will." She looked away and fed Mattie a few more bites. Her baby squeals of happiness were a stark contrast to the actual mood in the room. "Do you mind if I ask what you're afraid will happen if you see him, or talk to him even?"

I shrugged, then let out a large sigh. "It's hard to explain, Ella. When I think of Riot, all I can think about is how if I could have just let him go, if I hadn't been so wrapped up in everything with him, Marcus might still be alive."

"Honey, what happened to Marcus is not your fault. It's *no one's* fault. It was an accident. A terrible, horrible, sad, and tragic accident. But it's not your fault."

"There is a tiny part of me that can understand that. A tiny fraction of my mind knows what happened to him could have happened when I was with him, could have happened at any time. But still, I can't shake the majority of my thoughts that say if I were home he never would have even been at the park. He wouldn't have run from Nancy. He would still be here. We'd have stayed home and played Monopoly or video games. He'd still be alive, Riot and I would still be apart, but everyone would be *fine.*"

"But that's not what happened, Kalli. You're still here, though, and it's perfectly all right for you to be happy, or at least try to find happiness. You don't have to punish yourself forever. Marcus wouldn't want that."

My first thought was that Ella wouldn't know what Marcus would want; she'd never met him. But I knew that was a harsh thought, and I also knew the only reason she'd never met him was because I kept him from everyone. So I let that thought simmer in my mind. Ella was just trying to help and I knew what she was saying was true, but moving past Marcus' death was definitely something easier said than done.

I don't think anyone prepares for the death of a loved one. I certainly didn't. Sure, I'd considered the idea that one day, perhaps, Marcus would get sick and because of his mental disabilities, he'd have a harder time recovering. But only in my deepest, darkest moments of fear had I ever considered he'd be taken from me in that way. I'd always imagined growing old with him, taking care of him until I couldn't anymore, but even then, we'd still be together. I'd never imagined a life without him, so *being* without him was almost like living in a dream. A terrible nightmare.

"I can work on being happy, but that doesn't mean I need to contact Riot. He was just a blip on my screen. Inconsequential." The words stung as I spoke them because they were so far from the truth. "Being happy today means going shopping with the girls," I declared, plastering a fake smile on my face. I was glad to go out and spend the day with Ella, Mattie, and Megan, but I could tell that pretending to be okay for an entire day would be exhausting.

"All right," Ella agreed, although she didn't sound convinced. "I was thinking of leaving in about an hour. Will that work for you?"

"Yup. I'll be ready," I answered as I stood up, walking toward the stairs to get ready to spend the day pretending.

We were halfway to Portland and I was really proud of myself for resisting for the whole thirty minutes we'd been on the road, but I couldn't help myself any longer. I pulled out my phone and opened up a browser and googled "Riot Bentley."

I had never googled him before. At first, when we were together, it had been for authenticity reasons. Anything I knew about him, I wanted to know because he'd shared it with me. It wasn't normal for me to date semi-famous people and I didn't want our relationship to be different just because he was on the rise in the Hollywood scene.

In recent months, not googling him had been more for self-preservation purposes. I didn't really want to see him, whether it be on a phone screen or a TV screen—I didn't want to see him, period. I wasn't sure my heart could take any more pain than it had already been through. So I just never did it. But sitting in Ella's car as she drove down the freeway, with the seal already broken, thanks to the red carpet coverage, I decided there probably wasn't anything worse on the Internet than what I'd seen on the television that morning.

I'd been wrong.

So.

Very.

Wrong.

I was flooded with images of him. All kinds of images. Pictures of him walking down the street in LA, of him on set laughing with his co-stars, stills from his show, him holding up a gun, looking like a real cop.

My breath caught for a moment and then I flipped my phone over and put the screen against my thigh. I must have moved too quickly because Ella's head turned toward me.

"What is it?" she asked, concerned.

"I just googled Riot." I scrubbed my hands over my face, trying—unsuccessfully—to wipe the images from my mind.

"Oh," she replied, her voice worried. "That was brave."

"I think the word you're looking for is dumb. That was dumb."

"Maybe a little. What'd you find?"

"Oh, not much, just a bunch of pictures of him looking incredible."

"He's not hard on the eyes."

"No, he's not," I agreed as I picked up my phone and flipped it over, looking at the screen again. Like I said, I was into pain. "He makes a really hot cop," I muttered absently, my finger swiping across my screen quickly. I wasn't even really taking the pictures in, I was just gorging myself on him. Like a kid let into a candy store and told they could eat as much as they wanted. I just kept shoveling it down. "Oh, God," I groaned, and instantly made my screen go black and shoved the phone between my thighs.

"What?"

"I saw a picture of him surfing. Shirtless. Wet. God." I groaned again. "I didn't even know he *could* surf."

After a moment's pause, Ella asked, "What do you think he was doing with Lexi?"

"You mean besides *Lexi*? I think they were on a date. Obviously." I picked up my phone again, but tried to clear out of the images and look for just an article about them.

"Maybe they just went to the movie as friends." Ella sounded hopeful. Even Mattie gave a wail from the backseat that sounded frustrated.

I turned to Ella and gave her my best "you've got to be kidding me" face. "Come on now, Ella. You saw that music video. She's adorable. And sexy. And hot. And he's… well… he's Riot. They aren't just friends. You can't just be friends with either one of them. Especially considering they hadn't ever met each other before that video."

"But what about her director boyfriend?"

"I'm reading about it now." I thumbed through the article until I found what I was looking for. "Lebowitz was contacted to comment on his relationship with Black and he declined to make a statement, which isn't unusual for him. Both Black and Bentley's camps are keeping quiet, not offering to confirm or deny a relationship between the two. We at E! News aren't calling this one yet. Our guts are telling us this was a publicity stunt, but we'll keep our eyes peeled for more sightings." I scrunched up my face. "A publicity stunt? They were kissing."

"Things aren't always as they appear," Ella said with her new motherly, all-knowing voice.

"It doesn't even matter. He can date whoever he wants."

"He'd probably like to date you," Ella said carefully, giving me the side-eye from behind the steering wheel.

I decided not to respond. I could have agreed with her, or told her it couldn't be true. Either reality was too harsh to think about. So I tried not to. Instead, we spent the next thirty minutes in silence as we made our way to Portland.

I took a few quick steps to get to the door of Poppy before Ella, holding it open so she could push her stroller through with ease. She gave me a thankful smile as she passed, and then I saw her eyes go into boss mode. She looked around the sales floor and I could only imagine what was running through her mind. She was probably examining inventory levels, employee productivity, all kinds of things she'd learned to manage as the owner of a small business and assess with just a sweep of her eyes.

"Hey, Fella," Megan called before we were halfway through the store. "Kalli!" she nearly squealed when her eyes found me. "I'm so excited to see you." She came toward us, giving us each a hug. Then she bent down in front of the stroller and used her baby voice on Mattie. "Hello, sweet girl. How's my favorite niece?"

Mattie gurgled her response.

"Are you ready to go?" Ella asked, taking another sweep of her eyes through the store.

"Yeah, Brittany's here, so I'm good."

Almost as if she'd heard her name, Brittany came out of the back room and saw us.

"Hey guys. How's it going?"

"Just headed out for a girls' day," Ella said, smiling warmly at Brittany.

"Sounds fun."

"Could you take a minute to finalize the schedule so it can be posted by tomorrow?" Megan asked Brittany. "I've already looked it over, but if you can do it too, I'll feel more comfortable."

"Of course. Want me to post it before I leave?"

"That would be awesome. I probably won't be back today. After girls' day, Patrick is taking me out to dinner. It's our six-month wedding anniversary."

"Awww…" Brittany sighed.

"You guys are too cute," Ella said with a little bit of disgust in her voice.

"Oh, my God," I cried. "You have no room to talk, Ella. You and Porter are, like, sickening to be around. Let your sister celebrate her anniversary."

All four of us laughed.

"Okay, okay. Let's go," Ella said, shaking her head.

We spent the afternoon shopping downtown, taking frequent and needed breaks to tend to Mattie. She was a wonderful shopping partner, being a happy baby, but she needed attention more often than us. We'd found a cute coffee shop to stop at while Ella fed Mattie, and I enjoyed a few minutes of just chatting with my best friends.

"So, what are you working on right now, Kalli?" Megan asked.

"There's a small theatre company in Portland who lost their costume designer over the summer. She's on maternity leave. So I'm outfitting their fall production."

"That sounds fun."

"It's so fun," I said with enthusiasm. "Their budget is pretty good and I've been able to hand-make some of the pieces. Makes me feel like I'm back in the lab in college, designing pieces and then making them real. It's refreshing."

"Seems almost therapeutic," Ella added. "Like you could get a lot of thinking done at a sewing machine."

"Yeah. That's true," I said, taking a sip of my cold coffee drink. "My mind's pretty much running a million miles an hour anyway. But you're right, having to sit in a quiet room for hours on end does let me get a lot of thinking done."

"What's your mind been telling you?" Megan asked.

I sighed. If anyone deserved a glimpse into my mind, it was Ella and Megan. They'd been supporting me emotionally for months, even if that meant stepping away and letting me deal quietly. I knew they wanted in, wanted me to talk to them, and I figured I owed it to them.

"My mind tells me different things every day. One day I feel like I've finally gotten over the hardest part of all this, but then the next day I wake up crying and missing Marcus so much, it feels like he just passed yesterday." I shook my head. Grief was a nasty thing. "But lately, I've been feeling pretty solid."

"She even looked up Riot on the Internet today," Ella supplied, then looked at me with wide eyes, expecting me to be upset she'd mentioned it. I wasn't. This was girl talk. I was a little sad my friends thought they had to walk on eggshells around me. I made a mental note to try to be more open with them.

"Images even," I added, giving Ella a smile.

"Oh, lord," Megan said.

"She did great," Ella praised, giving my hand a quick squeeze.

"You know what? I totally did. I looked at those pictures and I responded the way any ex-girlfriend would, all swoony and full of regret, but he's hot and I couldn't help it. But you know what the most important part of this story is?" I looked back and forth between Megan and Ella expectantly. "Huh?" I asked again, more insistently.

"What?" Megan asked, giving me what I wanted—audience participation.

"I didn't cry. I didn't cry and I didn't have a woe-is-me pity party." I said those words with such pride and satisfaction. It was, indeed, a milestone. Any girl would attest to the fact that the day you could look at pictures of your ex-boyfriend without a breakdown was a good day.

"Well, hot damn, chica. If we didn't have a tiny baby with us, I'd take you to a bar and buy you a shot," Megan said with a laugh.

A wave of confidence rolled through me; something I hadn't felt in a while. For whatever reason, in that moment, I felt like I could take on the world. I could move forward with life and still be a productive member of society. I would miss Marcus forever, but being sad all the time would never bring him back. I had two choices: I could be sad forever, or I could try my hardest to be happy. I might not ever be as happy as I'd been in the last few months of his life, I might have hit my peak, but I could still lead a full and happy life. Or I could at least try.

That feeling lasted all of twenty-four hours.

Chapter Four

He's Looking Down On You

Kalli

The next day, as I was leaving the studio of the theatre company I was working for, I got a call from my agent, Lucy.

"Kalli, I've got the best news for you. Are you sitting down? You need to be sitting down for this."

"Okay, give me two seconds to get into my car," I said with a slight laugh. Her excitement had my belly flipping over with nerves. I had no idea what she had to say, but it sounded like good news. "All right," I said, right after closing the door. "I'm in my car. Lay it on me."

"You have just been offered a *permanent* position as *chief costume designer* on a new sitcom which will begin filming in a month!"

"What?" There's no way that was a true statement. I misheard her. Or she misspoke. Or I'd been drugged. I was high, obviously. "What did you say?"

"Full-time, long-term, permanent position as chief costume designer, Kalli. The holy grail of showbiz jobs. The triple crown. The giant belt thingy those wrestlers fake fight over."

"Holy shit," I whispered, breathing hard and rapidly.

"Holy shit is right, Kalli. You've been doing great work and the industry is noticing. If I were you, I'd try to negotiate the salary a little, but that's up to you. I think they'll budge a little."

"What are the terms?"

"They're offering full medical, pension, 401K, all that good stuff, $8,000 to cover relocation, and $100,000 a year salary. That $100,000 is contingent upon the show being picked up for a second season, and then in year two you'd be up for salary negotiations again. This is very common and straightforward. A good offer, Kal. But I think you can get one-twenty."

"But, $100,000 is a lot of money." Damn straight, it was a lot of money. I made a decent salary now. It was enough to cover the house and expenses. A trust Marcus had inherited when my parents died went a long way to cover the care Nancy provided, not all of it, but a good portion. Money had never been terribly tight. But $100,000 a year would be a vast pay increase. "Where is this job located?"

"LA."

Fuck. Of course it was in LA. I'd avoided LA like the plague since Marcus passed. Even though LA is a huge town, show business made it smaller than it seemed. Sure, I could potentially go there and never see Riot, but the odds were against that.

"Oh, I don't know about LA," I said, my voice trailing off at the end.

"Kalli, you can't avoid LA forever. Not with your job. Now, I believe in you and all that other supportive BS I'm supposed to say, but this is a job of a lifetime. If this show takes off, which it's got a good chance of doing considering the cast, this could set you up for life, honey."

I let her words sink in a little, thinking about how much my life would change if I moved to LA. I'd have to leave my friends behind, and that would suck, but there really wasn't anything holding me back. The money would be great, obviously, but the *job* would be amazing. To be offered that job, without even so much as a conversation with the producers, was huge, and I couldn't ignore the compliment. My agent was right; it could be the job that put me on the map. It could be the job that set me up for the rest of my life.

It could also be a huge flop—it was Hollywood after all.

But could I take all that goodness, all those pros, and weigh them against the con of possibly seeing Riot?

"When do they want an answer?"

"You're lucky they're even giving you time, which is another indication you should ask for more money. But you've got until Friday at 4:00 p.m."

"Okay. I probably don't need that much time, but I do need some. I'll let you know."

"Should I send them any kind of counteroffer? Ask for the one-twenty?"

"No. If I take the job, I'll take it as is."

I heard her sigh on the other end of the line. Sure, she wouldn't mind another $2,000, which would be her cut of an extra $20,000, but being greedy was not the way to make yourself a good name in this business. If I was worth more than the $100,000 they were offering, then I'd get a bigger offer in a year. And it would feel better too.

"Okay, Kal. Let me know soon, all right? This is huge. Congrats."

"Thanks, Lucy. I will."

I hung up and immediately sent a text to Ella.

I need some serious advice when I get home.

I waited for her response. It came after just a few moments.

Should I put a bottle of wine in the fridge now?

I smiled at her response.

I knew we were friends for a reason. Yes, please.

Although our conversation was stalled until Mattie went down, the poor baby was teething and wouldn't allow her mother and me a word—understandably. When Ella and I finally sat down on her big, comfortable couch, I was glad to have a glass of chilled white wine.

"Okay, now that we've got some silence," Ella said with an eye roll, "tell me what's up."

"I got a call from my agent today and she told me I've been offered a job. A really good job. An amazing job, actually."

"What? That's great news, Kalli!" Ella reached forward and clanked her wine glass against mine, saying, "Cheers!"

I smiled and clinked my glass against hers in return, took a sip, and then continued.

"The only thing is, it would mean moving to LA permanently. Or at least for six months. If the show gets picked up for a second season, it would then become permanent."

"Wait, a *show*? Like, a series?" Her eyes were wide and I could see the excitement building.

"Yeah, it's a new sitcom, a romantic comedy. Some pretty big names are supposedly signed on. I'd be the head costume designer. It comes with a really huge paycheck. But it's permanent. And in LA, of all places."

"Yeah, but, isn't LA kind of the mecca for all this stuff? Either LA or New York, I would imagine."

"Yeah, but LA is also where Riot is," I said.

"Right. Gotcha." She leaned forward and placed her wine glass on the coffee table, then turned back toward me. "Listen, I wouldn't blame you for turning down a job because you were afraid you were going to run into him. The way it ended with him was... painful... to say the least." She looked me right in the eyes when she said her next words. "But you shouldn't let your experience with Riot keep you from living your life." She placed her hand on my knee and gave me a few friendly pats. "If you want my opinion, I think you should consider the job as if he weren't a factor. If you have some other reason for turning the job down, then consider that. But don't let a failed relationship keep you from progressing in your career. Your career is *yours*, and you've worked hard to cultivate it. No one can take that away from you, and you shouldn't let someone else control where it goes."

I took her words in and thought hard about them. Ella had a point and if there was anyone who had sacrificed for her career, it was her. Hell, she'd even gone back to work at a store where she'd been shot. Because it was *her* store. She could have very well closed up shop and let the fear rule her actions, but she hadn't. And if Ella could go back after being shot, I could surely risk *maybe* seeing an ex-boyfriend.

"You're right," I said, then took a sip of my wine. "I would regret turning this job down for such a terrible reason."

"I think you would too," Ella agreed, her voice soft and understanding. "You're one of the bravest people I know,

Kal. If anyone can move to LA and become the head costume designer for a kick-ass sitcom, it's you."

"Thanks." Ella's affection for me always caught me off guard. Never before had I met someone and instantly known I was meant to be best friends with her. Megan was a bonus. The two of them had, in so many ways, held me up when I wasn't able to stand on my own two feet. The emotion was bubbling up in me and I drowned the lump in my throat with delicious wine, not wanting to cry on her couch like I had a million times in the months before.

After a moment of silent contemplation, I finally let out a large sigh. "I guess I'm moving to LA."

After I decided to accept the new job, life became unmanageable. I had three weeks left on the job I was working, and even though it was always temporary, the good-bye at that job flooded me with emotion. It was as if I were saying goodbye to an entire chapter of my life, not just some nice people I'd worked with for a few weeks. Ella and Megan even planned a big going away dinner. Even though Ella was a dear friend and would always support me, I knew she loved any reason to have people over to her beautiful house, designed and built by her fantastic husband.

The evening had been capped by Nancy and Bob surprising me by showing up. Nancy looked great and I knew Bob was taking good care of her. We'd found a moment to sneak onto Ella's back deck and talk, staying warm with the propane warmers Porter had installed for just such an occasion. She told me she'd found a new job at a nursing home with a pediatric unit. She was still helping to care for kids, but now it was on a broader scale. She said she couldn't imagine taking on another job where she was the main care provider for one child. She smiled softly and told me that Marcus had ruined her for any other kids.

We both smiled with tears in our eyes and then she hugged me, telling me she was proud of me for taking the next step.

"He's looking down on you and he's so proud, Kal. You have to believe this is what he wants for you."

I hugged her tighter, then we both pulled away and dried our eyes.

"Come on, Nance. Let's go back inside before people realize we're out here crying."

The party was amazing, but I still had things to wrap up, so the next day I drove to Seattle and made an appointment for a property management company to meet me at my house. I figured I may as well rent it out while I was in LA. That way, I could earn a little money on it, but still have a place to come back to should the job in LA not work out. I was determined to no longer be a drain on my friends.

I pulled up to my house and could almost imagine Marcus running out of the front door, Nancy behind him, yelling my name, excited to have me home. But instead, what I saw was a house that looked dark inside, a yard that definitely needed to be tended to, and a pile of weekly newspapers spread across the front walkway.

I grabbed my bag from the car and started toward the door when I heard someone yelling from across the street.

"Ma'am? Ma'am?"

I turned and saw a woman running toward me, looking both ways quickly before she crossed the road.

"Ma'am, do you live here?" She looked at me expectantly. My first reaction was a little rude. Who else would be coming up to the door with a suitcase? But then I calmed down and tried to remember that I hadn't been there in months and even before then, I wasn't here often. If Nancy had shown up, I'm sure the neighbor would have recognized her and probably would have even known her name.

"I own this house. My name is Kalli Rivers." I held my hand out to her, and she smiled when she shook it.

"Oh, good, an owner. I thought the house had been abandoned. Thought, you know, a foreclosure or something. There used to be people living here, but they cleared out quickly."

My heart lurched at her words. "You probably mean my brother, Marcus, and his caretaker, Nancy."

"Nancy, yes! Oh, I didn't realize Marcus had a sister. How is Marcus?" Her eyes were alight with warmth. Obviously, she'd met Marcus and thought he was just as delightful as anyone who'd come into contact with him.

"I'm sorry to tell you he passed away a few months ago." The words were never easy to say, but I did notice that when I told her, I didn't feel like I wanted to crawl into a black cave. Somehow, telling someone he'd passed had become less difficult. I wasn't less sad, it was just, I don't know, a part of me. Something I'd learned to deal with as time went on.

"Oh my, I'm so sorry," she said as she reached out and took my hand. Then she used my hand to pull me into a hug. I stiffened at first, unused to hugging strangers, but then I let her hug me and I leaned into it a little. Comfort was something I needed to learn to accept from those who offered it. People didn't offer comfort for selfish or insincere reasons. When people wanted to hug you, it was because they thought it would make your pain ease. So I let her ease my pain.

"Wait," she said, pulling away quickly. "You're Kalli?"

"That's right," I answered, my brows pulled together in confusion.

"I have something for you." She stepped away from me and hurried back to her house. I stood between my driveway and my front door, waiting for the woman to return. I finally saw her open her front door and scurry across the street again, holding something in her hand.

"These were delivered to your house, but no one ever came to get them. I hope you don't mind," she said, a little out of breath from her jaunt across the street. "They would sit out there for days, so I'd go and collect them. I eventually had to throw them away, but I always kept the cards." She held out a stack of small envelopes.

"What are these?"

"Cards. They came with the flowers."

"Flowers?"

"Yes. At least twice a month, sometimes more, flowers would get delivered to your house and sit on the bench on the porch for days. No one was coming to get them. I told the delivery driver one day that no one lived there, but he didn't seem to care much. They just kept coming. I hope I did the right thing. I didn't have anyone to contact…" Her voice trailed off and I just looked at the envelopes, stunned.

"No, it's fine, um, I never caught your name."

"Barbara. Barbara McKinley. From across the street."

"Barbara, thank you for keeping these. I'm sorry you went to all the trouble with the flowers. I had no idea they were coming."

"Someone was obviously extremely persistent." Her voice held a question, as if she were hoping I'd tell her all about who was sending me flowers. I didn't offer her any information.

"Yes, well, thank you again. I think I'll go inside and wait for my appointment."

"Oh, yes, don't let me keep you." She gave me another sympathetic smile and then turned to head back to her house. It struck me that I had no idea who lived across the street from me all those years. It was a little too late to try to build a relationship now, but I made a mental note to try and be more open in the future.

I made my way toward the house, the stack of envelopes burning in my hand the whole way. There was only one person who came to mind, and I wasn't sure I could handle reading what would undoubtedly be sweet and heartbreaking notes from Riot. I wish I'd asked Barbara when the last one had been delivered. Suddenly it became exceedingly important to know how long the flowers had been coming. Had the last bunch been delivered months ago, I might have been able to handle the information. But if some had come last week, well, that would throw my whole world off its axis.

I didn't have time to contemplate anything, though, because there was a knock on my door before I could even open the first envelope. I tucked them into my purse and went to answer the door.

"Are you Ms. Rivers?" the woman on the other side of the door asked.

"That's me," I said with a sigh, opening the door wide to let the woman in.

I spent the next hour discussing terms with the woman from the rental company. Luckily, the house was in good condition and only needed minimal work before it could be rented out. Even better, the woman said that for a fee they could take care of everything and have the house rented by the end of the month.

I signed the contract, handed over the keys, and we both left. She made her way to her sleek black Mercedes, and I stood in the driveway staring up at the house I could hardly bear standing in for too long, but cared too much about to sell. It was the last place I'd heard Marcus laugh, the last place I'd seen his smiling face. No, I couldn't sell it yet. Maybe not ever. For now, this would do. I'd let someone else live there. Maybe that would change the way the house felt to me. Perhaps, if I knew another family was there, making new and happy memories, I'd be able to move from this place of limbo. I didn't know what I'd do with it in the future, but for now, I'd keep it.

Chapter Five

Only Temporary

Riot

"You're needed on set in five, Mr. Bentley." Erin was an assistant assigned to our set. She always had a clipboard in her hand and a pencil behind her ear. And she almost always sounded like she was going to explode from stress. Even now, watching me walk away from our set, knowing I had only five minutes before we began shooting, she sounded like she wanted to strangle me.

"I'll be back in time. Promise." I winked at her and laughed when she blushed but pretended to be frustrated. She was young, still in college I believed, and she was definitely inexperienced in the business. None of that affected her ability to do a good job. Inexperienced or not, the will to succeed would take you farther in this business than anything. Hollywood had a reputation for being cutthroat, and it was to an extent, but there were plenty of people who wanted to work hard. Erin was one of them. Not only did she want to work hard, she wanted to do well. That would take her far.

I was, by no means, an expert on the ways of Hollywood. I'd only been here a few months, but it was easy to spot the kids who were here because mommy or daddy got them a spot and the ones who worked their way in with ingenuity and talent. Erin was the latter.

There were approximately one thousand Coffee Bean coffee shops on set. It was almost as if Coffee Bean, as a company, paid a premium to be so prevalent on the campus. You couldn't walk from one soundstage to another without encountering a shop. It was annoying at times, but most of the time it was convenient. Like now. I'd been up late reading through a script change that had come in last-minute, trying to familiarize myself with the new storyline, and I'd missed the sleep I needed. So, coffee it was. I wasn't famous enough for a personal assistant, so I got my own coffee.

I pulled my coat closed around my body. It was cold for a November day in LA. Not anywhere near as cold as it could get in San Francisco, but still chilly. My face was tilted down, looking at the pavement as I walked, trying to keep the wind from making my cheeks pink and giving Makeup a heart attack.

I made the walk to the closest Coffee Bean a few times a week, so I felt like I could walk there with my eyes closed. When I saw the curb that started right in front of the coffee shop I turned and started up their walkway. I pulled the door open and my nose took in all the smells. The bitter smell of the coffee and the sweet smell of the pastries in the case. I looked up once I was inside, taking my hands out of my coat pockets, and reaching into the back pocket of my jeans for my wallet.

Over the common, neutral buzz of voices that was normal, I heard one voice stand out. My head quickly turned to the left and I nearly choked on the breath I pulled in at the sight of the blonde woman sitting with her back to me.

It was her.

I knew it was her.

I could feel it.

What in the world was she doing here?

Every part of my body seized at the sight of her. Even though she was facing away from me, I *knew* it was Kalli.

I would recognize her voice in an instant, in any situation. We'd spent the majority of our relationship on the phone. Her voice, in those months, had become a salve to me, the light I looked forward to every day. It was like a drug to me. So I knew it was her when I heard her talking to whoever was on the other end of her phone.

I was stuck in place, the barista looking at me with confusion, probably wondering why I wasn't ordering my usual drink and was, instead, standing in the middle of the coffee shop with a dumbfounded look on my face.

I turned and nearly ran from the coffee shop. If Kalli was in LA and hadn't contacted me, it was probably because she didn't want to see me. And as much as I wanted to run to her, to touch her, to push her hair behind her ears and look her in the eyes, I wouldn't purposefully do anything to upset her.

I walked quickly back to set and found Erin, pencil still behind her ear, looking as determined as ever.

"Erin, I need a favor," I said quietly as I pulled her behind the wall of a set.

"I'm in the middle of something," she said, but looked concerned.

"Listen, I know it's asking a lot, but I need you to find out some information for me."

Her eyes drilled into mine, searching for something. Finally, she sighed and relented.

"What do you need?" she asked, sounding as if she were put out by my request, but I knew she liked feeling needed.

"There's a costume designer on the lot. I need to know what she's working on and how long she'll be here."

"Um, I'm pretty sure that's not information I have access to. I'm just an intern."

"I'm not asking you to hack into someone's computer. Just ask around. Talk to your intern friends. I just need to know why she's here."

"Okay. What's her name?"

"Kalli Rivers."

Erin took her pencil from behind her ear and started scribbling on her clipboard. "Okay, Kalli Rivers. Got it. I'll try to figure it out for you, but I've got actual work I have to get done too."

"I appreciate it, Erin." I tried to give her a smile, but I couldn't manage a convincing one. Instead, I think I gave her a smile that morphed into a frown halfway through. I turned away from her and walked back to my dressing room. I went straight to the vanity at the end of the room and just stood under the bright lights, staring back at my reflection.

I had told myself, since Marcus' funeral, that eventually she'd come back to me. I held on to the hope that eventually she'd heal enough to realize that I loved her more than anything. I didn't want her to forget that I was here, waiting for her. I'd not heard one word from her, but that only made me think she wasn't ready.

But seeing her in LA, at a coffee shop, holding a normal conversation — fuck, it hurt. It was painful in a way I couldn't fully appreciate in that moment. To think that she'd been in LA and not reached out to me, it hurt worse than hearing her yelling my name, screaming for me to leave her alone. Seeing her in LA meant she'd moved on in some way and didn't want to bring me along with her.

I scrubbed my hands down my face, trying to brush away the troubling thoughts. When I looked at the clock I realized I was late.

"Fuck," I whispered, and threw my coat onto the couch. I walked out the door, heading back to set, wondering how I was going to make it through filming with Kalli on my mind.

Throughout the day I caught sight of Erin, tried to make eye contact with her, wondering if she'd found anything out for me yet, but she never looked my way. She was running errands for the director, making calls for him, getting lunch for him, everything she was supposed to be doing. Every time I saw her and she didn't give me any information, I became more irritated.

"Riot, get in the game," my director hollered at me right after he'd yelled, "CUT!"

The overwhelming urge to punch something rocketed through me. I'd never had violent tendencies, but the electricity running through me, the anger I felt toward myself, needed an outlet.

"I got it," I said, just loud enough for the director to hear, looking at the ground, unable to meet his eyes.

"It doesn't really seem like you do, man. We've been running this scene for over an hour. Come on. Whatever is clouding your brain, man, leave it at the door."

His voice was teetering between angry and sympathetic. He was obviously frustrated with the way the day was going, as was I, but he knew it wasn't normal for me.

"I got it," I repeated, still looking at the floor.

I heard him sigh, then he bellowed, "Everyone take five so Riot can get his shit together!"

At his words, I walked back to my dressing room, slumping down on the couch, elbows on my knees and head in my hands. After just a few minutes I heard my door open.

"Riot?" Erin's face peeked through the opening.

"You find something out?" I asked, ignoring manners and demanding information.

"Yeah, turns out Kalli Rivers is the chief costume designer for the new sitcom they're filming over on Lot B. She's been here about three weeks. Not long."

"*Chief* costume designer?" I asked, a little surprised by her job title.

"Yup," Erin responded, sounding impatient. "Do you need anything else?"

I thought about what I needed and what Erin could provide. The answer was depressing because there wasn't anything else she could do. All the other questions I had, only Kalli could answer.

"No. Thank you, Erin. I appreciate the favor."

She gave me a small smile before her head disappeared and the door closed again.

Kalli had been in LA for at least three weeks, perhaps longer, and she hadn't tried to reach out to me. She was on my studio's lot, working here every day, and I hadn't heard a word from her. The new information was making me ill. My gut turned, actually ached with the news. This was not what I had expected. Not what I was holding out hope for.

I dragged my fingers through my hair, gripping the strands and pulling, trying to distract myself from the hole forming in my chest. *Fuck*. I had banked on the idea that she would contact me. Call me. Write me. Text me. Anything. I stood up and walked back to the vanity, staring at my own reflection, wondering where in the hell I was supposed to go from here.

I only had a minute or two until I needed to get back to set, so I needed to get back into the game. Kalli was a big distraction, but I couldn't let the new information cause a problem with my job. This job, so far, had been incredible, and I was grateful for the opportunity. I didn't want the director or producers to start thinking I was a high-maintenance actor. That reputation would follow me around throughout my entire career. No, I needed to calm the hell down and get back to work.

If Kalli truly was the costume designer for a show shooting here, I'd have my opportunity to confront her. It just wouldn't be today.

I stood up straighter, squared my shoulders, and turned to return to set. The entire time I was walking through the soundstage I was telling myself I'd have my chance, that I'd get the opportunity to speak with her, I just had to keep my cool until then.

When I walked up to the set, with its lights blazing and people standing around waiting for me to get my head on straight, my director turned to me and asked, "You ready to work?"

"I'm ready, boss. Sorry for the delay. It won't happen again."

He looked at me for a few seconds, seeming to decide if he believed me or not. But finally, he nodded and said,

"Glad to hear it." Then he yelled to everyone else on set, "Places. Let's roll, people."

And I was back in business.

It was dark when I left the studio that night. Scenes ran long, although thankfully I wasn't the only one holding up production, and the weight of the director's disdain landed on someone else not long after I'd tried to shrug it off. It had been a long day, full of mistakes and mishaps, having to reshoot scenes for idiotic reasons, and trying not to let aggravation seep into my performance. Sometimes I found myself thinking about how modeling was so much easier than acting. Modeling, although it came with its difficulties as well, sometimes was just as easy as standing in a certain pose and staring at the camera. Acting, especially on film, was a whole different animal and it came with an impressive list of difficulties, hurdles, and a steep learning curve.

I pulled my coat closed around me again, the chill in the air quite a bit more biting now that the sun had set. I thought that the next day I should wear a cap, or a scarf. I knew it wouldn't get too cold in LA—snow wasn't even on my radar—but the early mornings and late evenings warranted warmer clothing.

I made it to my truck, climbed in, and started the engine, blasting the heater. The windows fogged a little, showing the age of my truck, so I sat and leaned my head against the back of the cab.

Kalli was here. In LA. Working on the same studio lot as me.

Most of me wanted to be really happy about the news I'd learned, but the majority found a way to be crushed instead.

My mind thought back to the coffee shop that afternoon, remembered what I'd seen of her, just the golden trail of her long blonde hair falling down her back against the denim jacket she was wearing. I'd seen, poking out from under the table, a little brown high-heeled boot on her foot, and that image alone sparked hundreds I had stored inside my brain. Memories I'd only allowed myself to ponder in deep moments of complete masochism.

I remembered her blue eyes staring down at me, her hair making a veil around us as she hovered, both of us naked, me inside of her, watching as she moved. The pink of her lips matching the exact shade of her cheeks, her creamy skin with a hint of the flush caused by her arousal.

My eyes drifted closed as I remembered the way she felt wrapped around me, how her heat enveloped me, spurred me on, and made me lose control on more than one occasion. Sex with Kalli was addictive and she was so receptive to being taken, it was difficult to be around her and not simply want to take.

My dick grew hard as I sat in the parking lot of my job, and the realization that I was hitting a new low washed over me. I wanted her so badly, but it seemed I was the last thing she was interested in. My hands gripped the steering wheel and I watched my knuckles turn white. How stupid could I have been? She'd pushed me away months ago and I was still hanging on to hope that her rejection was only temporary. *Fuck me.* I swiped my hands down my face roughly, threw the truck in reverse, and hauled ass out of that parking lot. I aimed my truck at the bar down the street from my apartment, planning to walk home when I was good and drunk.

Chapter Six

Be Invisible

Kalli

I'd developed a routine since arriving in LA. I went to work and stayed on set when possible, ignoring my desire to explore the studio lot. I was afraid if I wandered, I'd wander right into Riot. Therefore, in an effort to avoid such an instance, I stayed on set or at the Coffee Bean right next to my soundstage.

I knew it was ridiculous. I knew eventually I'd run into him and things would be awkward. But I was willing to postpone the painful experience as long as possible. So I kept to my private studio, the set, and the Coffee Bean. When the day was finished I hauled it back to the studio apartment I'd rented.

November had brought some unusual rain to LA, so I was run-walking all the way into the coffee shop and didn't stop at the register to order. Instead, I headed directly to my table, which was usually empty because people on a studio lot in LA weren't there to sit and have a relaxing cup of coffee. People ordered to go and left with as much haste as they came in with.

I dropped my bag on the chair and shook out my coat, and only when I lifted my eyes to the tabletop did I see the piece of paper folded up and lying flat atop it. The paper had my name scrawled across it and I knew it was his handwriting.

I picked it up, then looked around. My eyes darted around the coffee shop, wondering if he was inside, or just outside. If he was watching me at that moment, or was someplace far away. My hands started to tremble, knowing that if I saw him I just might lose my composure. I wasn't ready to face him yet. Somewhere in the back of my mind it occurred to me that he must have known that, which was why he left me a note but didn't stick around to watch me read it.

I sat down, holding the paper in my hands, wondering if I had the will to even open it or not. I hadn't opened a single card that came with the flowers. I knew myself. I knew that if I opened the note, whatever was written inside would alter me. Would affect me. No matter what the note said, it would change me. I also knew myself well enough to know I wasn't over him. Sure, I was better off than I had been weeks ago, but there was a part of me that believed I would never truly be able to move past him. So his note would either break me by telling me to move on, or force me to take action by telling me he wasn't over me either. I wasn't comfortable with either one of those scenarios.

No, I liked the smooth sailing I'd encountered since moving to LA.

I went to work, I did my job, I went home. Wash, rinse, repeat.

Knowing Riot had been here, been right at this table, jostled something inside of me, and I found the courage to open the paper. My eyes drifted over the paper, catching single, insignificant words, then hopped around some more until I finally closed them, took a breath, and started reading the note from the beginning.

Kalli,

I saw you sitting at this table one day, and I've seen you almost every day since. I know why you sit in the back, facing away from the door, not near any windows, and I've tried to respect that. I've tried to allow you the invisibility you're obviously looking for. So, every day I come to this coffee shop, I take in the sight of you, and then I leave you to the solitary bubble you've created.

I get it.

I don't know if you knew I worked here or not, but, in case you didn't—I work here. Just on the next lot over, actually. It didn't take me long to figure out where you worked after I saw you, so I imagine it couldn't have been hard for you to find out the same information about me. That only leads me to believe you knew I worked here but were trying to avoid me.

Again, I get it.

But I don't like it.

So, I'm giving you fair warning. When I come in tomorrow, if I see you sitting here, I'm going to approach you. I'll sit down and say hi, and you can respond however you'd like, but I hope you'll talk to me, Kalli. If nothing else, I miss talking to you. We used to talk so often. I'm just asking to have a conversation with you.

If you don't want this to happen, I suggest you find somewhere else to be invisible.

But I'll find you there, too.

Love,

Riot

Shit.

I put the paper down, closing my eyes and leaning my head back to face the ceiling. If I was being really honest with myself, I knew this would happen. I knew coming to LA meant seeing Riot. I didn't, however, think that he'd contact me in quite that manner. It was just like him though, putting my needs first and giving me an out. Kind of. He told me I could find another place to go, to not come back to that coffee shop, but that he'd eventually find me and make it happen.

Somewhere in the back of my mind I knew that all along he'd just been biding his time.

That sent a shiver through me.

He couldn't be dissuaded. He could be put off, but only until he was done waiting. I knew that.

I pulled out my phone, and in just moments I heard Megan's voice on the other end.

"Kal, what's up, lady?"

"I got a note from Riot."

"What?" she asked, sounding genuinely shocked. "What did it say?"

"Basically, it says that he knows I'm here, and that he wants to talk to me, but he'll give me more time if I need it."

I expected at least *something* from Megan; she was rarely quiet. But all I got was thick silence.

"Meg? You there?"

"I think you should talk to him." Her words were firm, but also hesitant. She knew her opinion was going to possibly rub me the wrong way.

I sighed. "I kind of figured you were going to say that."

"Look at it this way, you might never be ready to talk to him. You might never feel ready. But he will wait forever. He will hang on to the hope of you until he breathes his last breath. And that's not fair to him. So, if you're not planning on talking to him, trying to work things out, at least tell him that much. Let him off the hook."

The thought of Riot waiting for me, silently watching me, standing by until he thought I was ready for him, made something clamp tight around my heart. The thought of telling him to move on, telling him I'd never be his again, well, day after day that thought caused me pain.

"I don't know if I'm ready to talk to him yet."

"Do you think you'll be ready soon?"

I shrugged then said, "Maybe."

"*Maybe*," she said with emphasis, "Riot is the one thing you need to move on completely."

"I don't know if you're right," I said slowly. "But I'm also not sure that you're wrong."

"When you see him, you'll know."

"You think?" I was hopeful. Even though I was unsure about seeing him, after months of being in the proverbial dark it would be nice to feel sure of something. Of anything.

"Is what you're doing now working? Are you thinking of him any less? Is avoiding him, even though you're in the same town, moving you forward? Listen," she said, her voice suddenly softer. "You don't have to jump back into a relationship with him. You don't have to do anything you're not ready for. But seeing him, talking to him, perhaps even talking about Marcus, that might help you, sweetie."

"Okay," I said, my voice matching her softness. "You're probably right."

"I usually am," she replied, her voice conveying the smile I knew was on her face.

"Your husband's a saint," I said, now laughing. "I don't know how he puts up with you."

"He totally is," she agreed. Then she sighed. "Patrick knows what he's got, and he knows he's got it good. And I feel lucky to have him too. That doesn't mean I'm wrong any less."

"I want what you have." My voice was suddenly a whisper. "I've wanted it for so long, Megs. I've just told myself it wasn't possible, that it would end badly, that I would hold someone else down and then they'd leave, and I'd be even more broken than I was when I started."

"Sweetie, I'm almost positive that Riot will give you whatever you want, but not if you keep hiding from him." Then, as she had a tendency to do, she lightened the mood. "I only hide from Patrick when there's some sort of sexual game going on, and even then I don't hide well enough for him to not find me."

I laughed, even as an errant tear slid down my face.

"What if I just end up pushing him away again?"

Megan let out a loud laugh. "Honey, you let Riot back in, there's no way he's going to let you push him away again. Not out of fear. Trust me, Kals. Just talk to him."

"Okay," I said, breathing the word out, hoping to push out some of the fear with it. "How is life in Portland?" I asked, trying to move the conversation away from me and the myriad of issues she and Ella were constantly helping me cope with.

"Oh, you know, same old. It's really rainy here, but that's no surprise. Getting colder. What are your plans for Thanksgiving?"

"I don't have any. I was just going to stay here, get some Chinese food."

"Do you get time off?"

"Yeah, I'm off Wednesday through Sunday."

"You should come to Lincoln City. Ella and Porter are hosting Thanksgiving at their beach house."

The last time I'd been in that house I'd slept with Riot. I'd fallen in love with him in that house. It would be torture to be there again if I didn't figure my life out.

"Maybe, I'll see what I can work out."

"Okay, well, we all want to see you."

I smiled because I knew she was being sincere. "I know, Megs. I want to see you guys too. I'll try to make it work."

"Okay. I've got to get back to the store now, Kal. Do you think you're gonna talk to Riot?"

"Yeah," I said softly.

"Good. Call me if you need me after."

"Will do."

"Love you, Kal."

"Bye, Megs."

It took me three days to work up the nerve to go back to the Coffee Bean I'd found the note in. I was a nervous wreck. I spent an inordinate amount of time picking the perfect outfit, I planned what I was going to say to him, and then I marched into the coffee shop, sat down, and I waited. I waited and I waited, but he never showed. Well, at least not in the two hours I sat there.

It hadn't occurred to me that he wouldn't come. He said if I was there, he'd find me. But then I started panicking. Perhaps he'd come the past three days, waited for me, but then assumed I wasn't coming back. Perhaps he thought I'd chosen to stay away, to avoid him. Suddenly, the apprehension I had about seeing him turned into fear that I would never see him again.

I grabbed my bag and headed for the door, walking with determination to the soundstage I knew he worked on. I opened the door and stalked down the hallways, looking frantically for Riot. I saw quite a few people, but none of them were the tall, dark-headed, and devastatingly handsome man I was looking for. I turned another corner and collided with a woman.

We both stumbled backward violently, and had I not fallen against the wall, I would have hit the floor.

"I'm so sorry," I said immediately. "Are you all right?" I righted myself and saw the other woman doing the same.

"I'm fine, are you okay?" she asked, not unkindly.

"Yeah. I'm sorry. I was just looking for someone."

She straightened her blouse and adjusted the pencil behind her ear, gripping her clipboard to her chest. "Maybe I can help. Who are you looking for?"

"Um, Riot Bentley. I think he works on this lot."

"He does. Are you Kalli?"

My chin came back in surprise. "How do you know my name?"

"Lucky guess," she said quickly, but then grabbed my elbow and started leading me down the hallway. I followed her through the maze of the soundstage. It looked similar to the lot I worked on, but there were differences. Different pictures hung on the walls, different people roamed the halls, different offices with different people. She led me on set and my mouth gaped a little. Even though I was in the business, even though I'd worked on movies, television, music videos, I never got tired of seeing a set in person. Something about a soundstage with the lights off, set unlit, almost like a page in a book not being read, gave me goose bumps.

"He's got to be on set in a few minutes, but I'll see if I can track him down."

"Um, okay. I don't want to get him in trouble. I can come back later."

"It's fine," she said, leading me back into a hallway, then turning into the first door on the left. Once inside I was overcome by his scent. It had to be his dressing room. It was almost annoying that my nose could identify him. It smelled spicy and clean, warm. Like Riot. I realized that, if given the opportunity, I could probably identify his smell in a blind nose test, and that was pitiful. "Wait here. I'll go find him."

"Wait, no, it's okay," I said to vapor as she disappeared down the hallway, walking faster than I thought was necessary, with purpose. I took a moment and slowly turned, looking around the room, trying to take it in. My eyes drifted from the couch against a wall to the brightly lit vanity, to the old-school coatrack with a familiar leather jacket draped over it. I knew if I walked to the coatrack I would not be able to keep myself from burying my face in his coat. So I didn't move.

I saw a pair of Converse sitting on the floor under the vanity and I smiled, thinking about how I loved him in those shoes. He wore them almost ironically. He wasn't trying to be a hipster. I knew he was trying to put off more of a rebel vibe, but he'd fallen victim to the hipster movement. He wore them before it was cool.

I heard loud, running footsteps coming down the hall, and my head snapped to face the doorway. When Riot appeared, hands braced against the doorframe, breathing heavily, a gorgeous and familiar smile across his face, my heart started beating triple-time.

"You're here," he said, panting.

I nodded, stuck standing still in the middle of his dressing room. My eyes took a moment to travel up and down him, taking stock of him, and my heart wondered if he was real, if he was truly just standing feet away. If my heart were in charge, my arms would be around his shoulders, my face buried in his neck. But my brain was currently in charge, so my eyes were the only part of me allowed to move.

His hair was still dark, styled a little differently, shorter on the sides but longer on top. He wore a black fitted t-shirt, tight in all the right places, all of which my eyes found. He had on faded jeans with a police badge clipped to the belt. Obviously, he was in costume.

"Hi," I said when my eyes were finally done taking him in. I couldn't move, couldn't find the way to make my brain communicate with my body, which was probably good. I wanted to run to him, run my hands over him, press myself into him, and take everything from him I'd been missing for so long.

"Hey," he said with a lopsided grin. "You get my note?"

"Yeah," I said, a smile finally sprouting, taking root, lighting me up.

"Good."

I startled when I heard, "Riot Bentley, Leah McCann, call to set B, three minutes."

"Shit," he murmured, but then he moved and was right in front of me, hands on either side of my neck. "I've got to go. I'm filming a scene. Can you wait? It might be a while."

I looked at the clock above the door and determined I had nowhere to be. I was technically done for the day and didn't need to be in the studio. I had my laptop and I could work in his dressing room.

"I can wait." His eyes lit up at my words and then they drifted down to my lips. My breath caught and his hands tightened just slightly, making my eyelids flutter. He couldn't kiss me right now; it was too soon. But knowing he was thinking about it, well, that was amazing. "Can I work here? Do you mind?"

"No," he said, giving me one last gentle squeeze then moving away. "Make yourself at home. Do you need anything?"

I needed so much. But I managed a simple, "No, I'm good."

"I'll be back as soon as I can."

"I'll be here."

He gave me one last smile and then turned and left.

"Holy crap," I mumbled to myself, willing my heart to stop beating so quickly. I rubbed my hands together, realizing they were clammy. He made me nervous. God, he looked good. Even better than I remembered, and I had a damn good memory. I turned and sat on the couch, hardly stopping my body from flopping down, my bag falling next to me. My head leaned back and I was looking at the ceiling, wondering if I'd made the right decision. My heart really wanted to see Riot—it had quite nearly leapt right out of my chest at just the sight of him. But my mind, now that the image of him was gone from right in front of me, was warring with my heart.

I took out my phone and sent a text to Ella.

**I'm in Riot's dressing room. **

I bit my bottom lip, running it through my teeth, waiting for her reply. Just as I knew it would, her reply came in just seconds.

What?! What happened? Are you horizontal?

**No, I'm not horizontal. I just worked up enough nerve to see him, so I went and found him. But he's working, so I'm waiting in his dressing room. **

**And then what? **

**I don't know. I'm hoping you can convince me to stay. The longer I sit here by myself, the stronger the urge to run gets. **

**Don't you dare run, Kalli. No more running. Give him a chance. You both deserve it. **

I sighed because I knew she was right. I also grinned because I knew I could count on her to help alleviate some of the uncertainty. So, instead of stewing and worrying about what might come when he walked through that door again, I pulled out my laptop and started working. I needed something really specific for a scene we would be shooting in a few weeks, and I hadn't managed to find it yet, so I was on the hunt.

Forty-five minutes later, I looked up from my screen when I heard footsteps enter.

There he was. Just as beautiful as he'd been earlier that day, still smiling.

"I was worried you'd leave."

"I almost did," I admitted, smiling. "Ella talked me down, told me to stay."

"I always liked her," he said softly.

"I think the feeling is mutual."

"Have you had dinner yet? Can I take you?"

I felt relief at his words. I needed to get out of this small confined space. A public dinner was a good idea.

"That sounds great."

He came farther into the room and closed the door behind him, then walked to his armoire and before I realized what was happening, he'd pulled his t-shirt up and over his head and I was left looking at the incredibly muscled back I could so vividly remember running my hands over. My mouth gaped and my eyes worked quickly to take him all in before the sight was taken from me. Just as quickly as he'd removed his shirt, he pulled another one on, and I made a silent plea to the ex-boyfriend gods that he'd leave his pants on. Thankfully, he bent and slipped off his shoes, exchanging them for the Converse I'd seen on the floor earlier, then removed his fake badge and left it on the counter of his vanity. Then he turned to me.

"Ready?"

"Sure," I said, closing the lid to my laptop and shoving it in my bag. I stood and followed him out of the building, walking straight to his truck. He opened the door for me and I smiled at him as I slid in, letting him close the door behind me. I took a deep breath as he rounded the bed, trying to calm my nerves.

Once it was started and we were on the move, I was able to relax a little.

"So, you got my note." He said it like a statement, only the tone of his voice indicating he wanted me to elaborate.

"I did. A few days ago."

"And yet you haven't been there since." He didn't sound angry, but maybe a little disappointed.

"I'd kind of been lying to myself since I moved here. I told myself that I probably wouldn't see you, and if by chance I did, I would be able to handle it." I saw his head turn toward me out of the corner of my eye, but couldn't bring myself to stare into his eyes while so close to him. Baby steps.

"So, you came and found me?"

"No. Well, yes, I guess so. I spent the last three days working up enough nerve to sit at that coffee shop and wait for you, and when you never showed I was a little pissed. So I went on a mission. Luckily, you weren't hard to find."

"Erin, the girl you bumped into with the clipboard? She helped me find out where you were working. You happened to literally run into the only person in the world who knew I was looking for you."

"You never came. To the coffee shop, I mean."

"I did," he said, his head turning to me once again, and that time I couldn't resist, so I turned to look at him as well. "I went there all three days, but you weren't there. No note in return. Nothing. But I hadn't given up. I just got caught at work shooting that scene. If I weren't in this truck with you right now, I'd be sitting in that coffee shop waiting for you. I'd have waited there forever if there was still hope you'd show up."

With his gaze darting between me and the road, I never got a clear look, but I knew his eyes had softened the way his voice did. The softness I heard there only went further to melting me on the inside.

A breathy, "Oh," was all I could manage in return.

"We'll talk about it at dinner."

"Okay," I said. Then he turned his head again and gave me that brilliant smile and my nerves came down another notch.

A few minutes later he pulled into a parking lot and made sure I knew to stay in my seat so he could open my door. I smiled as I climbed out, and then laughed when I saw his choice of restaurant.

"Pizza? What are you? Twelve?" I laughed and smiled at him, my belly flipping when I heard him laugh along with me.

"What can I say? I haven't gotten the lay of the land here in LA completely, but I do know this place has excellent pizza and beer."

"Well, in that case…." I laughed.

He opened the door for me and when we were led to our table he scooted in my chair. I wasn't surprised; Riot had always been rather chivalrous and thoughtful. But it also made me feel slightly uneasy. It was feeling too much like a date and I wasn't sure what was happening. Then suddenly, Riot Bentley was sitting across from me, smiling, and I didn't know if I'd be able to stay away from him any longer.

Chapter Seven

Beautiful Torture

Riot

The past three days, waiting for Kalli to show, had been tough. At first I was optimistic she'd come, hopeful she'd take my note as a sign that it was time to move forward. But as each day passed and I sat there for hours, I began to worry she'd disappeared again. Retreated back into the darkness I'd left her in months before. It was difficult, but I knew I would go back there until I was sure there was no point any longer.

So, when Erin told me Kalli was in my dressing room, I'd never sprinted anywhere so quickly. I'd gotten to my room out of breath, but deliriously happy to see her there. In the months since I'd seen her, I had moments of panic when the dark thoughts would take over and I'd give in to the fear that I'd never see her again. But there she'd been, waiting for me. It was something I never imagined would actually happen, and I wasn't about to let this opportunity go to waste.

Kalli was with me and it took every ounce of self-control I had not to reach over and take her hand, or brush her hair away from her face, which was so fucking beautiful. I wanted to hold her and touch her, but I couldn't scare her away. I could already tell she was skittish. She'd changed from the Kalli I'd first met so many months ago. She'd been feisty, snarky, and sassy. Obviously, the hurt she'd been through had buried some of that. I was going to enjoy bringing it out again.

She was looking around the pizza place, obviously trying to avoid eye contact, but I let her. I wanted her to be comfortable, so if it took some time to warm her up, so be it.

The waitress came and Kalli ordered a beer, which I loved. I loved that she could hang. She liked her girly cocktails, but wasn't afraid to drink a beer with her pizza. I ordered the same.

"So, how long have you been in LA?" I tried to open up the conversation with something light, something that felt like normal conversation.

"About four weeks. I started my new job about a week after I came to town."

"How are you liking it so far?"

"It's pretty crazy," she said, her sweet laugh mixing with her words. "I never thought I would live here. We talked about that once," she said, her hand motioning between us. Then she shrugged. "But the time was right and the job is amazing, so I made the leap."

"Even though you knew I would be here?" I asked, my smile widening, eyes locking on hers. I watched her throat dip as she swallowed. *Jesus.*

"Even though."

"I can't tell if you think it was a mistake or not, coming here and having to see me."

"If I thought it was a mistake, I wouldn't have come looking for you."

Jesus.

Her words shot through the air and hit me right in the chest, followed by a sweet burn I'd been longing for. Her, here, admitting she wanted to see me. It was the most beautiful torture. Beautiful because it was what I'd wanted for so long, ever since I'd met her, for her to want me just as much as I wanted her. Torture because she was still so fucking far away. Sure, she was sitting at my table, about to eat dinner with me, but she wasn't nearly as close as I needed her.

We'd work on that slowly.

"I'm glad you did," was my response.

She smiled and took a sip of her beer, her eyes wandering again. The waitress returned and I ordered us a pizza. "Can you also please make sure you bring a fork for her? She likes to eat her pizza with a fork." The waitress smiled then walked away, and Kalli was laughing.

"That was a little uncalled for," she said when her laughing tapered off.

"What? I just want you to have everything you need to eat your pizza."

"You just wanted an opportunity to make fun of me." She said the words with a smile so I knew she wasn't offended. She was also right, so I gave her that.

"You're still the only person I've ever met who eats pizza with a fork."

"I can eat it without," she said, as if she were challenging me.

I shrugged. "I think it's cute."

She blushed, and that was cute too.

"So, what have you been up to these past few months? I always thought about you, but wasn't sure you wanted to hear from me."

The smile she'd been wearing dimmed a little, which I hated, but I liked that she answered me anyway.

"I took some time off… after… but then I just tried to stay busy with work. I was staying either on location or with Megan and Ella, just working as much as I could." She paused for a moment and looked as though she was fighting an inner battle. Her hands were on her glass, turning it, as though she couldn't keep her fingers still. "I tried to distract myself from losing him. I couldn't go back to my house, couldn't really do anything that reminded me of him."

"I never got a chance to tell you how sorry I was, Kal."

I watched her stiffen at my words, but then slowly she let out a breath and I watched as some tension physically left her.

"I don't know when it will get easier to talk about him, but it's still really difficult. And even more difficult is knowing I was the reason you never got to tell me you were sorry. Because I pushed you away. And *I'm sorry* for that." Her eyes finally met mine and they were simply begging for forgiveness. I took a chance and reached for her hand, just gently laying mine over it, trying to calm it from its frantic movements.

"You have nothing to be sorry for, baby. Absolutely nothing. You did what you had to do in order to survive, I get that. And I'm glad you're here, now, giving us a chance to talk." I rubbed my thumb over the back of her knuckles, gently, but then pulled away, not wanting to push it.

The air between us was charged, but we were both silent for a few moments. Finally, her voice broke the silence.

"You were always so sweet," she whispered. "I'm glad to see some things never change." Her smile was back and it was blindingly beautiful.

"So, you're liking LA?" I asked, trying to bring the conversation back to a safe zone. I took a drink and watched as her face scrunched up.

"I like the weather and the job, but I still don't feel like I fit in very well."

I laughed. "I like the weather too, but it's fall. Wait until spring and summer roll around. The heat gets brutal."

"Yeah, November in LA is a lot like late summer in Washington," she said, laughing along with me. "Are you still in the same apartment?" Her eyebrows rose with her question.

"Um, yeah. I never really got the urge to leave, so I stayed." I didn't tell her the only reason I stayed was because she'd been there, in my bed, with me. It was the only part of her I had left, the only piece of my life she'd touched, and I wanted to hold on to it as long as I could.

"Sometimes when you've got something you want, you've got to hold on to it." Kalli's voice was thoughtful and soft, and I'd be damned if she wasn't looking right in my eyes as she said those words. That one sentence, that one remark, lifted me up and gave me hope for something more. It also solidified my game plan. I wanted her and I wasn't going to let go of her again. This time, I wasn't going to fade into the background and hope she eventually came around. I was going to be gentle and considerate of her emotional state, but I wasn't going to let her make decisions that tore us apart. Not anymore.

She looked back at her glass, started spinning it again, and bit her lower lip. "So, how are things with Lexi?"

"Lexi?" I asked, my head rearing back, caught completely off guard by her question.

"I saw you with her on the news. She looked really happy."

I could feel my eyebrows bunching in confusion, mouth gaping open, looking for any kind of explanation for her statement. After a few moments it dawned on me. Lexi. The movie premiere. *Shit*. It had been weeks since that happened and the gossip had died down shortly after.

"Kal," I said, reaching out to her again, "I was never with Lexi. Her publicist and my agent set us up on that stunt. I didn't even realize what was going on until I was on the red carpet with her." I squeezed her hand gently, trying to urge her to understand. I could feel the tiniest burn in my chest, anger suddenly hot inside me, at the idea of Kal watching Lexi and me on TV, thinking we were an item. "I promise, Kalli. There's nothing going on between us."

She didn't take her hand away, but she dropped her gaze from me, looking back at the table.

"It's none of my business if you're with her, Riot. You make a great-looking couple."

"We're not a couple," I said, my voice deeper, more insistent. "Kal, look at me, please." She slowly raised her eyes to meet mine, but she looked sadder than she'd been just five minutes ago. After everything she'd been through, I was pissed that Lexi had caused her more pain needlessly. "We're not together. We never have been. I haven't been with anyone since you, and I don't plan on being with anyone *except* you. Ever."

I watched her eyes widen at my words, her lips part slightly, heard her breath catch. I hadn't meant to come on so strong, had wanted to play this evening cool, become friends with her again, ease my way back into her life. Claiming her hadn't been on my short list of things to do.

She finally let out the breath she'd been holding, but she only nodded slightly, pulling her hand from mine to take a drink. She was retreating and all I wanted to do was grab her, shake her, kiss her, and prove I was hers. Only.

"Babe," I said quietly. "Look at me." Her eyes found mine almost immediately. "I'm not with Lexi. I'm here. With you. I'm all yours for whatever purpose you want. You want to be friends? That's cool. You want to be more than that? I'm down with that too, dying for that. But I can't let you sit there thinking I'm with someone else. That I could have moved on so easily from you. I couldn't. I didn't. I haven't been able to think of anyone else but you, let alone date someone else. I've just been here, biding my time, trying to give you the space you wanted. But I never let you go, Kal."

"Okay," she whispered, after a brutally long moment of silence. She took in a deep breath, then let it out. "I haven't been with anyone either." Her words were small and quiet, but she might as well have written them across the sky, laid them out in the stars, for what they did to me. My heart thundered in my chest and any oxygen I'd taken in disappeared. "You have to know," she continued, still quiet as summer rain, "I didn't make you go because I didn't love you. I pushed you away because it hurt too much to love anyone other than Marcus. I know it sounds silly, but loving you, being with you, only made me feel guilty about what happened to him."

"It's not silly. It's grief. Whatever you felt, or feel, you're entitled to that. I'd never tell you anything different."

"Thank you, I appreciate that. But I still want to explain. I owe you that much."

I didn't think she owed me anything, but I could tell it was important to her to get the words out. She looked as though she was ready to burst, keeping them inside. Right before she opened her mouth though, the waitress brought our pizza to our table, completely unaware of the awkward pause she'd caused us to take in a monumental conversation that was months in the making. The waitress smiled at me as she placed two forks in the middle of the table. After she walked away, I folded my arms on the edge of the table in front of me and gave my attention to Kalli, letting her know I was listening, waiting to hear whatever she needed to tell me.

"When the accident with Marcus happened, the first thing I did was blame myself. All I could think was that, had I been home, it never would have happened. Enough time has passed that I'm able to let that go a little. Not fully, though, because Lord knows I'll always wonder if I could have saved him if I'd been there. But," she said, shaking her head a little, "I can accept that his death wasn't my fault. Or yours," she said, her eyes meeting mine. "The fact of the matter is, Marky would be really upset with me if he knew I was using his death as an excuse to be unhappy. So I'm trying to move past it. And mostly I think I'm doing a good job. I still have rough days, still miss him tremendously, but I'm coping." She gave me a smile and, even though it was small, it could have lit up an entire soundstage, it was so brilliant. "I'm sorry I pushed you away, but unfortunately, it was just how I dealt with everything. I hope one day you can forgive me."

"There's nothing to forgive. But if you need the words, then hear them. I forgive you."

Our eyes were trained on each other and I watched as my words washed over her. She smiled, but it was sad, then her eyes welled and I knew she was close to tears. Without thinking I stood and walked to her, grabbed her hand, and pulled her up to me. She came without any argument and buried her face in my chest. We stood in the middle of the pizza parlor, our meal cooling, people eating all around us, sharing the first embrace since before her brother died.

I wanted to rush her from the restaurant, take her to my apartment, and just hold her. I wanted privacy to show her the comfort I could offer, the comfort she'd kept herself from for so long, but I had to settle for wrapping my arms around her in the middle of everyone's dinner.

"I know we've been apart, Kal, but I'm here and I never really left. I've just been waiting for you." Her face tilted up to look at me and I could see the wet tracks from the tears falling down her cheeks. I clasped my hands behind her, at the small of her back, holding her in place. All I wanted was to lean down and kiss her, but I knew the timing wasn't right.

"I'm grateful you waited," she whispered, trying to smile through the tears, so I pulled her closer to me. When her cheek rested against my chest again, I kissed the top of her head and heard her sigh. No, I wouldn't push her. I'd let her come to me. It had worked so far.

Chapter Eight

Gratifying Ogling

Kalli

The alarm on my phone blared and I swiped my finger across the screen, then moved my hand back to rest under my cheek where it had been all night. I knew it had been there all night because I hadn't slept. Not at all. Not even a little.

Riot had brought me back to the studio lot, parked right next to my Rover, and we said good-bye. It was ten whole seconds riddled with angst and tension. I wanted so badly to scoot across the bench of his truck, pull his face to mine, and remind myself what it was like to taste him, but I could tell he wanted to leave things platonic. He made no move to touch me, even though I could have sworn he was battling the same desires I was. If he was, he hid it well. I left him and my whole body was buzzing with unreleased tension, which kept me awake all night.

My mind drifted constantly through images of what would happen next. I saw us on dates, I saw him kissing me, could practically feel his fingers brushing over my skin as his lips pressed against mine. Then I would blink and realize I was still in bed and still awake, very much unkissed and entirely untouched.

The last time I'd spent the night awake and daydreaming about a boy I'd been seventeen and the captain of the football team had asked me on a date. I was all aflutter with anticipation and hopeful wishes for a romance to rival fairy tales. And even though our history was far from fairy tale status, I still hoped there was a happy ending waiting for Riot and me. What that happy ending would entail, I wasn't quite sure. But as long as we were both happy I didn't think it mattered much.

I flung down the blanket covering me and swung my legs out of the bed, stretched, and then headed to the kitchen. Coffee was on my list of things necessary to get through my day. As I stood by the coffee pot, hip cocked and leaning against the counter, my phone pinged, signaling I'd gotten a text message.

I hope you're as tired as I am. I didn't sleep a wink.

I smiled at Riot's message. I smiled because it was sweet he was messaging the morning after our dinner, but also smiling because he'd been up all night too. I couldn't help but hope his mind had kept him up with thoughts of me.

My thumbs moved swiftly over the keypad on my phone as I replied.

I'll probably need lots of coffee today. Good thing I know of a coffee shop that's close to my set.

I like the way you think. I'm free around noon. Any chance you want to meet me there for a pick-me-up?

I smiled down at my phone, running my bottom lip between my teeth. We were flirting. I was smiling. This was good.

I think that can be arranged.

I held my breath waiting for his reply.

See you then. Can't wait.

My morning, although it would be a rough one, was exponentially better now that I knew I'd be seeing Riot in just a few short hours.

I poured my cup of coffee and went to the bathroom to get ready for the day.

Hours later I opened the door to the Coffee Bean and let out a relieved sigh when I saw Riot sitting at our table. He had a script on the table in front of him and he was wearing a backward baseball hat. When he heard me coming his head tilted up and his eyes met mine. Having all his hair pushed back gave me an unobstructed view of his beautiful face and it sent butterflies soaring in my belly.

His dark eyes, which were usually complemented by his dark hair, were like beacons and my eyes zeroed in on them without hesitation. His smile widened as I came closer. As I approached the table he used his foot to push out the chair across from him. I took the seat and wasn't upset that I'd have to look at his beautiful face.

"Hey," I said with a smile, sitting and placing my purse on the empty chair next to me.

"Hey, yourself."

"I don't know about you, but I need to be caffeinated."

"I was just waiting for you. What would you like?" he asked as he stood from his chair, his eyes never leaving mine.

"I'll take an iced latte, please."

"Coming up." He headed toward the counter and I took the opportunity to watch him walk away. He was dressed casually, jeans and a t-shirt, but the jeans made his ass look amazing. After a few moments of completely selfish, yet gratifying, ogling, I turned back to the table and eyed the script lying atop it. I peeked at the paper, then used a finger to swing it to face me, letting my eyes peruse it.

It seemed to be a scene between Riot's character and the person who played his rookie partner. I read it for a few pages and surmised the two characters were trying to out a dirty cop who was high up in the ranks.

"I'd get in a lot of trouble if my producer knew I'd let you read my script. That's the midseason cliffhanger you're sneaking a peek at."

I smiled and turned his script back to him. "Looks exciting."

"You know, I really like the writers. They've got a good storyline going, or as far as I can tell they do, anyway." He put my coffee in front of me and I felt like Pavlov's dog, nearly drooling at the sight of the cup.

"Thank you," I sighed, then took a satisfying drink.

"You're welcome," he said, a smile tugging at his lips as he sat down across from me again. "I'll buy you coffee every day if I get to watch you take that dreamy first sip."

I gave him a flirty smile, but then took one more sip. "I slept for crap last night. This coffee is going to get me through the fittings I have scheduled this afternoon."

"Measuring more inseams?" He waggled his eyebrows at me and I couldn't help the laugh that escaped me.

"No, no inseams." I blushed at the memory of kneeling in front of Riot, measuring tape in hand, praying he couldn't see my hand shaking as I took his measurement. That was the day that had started everything between us, and I was glad I could look back on the memory with a smile. For the last couple of months, every memory that included Riot had sent me into a panic. I loved thinking about him, remembering the good moments between us, and having no apprehension.

"Do you have any plans this weekend?"

I shook my head. "None. I was just going to stay home and get some work done."

A slow and easy smile spread across his face. "My little sister's birthday is this weekend and my family is having a party. Would you like to take a trip to San Francisco with me?"

Suddenly, I didn't need coffee to wake me up. Riot was asking me to go away with him for the weekend. One day after we'd started talking to each other again. I was wide awake. My heart rate picked up and my mind started working overtime. Sure, I wanted to spend time with him, wanted to explore where our relationship could go from here, but I didn't think it would be going to San Francisco for the weekend. He must have seen the panic in my face, or noticed the way my entire body tensed at his question, because he immediately tried to soothe me.

"Hey, Kal, listen. It was just a suggestion. I thought it would be fun to get away. No pressure."

"I'm sorry. That just really surprised me." I felt terrible. First, because I didn't want him to think I didn't want to spend time with him, and second, because as soon as he started to tell me it was okay if I didn't want to go, I wanted to go. Sure, my first reaction was terror, but once I thought about it for a moment, spending a weekend with Riot somewhere new sounded like the perfect way to ease back into whatever it was we were trying to build between us. "So, does your family know you're inviting a woman to the family gathering?"

"No. But they'd love to meet you, so I'm sure it wouldn't be a problem." He eyed me warily, which made me feel even worse.

"Where would we stay? At your parents' house?" The idea of seeing the house Riot grew up in made my belly warm, then the feeling spread throughout my body. Even though I'd fallen totally and madly in love with Riot months before, we'd actually learned quite little about each other. All he really knew of me was what I showed him, and all I knew of him was what I was able to surmise from a brief yet entirely passionate long-distance relationship.

"Well, unfortunately, since I haven't RSVP'd yet, all the rooms are spoken for, so we'd have to stay at a hotel. Obviously, we can get two rooms... if you're worried about..."

His voice trailed off and I wanted to end his misery. "I think it'd be really fun to go to San Francisco with you."

"Great," he said on a sigh, obviously relieved. He smiled as he brought his coffee to his lips, and I couldn't help but smile back.

"How old is your sister turning? What is she into? I need gift ideas."

"She's kind of a nerd," he said in a big brother, teasing-with-love kind of way. "I usually just get her a gift card to her favorite bookstore and call it good."

"That's very male of you." I rolled my eyes at him, but then I smiled as a small laugh escaped my lips.

"What's wrong with a gift card?" he asked, feigning offense.

"Nothing is wrong with a gift card, if you're going for a completely impersonal gift. But if I'm meeting your family for the first time, I want to bring something that doesn't scream, 'I stopped at a grocery store five minutes ago to get your birthday present.'"

"Ouch." His hand came up to cover his heart and the wounded look he wore, with just one edge of his mouth tipped up, was absolutely adorable. Then his face went blank as he picked up his coffee again. "My sister loves my gift cards."

I laughed, then lifted one shoulder in a shrug. "I'm sure she does."

"I don't want to monopolize all your time, but do you have plans on Wednesday evening? They're playing that new scary thriller movie at the lot theatre. Wanna go see it with me?" His eyebrows were raised, eyes trained on me as he waited for my answer. Generally, I hated scary movies. When I was a teenager I'd loved them, enjoyed scaring myself silly with my friends at the movie theatre or late at night during a sleepover. But once I hit adulthood, I realized serial killers and ghosts were just one more thing to fear that I didn't need, and found myself hating the entire genre of film. However, sitting in the studio's movie theatre plush seats, built like love seats, didn't sound like a bad way to spend an evening. Especially if it meant I could be close to Riot.

"I think I could make time to see a movie with you," I answered, trying not to sound too eager.

"Great," he said, his smile just as brilliant and beaming as I knew mine was.

"Great," I mimicked.

"I guess we should both get back to work soon." His eyes didn't leave mine as he said the words and his smile didn't dim at all either.

"I guess we should."

"Have I mentioned how glad I am that you're here?"

The sudden change in topic and also the rawness of his words caught me off guard. My breath faltered, the last lungful of air stopped, waiting for me to relieve the tension and exhale. I opened my mouth to try to respond, to fill the empty space between us, but he spoke first.

"I don't know where this is headed, and I'm trying to not expect anything, but Kal, it's nice to just sit here with you and see you smiling. Come what may, I'm glad you're here."

"I'm glad I'm here too," was all I could manage, and even that was whispered and gravelly. The breath that had been stalled was now a slightly painful lump in my throat and I tried to push it down, not wanting to ruin our happy moment with tears. But Riot's words had done something to me, opened something up. I didn't want to expect anything either, but I wanted to be happy, to be hopeful. This was the first time in eight years I'd been stationary, the first time I'd been standing still. I had a long-term job, a home in the same city as my job; nothing about my life in that moment was temporary. Everything felt heavier, weighed me down, held me in place.

Months ago, that feeling—the weight of all the connections, obligations, and expectations—would have caused me to panic, sent me into a tailspin and I would have picked up, moved, and run away. But sitting in that coffee shop with Riot, making plans to see his family, knowing he'd be there in a week, or a month, well, it lit me up. It warmed me. Caused parts of me that had been frozen for so long to thaw and melt away. The heat, both the heat I felt coming from him and the heat I felt inside myself, was breathtaking. This was the second time Riot had chased away my anxiety, fought the darkness and brought me into the light, and both times he'd done it with so much compassion and understanding, it was beyond amazing. It also wasn't a coincidence. It wasn't a coincidence that Riot had been the only man to make me safe and secure enough to *feel*. It was fate.

I opened my mouth again, hoping my brain could form words enough to explain to him how, in that moment, I was beyond grateful for the unyielding support he'd always offered, even when that support came in the form of leaving me alone. But before I could tell him anything, before I could explain the enormity of what I was feeling, he stood up and smiled at me. He waited for me to follow, his expression telling me that he already knew everything I was feeling, that words weren't necessary, that my being there was enough explanation.

So I stood too. And I shivered when his hand met the small of my back as he guided me toward the exit, relishing the fact that my body was literally shivering just from one touch of his hand. We were both trying to play it smart, keep our hearts safe, but my body was leaps and bounds ahead of my head, and my body wanted his. He walked me to the entrance of my soundstage and I felt his hand leave my back only to gently grip my arm at the elbow. He turned me toward him, then his hands moved up my arm, over my shoulder, and stopped with his fingers tenderly wrapping around the side of my neck. He was just inches away and his scent was swirling around me, and my body went from wanting his, to aching for it.

I couldn't help the sigh the escaped me when he pressed his lips to the crown of my head. My eyes closed, I exhaled, and my body melted into his. My front pressed into his, my free hand coming to rest on his hip, and I let the connection between us wash over me. Even after all the months apart, he was my home.

"I'll text you," he said quietly against my hair.

"Okay," I whispered, my fingers curling in at his waist, his t-shirt gathering in my clutch. He pressed a chaste kiss to my head again, then pulled away, taking his body and his shirt with him, even if I silently objected.

"Later," he said coolly, as he backed away from me.

"Bye." I brought my eyes up to meet his. He winked at me and I nearly passed out as all the blood rushed down from my head and left me dizzy.

The light-headed feeling stayed with me until Wednesday, only exacerbated by the frequent texting happening between us, which was filled with flirting and sexual tension. When I met him outside the theater on the lot, the dizziness was still present but one smile from him and I was spinning.

"You made it," he said with a smile as I stopped just a step or two away from him.

"I'm here. Ready to be scared to death."

He tilted his head to the side and furrowed his brow. "You don't like scary movies?"

"Used to, but then life got real and I didn't need anything else to be afraid of." The honest words flowed, surprising even me. I couldn't help but feel lighter after I'd said them, almost enjoying that I'd shared something with him I normally wouldn't have, and wasn't panicking about it. I'd told him something real. Something true. I'd given him a tiny piece of me to hold on to.

It made it all worth it when he seemed to mentally tuck the information away, turned toward me, wrapped his arm lightly around my shoulder, and said, "I'll be sure to protect you."

The studio built an incredibly plush theatre, which was free and open to anyone who worked on the lot. It was fancy. That was really the only way it could be described. The studio understood the people who made the movies didn't always have time to see them, so they built a theatre to make the movies more accessible. Also, sometimes the big Hollywood actors couldn't just go to a movie theatre. Not that I expected to see someone famous. Usually the theatre was used by poor interns or other employees who couldn't really *afford* to go to the movies in LA, as it was nearly as expensive as putting a down payment on a house.

Plus, the popcorn was free and loaded with salt and butter.

We found our seats, not too close to the front, and I started the process of getting comfortable. The seats, which weren't like the ones in a normal theatre, were like soft, fluffy love seats. They were just big enough for two people to have enough space, but small enough that you were forced to share your personal space anyway. I had no qualms making myself at home. I stripped off my jacket, laying it over the arm of the seat, then took my shoes off. Riot looked at me with one eyebrow raised.

"Did you bring your favorite pajamas too?"

He was mocking me.

"They pretty much invite you to pretend you're at home with these chairs. I don't want to be uncomfortable. I want to lounge. Especially if I'm going to watch a scary movie."

He held up both his hands in defense, but a smile was playing on his lips. "Hey, I wouldn't want to stand in the way of your comfort. By all means, make yourself at home."

"I intend to," I said, raising my chin in defiance. He was laughing at me, but he stopped when I settled next to him, my hips touching his. My feet were curled up under me to the side, forcing me to lean against him. No, he wasn't laughing any longer. He was, however, smiling when he lifted his arm and coolly laid it behind me, his hand coming to rest on my shoulder. I let my body lean farther into him, taking the space his arm had vacated. I snuggled in a little closer and whispered, "Smooth."

I felt him laugh, but didn't hear him. I did see his smile hiding behind his hand as his fingers covered his mouth. He was busted. I just smiled though, and leaned in a little farther, dipping my hand to pull a few popcorn kernels out of our tub and toss them in my mouth.

"Hey," he said quietly. I turned my head slightly to look up at him. "Hit me." His mouth opened wide and stayed that way. I laughed, but relented, placing a few kernels in his mouth. He smiled as he started chewing. The theatre was pretty empty, typical for a Wednesday night, but in that moment it felt like we were the only ones in the room. I stared at his jaw as he chewed, watched his Adam's apple dip when he swallowed, and couldn't tear my eyes away from him for anything. He made popcorn sexy.

He gave me a sharp nod. "One more hit, babe." My hands were on autopilot and I deposited a few more pieces of popcorn in his mouth. He closed his lips around my finger before I had a chance to pull away. I drew in a faltering breath as he took his time sucking the salt and butter from my finger, his eyes never leaving mine. It was anything but innocent. It was raw, carnal, and only brought on images of Riot sucking on other parts of my body. Images I'd tried to bury for months, that hurt too much to think about for so long. Now, however, those pictures flooded my mind and I not only welcomed them, my mind took them farther, put him and me in new and equally hot scenarios where his mouth was latched on to my body for a variety of reasons in a variety of places.

He pulled his mouth to the end of my finger, his tongue flat and dragging along the bottom of it, and just before my finger fell away, he pressed a kiss to the very end of it. It was, possibly, the most erotic thing I'd ever witnessed firsthand. And we were in a movie theatre. Surrounded by other people. I let out a shuddering breath and felt the crimson blush heat up my cheeks. He smiled at my obvious mortification, but pulled my shoulder closer to him. My lungs tripped again when I felt his breath feather over the skin just below my ear.

"You taste good," he growled, so low it was almost a whisper.

"It's the butter from the popcorn," I stupidly responded, my words rushing out with the only breath I'd been able to take in since he'd fucked my finger with his mouth.

"I give credit where it's due, baby. You. Taste. Good."

He might as well have been talking directly to my vagina for all the clenching he was causing. Riot and I had always done sexual tension well. It had been built up over the phone and explosive anytime we were physically near each other. It had been capped for so long, our desire for one another put on hold, forced into a proverbial darkness. Now that we'd kind of lifted the ban, I was afraid the passion we'd always had for each other was going to sweep us away on a wave of lust and potentially bad decisions.

All those thoughts didn't stop me from melting into him when he pulled my shoulder closer to him. It didn't stop me from watching that horrifying movie, pressing my face into his chest when I wanted to scream. And it didn't stop me from loving the way it felt to let him hold me, his thumb absently rubbing up and down the side of my shoulder, causing goose bumps to spread all over.

When the lights came up and I heard the people around us shuffling to gather their belongings and leave the theatre, I frowned into him, not wanting to leave the little bubble of warmth we'd created. I was comfortable. More than that, I'd not had one heavy thought for two solid hours as I leaned against him, watching that scary excuse for a film.

His arm gave me a gentle squeeze and I knew it was time to get up. I frowned again, but moved away from him, leaning down to grab my shoes. We didn't say anything as we stood, but he reached down and took my hand, linking our fingers, and leading the way.

It had been so long since I held his hand; all the schoolgirl butterflies came back, flooding my belly. Instinctively, my free hand wrapped around his arm, holding that sexy, strong part of him close to me.

He walked me all the way to my car, taking my keys from me and opening my door. I smiled at his familiar chivalrous ways, then turned to tell him thank you. I was startled by his body pressing into mine, forcing me to back up into the side of my car. His hands were suddenly resting on the curve of my hips, mine finding their natural resting place against his chest, and my face turning up to look at him. My breathing sped up and my eyes searched his, hoping I'd see something in them that would give me answers to the questions spinning in my head with his body pressed so firmly against mine.

"I miss you." His voice was low and raspy, as if he didn't want anyone else in the world to hear his words except me. "I like this, spending time with you, but I still feel like you're an arm's length away." His tender eyes moved back and forth as he took mine in. Perhaps he was searching for answers too. I wanted to give him everything I could.

"I'm right here," I replied, my voice just as low, just as full of emotion. "I know you've been waiting, and we're nearly there. I just don't want to fall back into something to have it blow up in my face. I want to be sure."

His hands moved from my waist, traveling up my back, putting gentle pressure on me, pushing my chest into his, forcing my hands to wind around his neck. We were so close; his nose was touching mine, our breaths intermingling. I could feel the rapid thumping of his heart through the thin cotton of his t-shirt, the buckle of his belt pressing into my belly. I was on my tiptoes, stretching, reaching, arching to him, trying to give him as much of me as I could in that moment. His hands spread wide across my shoulder blades, hot and wild, pulling me in to him.

And then his lips were on mine. It was soft at first; hesitant. Slow and fragile. He kissed me as if he were afraid I was going to dissolve around him. His plush lips brushed over mine and I couldn't move. I was frozen, hoping this wasn't one of my many dreams where Riot held and kissed me through the night, only to wake up and find he wasn't there. I whimpered as his lips pressed against mine with just a fraction more pressure, then nearly collapsed when his tongue traced my bottom lip.

I slowly opened, tentatively dipped my tongue out to meet his, and then we both cracked.

We fractured.

We exploded.

Suddenly, kissing him was more important than breathing. More important than living and seeing and *being*. All that mattered was his mouth pressed against mine.

Hands grasped at each other, trying to hold on to any part they could find purchase on. My fingers ran through the soft, short hair at his nape, and one of my legs lifted to wrap around his hip. He immediately wrapped one hand around the back of my knee, pulling our centers closer, and then, without warning, he slowly thrust against me.

All I could feel, all I could process, was the ridiculously hard and delicious pressure of his denim-clad cock pressing against my center. Slowly dragging up, causing every nerve in my body to shoot into overdrive, every synapse to fire, every sensory indicator to short circuit. I pulled my mouth away to moan, unable to keep quiet, unable to pretend the contact hadn't just totally incinerated me from the inside out.

It had been months since my body had felt anything outside of despair and grief, so to suddenly be thrust into sexual overdrive, well, it was a lot to handle. I couldn't take in enough air, couldn't hold my hands steady, as they were shaking with need. My heart was thundering in my chest, racing toward oblivion. And it all felt wonderful.

Riot thrust against me one more time, my moan a little louder and a lot needier when his mouth moved down my throat, leaving kisses like breadcrumbs.

"Riot," I groaned, loving the way his lips trailed along my skin. "Someone could see us out here."

"I don't fucking care," he said, his hand moving from the back of my knee up to grab my ass, pressing our centers together even more. I let him. I let him feast for just a moment more because I was in love with the way I was feeling just then. I felt light, wanted, and free. I felt as though I were floating above us, as if I were watching someone else because, certainly, this was not me. I didn't live a life where I pushed a man away and he understood why. Where I yelled and screamed at him, blamed him for something so terrible, and he waited patiently, knowing I'd loved him all along. This had to be someone else's life.

So I let him kiss every part of my skin available to him in that parking lot, let his hands roam over my clothed body, and I loved every single second of it.

Just as I knew he would, he finally came back from the momentary lust-induced insanity, dropped my leg, and simply returned to sweet kisses laid softly on my mouth.

"Fuck, I missed you, Kal."

The way he said my name, the way his thumb moved over my bottom lip, the heavy way he held me as he said those words, it all swirled around me and I melted into him a little bit more.

"I missed you too."

"Have I got you back now? Is this for real? I want this. I want us."

His words went from sweet and meaningful to rushed and a little scared, and I knew it was because he was afraid I would push him away again.

I stared up at him, looking into his eyes, trying to see past the hurt lingering there, past the nearly feral man who just practically took me up against my car in a parking lot, and I looked for the man I fell in love with so many months ago. The man who was gentle and caring, who handled me with exactly the right amount of tenderness, but took charge when I needed that from him. He was still there; I could feel him. And I had to believe if the Riot I fell in love with was still there, waiting for me, then the Kalli he fell in love with had to be somewhere inside me as well.

I fell against him, leaning my forehead into his chest. "I want this too." I took in a deep breath then exhaled, looking up at him. "I want us. I want you. But..." I felt my bottom lip become trapped between my teeth. "I don't think I can handle losing you again."

"Hey," he said, his hands coming to frame my face. "You never lost me. I know I disappeared, but you didn't lose me. You understand that, right? I would never abandon you. Not ever. I did what I thought was best for you, but I didn't want to leave you, Kalli. Not then, not now. Never."

"I know," I whispered, wrapping my arms around his neck, letting him hold me. A part of me died to hear the desperation in his voice, the sadness in his words. I'd done that to him. I'd been the one to make him leave, and even though it hurt him, he did it. For me. He was so *good*. "I just need you to be patient with me."

"There's no rush here. I promise. Even though I basically just pushed you up against your car and felt you up, I promise it won't happen again." He stepped back, making me want to pull him to me again, but I let him go, watching as he ran the back of his hand over the stubble at his jaw.

Damn.

"Then," I said with a smile, nearly drunk on happiness, "I'm all yours."

His sexy smile spread quickly over his face, his dark eyes sparkling in the overhead lights of the parking lot, and in just one second I was back in his arms. He picked me up and spun me around playfully, my laugh ringing out. I sounded happy. I was happy. It was some sort of miracle.

When he finally placed me back on the ground, he kissed me again, but this time it was sweet and innocent. Just happy lips pressed against happy lips. He was still smiling when he pulled away.

"I knew you'd come back to me."

I kept looking in his eyes as he tucked a lock of wayward hair behind my ear, marveling at how wonderful a man he was.

"I think I knew I'd come back to you too. It's always been you, Riot."

Chapter Nine

Give Her The World

Riot

Memories flooded my mind while I leaned up against Kalli's Range Rover, which was parked in the same spot it had been two nights ago when I had her body pressed against it. When I'd been able to feel her under my hands, kiss her, and her body had been pushed up against mine. I'd always had a hard time controlling myself when it came to Kalli. And now, well, I was taking her to my hometown for the weekend. We'd be surrounded by my mom, dad, and sister for some of the time, and I'd spend the rest of the time trying not to rid her of all her clothes and let my body sink into hers.

Perhaps this was a bad idea.

Months.

Months I'd gone with just the memories of what it felt like to be with her, to have her body wrapped around mine, or to feel her pulse beneath my hand as I kissed her. Then, last night, we both let down our guards for just a little while, and I was reminded of how perfectly her body was made for mine. Not that I'd forgotten.

This was what I imagined someone felt like when stranded on a deserted island, dreaming about all the food they wished they had. I'd been trapped on my own personal island of hell, wishing she were next to me so many nights, and now that she was within my grasp, and letting me touch her, it was going to take all my self-control to not lay her out on any available flat surface.

I heard the unmistakable sounds of footfalls and turned to see Kalli walking toward me, smiling brightly. I hadn't seen her since Wednesday, but we'd been texting nonstop. I knew if I went to her my self-control would be tested, and I didn't want to put either of us in that situation. I wanted the exact moment I was having then: Kalli, without worry lines marring her beautiful face, walking toward me looking happy, radiant, and sexy as fucking hell.

Her blonde hair cascaded over her shoulder in a thick, loose, crazy braid. She wore a long sweater that looked to be a dress, as it came down to the middle of her thighs. It was a deep maroon color and was slouching off one of her shoulders, giving me a peek at her collarbone. She wore black leggings that disappeared into the black boots, which were currently making the clacking noises.

She looked incredible. She looked like she was ready to curl up on a couch and read a book, or curl into my side and watch a movie. Perhaps she'd purposefully made herself look soft and comfortable. Either way, it worked. I wanted to feel the sweater under my hands, and I needed to feel it bunching as I slid it up her torso and pulled it over her head.

"Hey," I said through the smile that wouldn't leave my face. She continued toward me, but didn't respond. She did, however, walk confidently to me, not stopping until her hand was at my cheek and her lips were pressed against mine. I was surprised by her approach, but only let a second pass before I engaged in the kiss. My hand found the back of her neck, loving the feel of her silky hair wound between my fingers, and I gave her a firm squeeze there.

"Hey, yourself," she said with a smirk after pulling away.

"You ready to go?" I asked, as my eyes took their time wandering down her body. The top she was wearing was meant to be loose and baggy, but I knew what curves lay beneath it and the façade drove me mad.

"Yup," she said, smiling as she swung her keyring around on one finger. She turned and walked to the back of her Rover, opening the trunk to allow me to place my duffle bag inside. Once the trunk was closed, I held my hand out to her.

"Keys."

Her forehead scrunched in confusion, eyebrows drawing together. It was adorable. "You're not driving my Rover."

"Babe, when's the last time you drove through San Francisco? It'll be easier if you just let me drive. It'll be late by the time we get there anyway, and dark."

"I can drive in the dark, Riot. I've been driving myself all over the west coast for years. You just want to drive my Rover."

"You're not wrong. Come on, babe," I moved closer to her, wrapping my arms around her waist. "I just want to drive my girl home and hold her hand." I blinked down at her, using some overly exaggerated pouty lips and batting my eyelashes. It was over the top and I knew I looked ridiculous, but I also knew it would work.

"Fine," she groaned, pulling away and slapping her keys in my hand. "But if you're driving, I get to pick the music."

"Deal," I said, dropping a kiss on her lips, enjoying the way I could feel her smile against my mouth. I walked her to the passenger side, opened her door, and watched her climb in.

When we were on the road, music selected, her hand loosely gripping mine, it was as if we were finally back to normal. Finally back to a place where there weren't dark clouds hanging over us, or guilt. I knew there would be many instances in our future where Kalli had setbacks, or bad days where Marcus would be at the front of her mind and she'd need me to hold her, or tell her funny memories I had of him and the few days I was lucky enough to spend with him, but for now she was happy.

We fought our way out of LA traffic and started climbing the grapevine, which was essentially a ridiculously large, tall, and windy road that went over a mountain. It was dry and a brownish-red color in the day, but with the sun already set, all we could see were the lights of the other cars on the road.

"I have a question," Kalli finally said, breaking our comfortable silence. "I thought your sister worked on a cruise ship? What is she doing in town?"

"Well, that's kind of why my parents' house is full. Halah came home for vacation and it just happened to be during her birthday. She hasn't been home in over two years, so my parents are throwing her a party. There's family coming in from out of town."

"So, I'm not just meeting your immediate family?" she asked nervously.

"No, babe, sorry. You're pretty much going to meet every family member I have who lives west of the Mississippi. Which is pretty much all of them."

"Are any of your family members from Lebanon going to be there?"

I shook my head. "No, we don't really see the family who's left there. It's mostly distant relatives now, as my grandparents have both passed away. But my mom's sister will be there. She lives in Montana. Seems my mother and her sister both fell for American men."

"I can't wait to meet your parents. I mean, I'm nervous, but from what you've told me about the way they met, they seem like people from a fairy tale. And I bet your mother is just beautiful."

Kalli was looking out her window, but her voice was wistful and genuine. I couldn't imagine what it would be like to lose your mother at such a young age, and I wanted her to feel like my family was her family.

"They're going to love you," I said, bringing the back of her hand up to my mouth and pressing a kiss against it. I wanted to tell her I loved her, too, to make sure she knew it, but I didn't push it. We were just getting back to being comfortable with each other, and I didn't need to ruin it by moving too quickly with her. She gave me her beautiful, carefree smile, but then turned back to the window.

When we drove through San Francisco proper, I was glad I'd forced her to let me drive. Her eyes were wide, taking in all the lights of the city. I wanted to stare at her, watch as she took in the beauty of the city skyline. I'd seen the city a thousand times, but it was all brand new watching it through her eyes.

We headed north through the city and I took a few opportunities to point out special places you could see from the freeway; places that had relevance to a special time in my life or a specific occasion.

"Before we head back home I want to take you to the pier."

"That's one place I've never been able to see when I've been here."

"Well, then it's settled." We drove in silence for a few more minutes. "Okay, so, I have reservations for us at the Palace Hotel, but my mom was hoping we could stop by her house before we check-in for the night." I turned my head for just a moment to look at her, hopeful she'd agree. I wanted nothing more than to introduce her to my family, to make her real in that way, make our relationship that much more solid.

"Riot, it's almost ten. Won't your family be asleep?"

I gave her a grin. "When you get my whole family together, they're a little rowdy. Especially with Halah home. They'll be up." I winked at her, trying to ease her apprehension.

"I'd love to meet them."

I kissed her hand again, unable to stop myself.

A minute later we were driving over the Golden Gate Bridge.

"This is so beautiful, Riot," she said in an almost whisper.

"It is," I agreed, but couldn't take my eyes off her.

Forty minutes later she read the road sign alerting her to my hometown.

"You grew up in Sausalito?" Her voice was high and she sounded astonished.

"I did. Well, just outside it in Muir Beach."

I had barely gotten Kalli out of the Rover before the front door opened and my mother's voice rang out into the night.

"Riot Bentley, you'd better get up here and give your mother a hug. And bring your beautiful girlfriend with you."

"You ready for this?" I asked Kalli, bringing my face just a breath away from hers.

"Ready when you are," she replied, sounding just a little nervous.

"They already love you," I whispered, just before I pressed a small, chaste kiss against her lips. I took her hand and walked her to the porch where my mother stood, just as breathtaking as she always had been. If Halah aged even half as beautifully as my mother, the man in her life would be the envy of all his friends.

"My baby." My mother held my face between her hands and pressed a kiss to each cheek. "You move away from home and you never come back to visit."

"Sorry, Ma." I took a step back and wrapped my arm around Kalli's waist. "Ma, this is my girlfriend, Kalli Rivers. Kal, this is my mom, Samarah Bentley."

"It is so good to finally meet you, my sweet girl." I watched as my mother wrapped Kalli in a tight and familiar hug. Kalli stiffened at first, but then I watched as she melted into my mother's embrace, and nearly hugged my mother again when she winked at me over Kalli's shoulder.

"I'm glad to meet you too," Kal said as they pulled apart.

"Mara, are you holding those kids hostage out there?" I heard my father's deep voice call from the house.

"Your father is anxious to see you," Ma said, urging us into the house. I took Kal's hand and led her into my childhood home. I'd never brought a girl home before, so even though I didn't want to stress Kalli out with that bit of information, this was kind of a big deal for my family. Halah had brought a few guys home to meet our parents, but life was different on a cruise ship. It seemed like she fell in and out of really intense relationships quite frequently. I guess when you're forced to live on a boat with someone, normal dating timelines go out the window.

I didn't stop to give Kal a tour. I could still hear my dad grumbling from the kitchen, so I headed straight there.

I saw Pops sitting in his usual place at the head of the table, cards in his hands, and sitting around the table were other members of my family. Pops half-stood when I made it to him, and I dropped Kal's hand to pat my dad on the back.

"Pops, this is Kalli, my girlfriend."

"Nice to meet you," Kalli said, her sweet voice a little unsure. I moved back to her, pressing my hand to the small of her back, trying to remind her physically that I was right with her, that she didn't need to be nervous. I watched as my dad took her outstretched hand, but only used it to pull her into a hug.

"Kalli, it's nice to meet you, too," he said, releasing her and giving her a warm smile. "We were starting to question Riot's character, wondering how he was treating the ladies seeing as how none of them would come home with him to visit."

"Pops," I said with a groan.

"You've never brought a girl home?" Kalli asked. I shook my head at her. Her eyes softened when she understood my answer, so I wrapped my arm around her shoulders and pressed a kiss to her temple.

"Kalli, my name's Chad. If you call me Mr. Bentley I'll be looking around for my own father, God rest his soul. You call me Chad, and her Mara," he said, nodding his head toward Ma, who'd just come into the kitchen with Halah. "And that's the birthday girl herself, Halah."

"Oh, my gosh, hi," Kalli opened her arms to Halah.

I watched as my baby sister hugged Kalli, and something inside me shifted, was nudged right into place. Something that had been off-kilter for so long I hadn't even realized it. In that moment, watching Kalli hug my sister, surrounded by my whole family, I knew it was the first time of many, and that brought me peace.

"Ri-Ri told me you were pretty, but he didn't do you justice," my sister said as she pulled back and looked at Kalli. I agreed. There was no way to tell someone how beautiful Kalli was. I could talk about her for hours, describe every single freckle, but I'd never be able to tell anyone how devastatingly beautiful she was. It was something you had to see to understand.

"Your whole family is beautiful," Kalli murmured on a breathy whisper. She wasn't wrong. My mother could have played an Arabian princess in an old fifties black-and-white movie, and my sister was more attractive than I'd like to admit. It was hard to grow up with her as my baby sister, especially in her teen years, because I wanted to punch in the face of every guy who even looked her way—which was a lot.

"Hey Hala-balloo," I said, hugging my sister, relieved to finally lay eyes on her. "I'm so glad you decided to come home for once." She pulled back and slapped my arm.

"You should talk."

"No fighting," Ma said, coming to stand between us, one arm around each of our waists. "My babies," she said, her voice soft and quiet. "It's been too long." I looked at Halah and she rolled her eyes, but more in a loving than sassy way. We both knew our mom would be emotional if we were in the same room together—it's the way of mothers. After a long embrace, Ma pulled away and headed into the kitchen, which was only divided from the dining room by an island. "Riot, Kalli, are either of you hungry?"

"We ate on the road," I said, sitting down at the table.

"Oh," Ma said, her voice deflated.

"But I'd really appreciate something to drink," Kalli said, reading my mom like a freaking book. Ma needed to fuss over us. Kalli walked to the island and even though she was just a few feet away, I wanted her back by my side.

Ma took great pleasure in getting Kalli a glass of water and I watched as Halah joined her at the island, both of them sitting, seeming to start up a conversation.

"She's a looker."

I turned to see Pops nod toward Kal. I couldn't help the grin that spread over my face.

"Yeah, I know."

"She important?"

"Yeah."

"Then treat her right, son. Give her the world and treat her right."

"On it, Pops. Got it covered."

"You happy? With her, I mean. She makes you happy?"

"Yeah." My dad had always been present, always been involved, but we'd never had a serious talk about someone I dated. That was largely due to the fact that since I'd moved out, I'd never brought a woman home, but even in high school, all I'd ever really gotten out of my father was the safe sex talk, followed by the "respect women" lecture.

He nodded at my response. "Don't let her go then."

I laughed a little and rubbed my hand over the stubble on the underside of my chin. "Noted." I didn't bother telling my dad that I'd already let her go once before, holding out hope that she'd return. Luckily for me, she had. I didn't have any intention of doing it again though. Once was more than enough for me. I was in this for the long haul. It was going to be forever this time.

"Riot," I heard my mom call from the kitchen. "Are you sure you don't want a sandwich?"

"Your mother wants to feed you. Humor her," my dad said under his breath, making sure it was low enough she couldn't hear him.

"Sure, Ma. I'd love a sandwich."

Eventually the women moved to the dining table and my mom brought me a sandwich. I ate it, even though I wasn't hungry, but I didn't mind because Kalli sat right next to me and took bites when I offered them to her. I had one hand on her thigh under the table, one hand on the sandwich Ma had made for me, and my eyes on my little sister. The evening couldn't have ended any better. Or so I thought.

After about an hour of small talk, Kalli and I made our way out to the car, promising we'd be back early enough the next day to help set up for the big party. I could tell my mother and sister were anxious to get Kalli away from me, to talk to her about our relationship and find out more about her, but I pried her away, telling them I was exhausted.

I wrapped my fingers through Kalli's as soon as we were back on the road.

"Your family is really nice." Her voice was soft again, thoughtful.

"They seemed to like you a lot." She turned her head toward me and smiled.

"I'm not going to lie, Riot. It's a little strange to be around a family." Her smile faded and her voice was suddenly heavier. Something inside my chest tightened and I gave her hand a gentle squeeze.

"Babe, whatever you need, just let me know. If you want to stay in the hotel tomorrow, I can go to the party by myself. If you're there and you need a minute to yourself, just tell me. I'll find a quiet place for you."

This time it was Kalli who brought my hand up, kissing it sweetly.

"I don't think it'll come to that, but just so you know, if I'm quiet, I'm not trying to be rude."

"Just promise you'll let me help you if you need it." The last thing I wanted was for her to be uncomfortable. I loved my sister, but I'd leave her party in a second if it was causing Kalli pain being there.

"I promise."

We pulled up to our hotel at nearly midnight. Kalli couldn't stop yawning and I was trying hard to stifle them as well. I handed the valet her keys and took both our bags out of the trunk, waving off the attendant. Kalli threaded her arm through the crook of my elbow and leaned heavily against me as we walked to the front counter to check in. Just before we got there, she pulled on my arm and stopped me, turning me to face her. She was biting her bottom lip and was obviously worried about something.

"What's wrong?" Her eyes met mine, but I couldn't read what was bothering her.

"Did you reserve two rooms?"

"Yeah," I said softly. "I told you I would. Don't worry, Kalli, I'm not going to pressure you in any way. I promise."

"No," she said quickly, interrupting me. "I'm not worried about that. I just, well, I think I only want us to get one room." She said the words as though she was worried about how I would react.

"Okay," I said, drawing the word out, wanting more of an explanation from her.

"I don't want to, I mean, I don't think I'm ready to have sex with you." She pulled her arm away from me and I could tell she was getting upset.

"Kalli, whatever you need, just tell me." I placed my bag on the floor and ran my free hand up and down her arm, trying to soothe her. She eased my fears a little when her hands came to my stomach then ran up my chest.

"I just want to sleep in your arms. Is that okay?" Her eyes were full of worry, as though she were afraid to ask that of me. My hand slipped from her arm to wrap around her waist, pulling her closer to me. I pressed my lips to hers gently, for just a moment.

"I'd love nothing more than to hold you tonight."

She gave me a relieved smile and nodded. I bent to pick up my bag, then headed to the front desk to check us in to just one room.

Chapter Ten

It Never Left

Kalli

I woke up warm. I was warm and cozy and so damn comfortable. I was also in a bed with Riot Bentley. I'd been in bed with Riot Bentley before, but for a while, there was a part of me that didn't think I'd ever share a bed with him again. And I'd missed being in bed with him.

We'd fallen asleep facing each other, feet and calves tangled together, holding hands between us. I'd awoken as the little spoon with his big, comfortable, warm, fantastic-smelling body pressed up against my back. His arm was wrapped tightly around my waist, while his other arm acted as my pillow. We were still holding hands. I don't remember moving around, but I didn't stop the smile that came over my face knowing all through the night we'd been connected in some way or another.

I heard a muffled groan come from him and then his arm tightened around my waist, pulling me even closer. I tried to be still when his obvious erection pressed against my ass, not wanting to further complicate the intricate nature of our current snuggling, but he must have done himself in because as soon as he moved, *he* felt his erection up against my ass. This was a common occurrence in our months together and, quite frankly, was responsible for many *many* wonderful instances of sleepy morning sex.

He groaned again and thrust against me.

Oh. God.

I bit my bottom lip to keep from matching his sounds. It had been so long since I'd been with him and in that moment I remembered all the fantastic mornings I'd spent wrapped up in him. Before I could stop myself I arched my back, pressing my ass right into the stiffness of his cock.

The arm I was lying on rolled up, wrapping around my head, pulling my face toward the mattress, and then his lips were on my neck. His other hand disentangled from mine and was flinging the covers off our bodies, his palm spread over my thigh, grabbing and kneading. His mouth roamed over the side of my neck, nipping at my ear, breathing heavily against the already sensitive skin.

"This is like a dream," he growled against me. "Waking up, your smell all over me, hair spilling onto my pillow, ass pressing into my dick. It's like a fucking dream."

Oh. God.

His hand gripped my hip and held me still as he ground himself into me again. I totally let him. I did. I let him hold me still while he used my ass to get himself off. And I loved it. I even pressed myself into him for even more friction. There was nothing I could do to stop him or me, it was natural and we were moving instinctively.

As our bodies writhed and breaths panted, his hand moved from my hip, up over my stomach, and then slid below the cotton tank top I was wearing. I gasped as his hand smoothed over my breast, cupping it, then gently palmed it. My hand reached back and took hold of his hip, which was still thrusting against me.

I was drowning in the need to be with him. The lust and electricity between us were stifling and yet, I wanted to live in them forever. This feeling, this frantic and hazy state of being where all I could focus on was his body pressing against mine and how my body was reacting, it was enough to last me for the rest of forever. I didn't need anything else in the world as long as Riot's hands were feeding me.

Suddenly, as if something snapped inside him, I was rolled to my back and he was over me, his delicious weight pressing me down into the mattress. My hands were pinned to the pillows above my head, my body covered by his, immobilized. Then his mouth was on mine. All thoughts of lazy, sleepy sex went out the proverbial window. It was not a sleepy kiss. It was like lightning. Hot. Fast. Electric.

My legs wrapped around his waist and my hips moved up, shamelessly grinding against him, searching for the ultimate release I'd denied myself for so long. He didn't need any provocation and got right in line, pressing his hard cock right against my throbbing center, holding absolutely nothing back. We might as well have been fucking. There was no pretense here, no question about what we both wanted. I wanted him. All of him. Inside me. Around me. On top of me.

Because my hands were still very much pinned above my head, I used my feet to try to pull off his boxers, but he shifted his hips away from me. His mouth pulled away and his eyes were looking directly into mine.

He was breathing hard but managed to say, "I'm going to go take a cold shower."

My face scrunched up in confusion, and also offense. "You're *what*?"

"This isn't going to happen right now, Kalli. I shouldn't have started it. I'm sorry."

"You're sorry?" I asked, still confused. "Riot, it's okay. Please. I want this." I lifted my head and pressed my mouth over his, urging his to open, tracing his lips with my tongue. He obliged and we started kissing again, albeit more slowly this time and less frantic. His hands moved from my wrists and came to caress my face as his tongue moved lazily and leisurely through my mouth.

"I want you more than anything," he whispered after he'd finally pulled away, leaning his forehead lightly against mine. "But not this morning. Not when you asked me just to hold you." He pressed another small kiss against my lips. "I hope it's soon, Kal, because I want *us* back. I want that part of you. But we need the rest back first."

Looking into his eyes, hearing his words, I knew he was right. I knew it would be smarter to wait until I was completely sure and we'd spent more than just a few hours together. But it was hard to tell my body no.

He rolled off me and started walking toward the bathroom.

"If you want you can order us breakfast. I shouldn't be too long."

"All right," I replied, trying not to sound like a child denied her favorite candy.

I ordered us both pancakes and juice, then flopped back onto the bed, thinking about the last thirty minutes.

I'd forgotten what it felt like to have my body at the command of Riot's hands. It was as if he'd put me together, designed me. He knew my body better than I did, and was the master of finding every part of me and simply flipping a switch that sent me reeling. And just like most deities, he used his powers to give and also take away. No one, ever, had been able to send me from sleepy to frantic with such intensity as Riot. And no one ever would. Because he'd claimed me and now I was ruined for anyone else.

A while later we were in the car headed back to his parents' house. The night before had been pretty nerve-racking, but Riot's parents were fantastic people. I loved that he called his mom and dad Ma and Pops. It seemed contradictory to him in nature, but somehow also fit him perfectly. It made me feel like he was close with his parents, and that, for some reason it didn't take Freud to deduce, made me feel closer to him.

I'd been astonished by his mother's beauty, and then completely destroyed by his sister's. They were both stunningly gorgeous. Distractingly so. But then, after meeting them and realizing they were the most beautiful women I'd ever seen, I fell even more in love with them when they turned out to also be the nicest and sweetest. His dad was like a big teddy bear, his mom was the quintessential mother, and his sister was like, well, the sister I never had. For the most part, it had always felt *right* to be with Riot, but spending time with his family only made me feel like I belonged with him even more, feel as though if we were together, he'd be giving me so much more than just himself.

It had been dark the night before when we'd finally arrived at his house, and I'd been so nervous I didn't have a chance to really take in my surroundings. But now, in the light of the late morning, I was astounded by what I saw.

The house was large and white, with maroon trim and lattice up one large panel. There were planter boxes beneath the windows that matched the trim, and each of the windows on the second floor had gables above them. The detail was incredible. He parked the car right next to the detached garage, like he had last night, but there were many more cars in the circular driveway than the night before. When I opened my door I heard something I hadn't noticed last night: water.

"Do I hear waves?" I asked, turning toward him.

"Yeah, babe. I'll show you in a minute." His smile was huge and he took my hand in his, leading the way to the house. When we got close to the front door, it opened wide and we were greeted by a shorter, robust man.

"Riot! The big-time television star has decided to grace us with his presence!" The words were said with a laugh and a smile, and I knew whoever the man was, he thought highly of Riot.

"Uncle Sal, good to see you." Riot walked up to his uncle and they hugged, slapping each other's backs. When Riot stepped away, Uncle Sal's eyes fell on me.

"You're new," he said, still smiling. "We don't get many blondes around here."

"For that I'm glad. I can't compete with the beautiful brunettes." I laughed, but Sal tilted his head at me.

"I think you can hold your own, sweetheart."

Riot let out a nervous laugh at the man's forward comment, but then his hand came back to me and wrapped around my waist. "Uncle Sal, this is my girlfriend, Kalli Rivers."

"It's nice to meet you, Kalli," he said politely, reaching his hand out to me.

"Likewise," I stated.

"Sal is married to my mom's sister."

"Ah ha," I muttered. Sal took a few steps back, opening the door wider, allowing us in.

"I hope you guys are ready to get pounced on. Once the family sees you," he said, looking at Riot and placing a friendly hand on his shoulder, "they're gonna go ballistic. You're like Hollywood royalty."

I smiled at his uncle's blatant admiration. Then I blushed when Riot's hand came up and scrubbed over the stubble on the underside of his chin. That same stubble had been stinging along the sensitive skin of my neck just hours before. It was a habit of his, running his hand over his chin, but it felt more intimate than that to me. Every time he touched it, I wanted to touch it too. Wanted to feel it against my skin.

"It's just a job," he said, by way of brushing off his uncle's comments.

"Oh, really? So, you don't have to be good-looking and talented to get your job?" Riot's uncle puffed out his chest and crossed his arms over it, looking at him with skeptical eyes.

"It's really just about luck. Being at the right place at the right time, knowing the right people—stuff like that."

"You're not giving yourself enough credit," I interjected before I could think about it.

"I knew I'd like her," Sal said. Riot turned his head toward me and gave me his sweet smile.

"Let's go inside and meet everyone else." Riot took my hand and led me through the house I did not get a good enough look at the night before. It was beautiful inside, but not intimidating. It was homey. It looked as though really happy people lived there.

There were exposed beams in the ceiling, and the walls were all painted light, happy colors. We walked through the living room and all I could hear were loud voices, some speaking a language I didn't understand, and laughter. High, trilling, infectious laughter. The room was packed full—built-in bookshelves were completely filled with books, knickknacks, beautiful vases, and a few beachy touches. The whole room reminded me of an extremely high-end beach house, one you'd rent on your honeymoon, when no expense was spared.

Riot, still holding my hand, led me past a wall of windows and my eyes, were they not connected to me, would have rolled right onto the ground when I looked at the view. Chad and Mara's house sat atop a bluff on the Pacific coastline. I was looking at the most serene, peaceful, and breathtaking view I had ever seen. We were hundreds of feet above sea level, surrounded by trees and greenery, but there was a clear view of roaring waves crashing against jagged rocks.

"Oh, my God," I said, stalling in the hallway, which was also lined floor to ceiling with windows. "Riot," I whispered, unsure of what else to say. It was simply too beautiful.

"It's incredible, isn't it?"

I turned to look at him and felt my heart soften when I saw the happy look on his face, as if he were so happy to be back in his childhood home. "You grew up here?"

He nodded. "Yeah. I saw this view every day from the time I was seven years old until I moved out. I'll admit, when I was younger I totally took it for granted. But the older I get, the longer I want to stand here and look at it." He squeezed my hand gently. "I could never tire of looking at beautiful things."

I melted a little bit more.

"Okay," he said quietly, almost as if he didn't want anyone else to hear. "My family will freak out when I go into the kitchen. They're all in there, most of them from out of state, and they haven't seen me since I started showing up on their televisions. I just want to warn you, it's going to get loud and embarrassing." His eyes lit up with his smile. "And they're probably going to lay it on extra thick since you're here, too."

"I can't wait," I said with a wink. He pressed a fast and chaste kiss to my lips, then led me into the kitchen.

We were met with a loud eruption of noise. So many voices rang out with so many different greetings and exclamations. Mara was the first to embrace him, followed by the woman who was obviously her sister, as they looked nearly identical. Both could pass for women half their age, and both were drop-dead gorgeous. When more family members approached, Riot's hold on my hand grew tighter and I was embraced right along with him. His family was congratulating him on his success in Hollywood, telling him they couldn't believe how much he'd grown, and more than a few of them took a moment to size me up and make quite obvious and very vocal gestures of their approval. One or two of the women held up my left hand, looking for an engagement ring, then berated Riot, questioning him about why we weren't headed toward marriage.

Halfway through the entire introduction, I caught Halah's eye. She was standing in the back of the room watching her brother endure the third degree, and she was clearly enjoying it. Her smile was wide and she gave me a little finger wave. I smiled back and then I saw her chuckle.

After what seemed like an endless line of relatives had welcomed Riot home, we were finally released and led to the kitchen table, which was covered with food and surrounded by people talking with each other. Mara led Riot to the head of the table, forced him to sit there, then motioned for me to take the seat just to his left. Thankfully, Halah came and sat next to me.

"Isn't this supposed to be your birthday party?" I whispered to her.

She waved her hand in the air. "I have birthdays every year. It's not every day your brother becomes a big Hollywood star."

It seemed like she sincerely wasn't bothered by Riot hijacking her birthday party, and that spoke to me, showed me how she felt about her brother. "Besides," she said, her voice lower as she leaned to whisper in my ear, "the more they are distracted by my brother, the less they will harp on me for being gone for so long." She leaned away from me, smiling, then winked. I couldn't help but laugh out loud.

I listened to Riot answer many questions about his life and his job, and he was patient, answering each question with sincerity and a smile. It didn't take long for the conversation to steer toward our relationship.

"How did you and Kalli meet?" The question was asked by a woman in her fifties. I wasn't sure how she was related to Riot, but she was warm and friendly.

"Kalli was the costume designer on one of my jobs," he answered as he placed his hand on my knee under the table, giving it a gentle squeeze.

Mara's eyes went wide when she heard his answer. "You work in the business too?"

"Well," I started, smiling at her enthusiasm, "I work more behind the scenes. I just prepare costumes and manage wardrobe. That kind of thing."

"She makes clothes too," Riot offered, squeezing my leg again.

"Only when I can't find exactly what I'm looking for. And I'm actually pretty terrible at it."

"Which job did you meet on?" Halah asked, looking interested.

"The music video I did with Lexi Black."

A bunch of knowing *ah-has* and *ohs* floated through the room, and it was then I saw Halah's eyes light up with intrigue.

"Wait, didn't you go to that movie premiere with her? The tabloids said you were dating."

I tried to keep the smile on my face at the mention of the movie premiere, but I could feel it getting tight and strained. I probably looked tense and angry. I was a terrible actress.

"I never dated Lexi," Riot responded with a little bit of bite to his words. I reached below the table and gave his hand a squeeze. I didn't want him to get upset over Lexi in front of his family. And honestly, I didn't want to talk about Lexi at all. She was a part of our past, but I still remember how much it stung to see her lips on his. I did the only thing I could think of and changed the topic of conversation.

"So, Halah, do you ever get celebrities on your cruises?" Her eyes lit up at my question and she launched into stories of all the famous people she'd ever encountered, including accounts of their drunken escapades. In the middle of one of her stories Riot slowly stood up, took my hand, and urged me to follow him.

We snuck out of the room, but I noticed Mara's eyes on us, her smile widening across her face.

Riot led me to the library, a cozy little room with shelves built into the walls and benches with thick cushions for reading. He went straight for the French doors, opened one, and took us onto the deck.

If I hadn't been completely blown away by his parents' house before, the deck would have done me in. The wooden planks jutted out away from the hill the house was on and made you feel like you were floating in the sky, or in a fort high up in the treetops. It was big and sturdy. There was a built-in fire pit with surrounding chairs that looked like an amazing place to spend a chilly fall evening.

The best part, however, came when Riot walked me to the edge of the deck and took me down a long, steep, zig-zagging staircase that led all the way down to the cluster of jagged rocks where land met sea. At this particular point of the Pacific Coast, there were no beaches, no sandy shores. There were just rocks and waves.

"Wow," was all I could mutter as I made my way onto the rocks.

"I haven't been down here in forever," Riot said, his voice wistful and deep. I pulled my hand from his grasp, but only so I could wrap both my hands around his waist and lean into his side. His arm came around my shoulders and he pressed a kiss to my temple. We stood on the rocks watching the waves crash up around us for a while. I loved his family, loved meeting all the important people in his life, but just standing together and staring out at the ocean was my favorite part of the day so far.

"Hey," he said softly, causing me to lift my chin to meet his eyes. He turned, now facing me, and pulled me tightly to him. "It means a lot that you would come here and spend the weekend with my family."

"They're great. I've loved meeting them."

His eyes darted back and forth between mine for a moment, but then he spoke again. "I've never even been inclined to bring someone home, Kalli. I've never wanted my family to get to know someone I was dating. The thought never even crossed my mind. And then I met you, and you're here, and you're perfect, and they love you, and…." His voice trailed off and he looked flustered. I leaned up on my tiptoes and caught his lips with mine, hoping my kiss could convey exactly what I was feeling.

"I love you, Kalli," Riot whispered, pulling his lips away from mine. "I never stopped. It never went away. It never will." He wrapped his arms around my shoulders and pulled me closer to him. I rested my cheek against his chest and let his words wash over me. After everything I had put him through, after every time I had pushed him away, he'd always been right there waiting for me. It was hard for me, in the past, to imagine a man would want me, even just for a little while, let alone forever. Every single man in my life had left—in one way or another. But I knew, and had known for a while, Riot was unlike any man I'd ever met.

"I love you too," I said against his broad chest, squeezing him with my arms. I felt his chest seize at my words, his breathing stop, his heart race. I pulled away slightly to look up at him. His mouth was partly open and he looked sincerely shocked. Apparently he wasn't expecting me to say the words back to him. That made me love him even more. I reached up, cupped his beautiful face, and pulled his mouth down to mine. I melted into him, his hand tangling in the hair at my nape, his other arm wrapping around my waist.

His tongue swept inside my mouth and tasted me. It was primal, the way he seemed to devour me. With just lips and tongue I was left to his mercy, wishing to feel his need for me always. I wanted to give him everything and feel like I was getting everything from him in return. It was new, this feeling of being 100 percent sure, but I was. And every time his lips caressed mine, it only solidified that I was making the right choice.

"You don't know how happy you make me," he said as he pressed his mouth to my neck, breathing me in.

"I could say the same thing to you," I replied, my voice raspy and shaking, emotion making every part of me tremble.

"There's nothing in the world, from this moment on, that's going to keep me from you, Kal. Understand that. I get why you needed time, why you needed space, but I'm done giving it to you."

I felt the sting of tears as they started to well in my eyes. I knew Marcus would want this for me, would want me to be happy with Riot. But sometimes, it hurt to be happy, to feel joy, knowing he wasn't here to experience life at all.

"Babe," he said, pulling me closer, wrapping his arms around my shoulders. "Marcus is up there, running around, and he's happy. He's free up there, Kal. You'll see him again someday, and he'll run to you with open arms, just like he used to, and he'll be so glad you didn't spend your whole life sad for him."

"I know," I said, my words muffled against his chest.

"Hey." He pulled away and placed a finger just below my chin, pulling my face up to meet his eyes. "I don't mean you can't be sad anymore. I just want to make sure you know that you can be sad *with me*. If you're missing him, tell me a story about him." He pushed some of my hair behind my ear and then his fingers trailed down my neck until he was holding me around my nape, firmly gripping me, squeezing gently. "I want you to lean on me, let me in. I'll always listen."

"I love you," I whispered. He didn't answer me, just leaned down and pressed his lips to mine in a soft, lingering kiss.

Chapter Eleven

I'm Asking to Come Home

Riot

The rest of the day passed uneventfully. I never let Kalli out of my sight, always keeping a hand on her in some way or another. The words we'd exchanged on the rocks by the ocean were real to me; they meant something. I could tell they meant a lot to her as well, but I wasn't ready to let her go yet, wasn't ready to be away from her where I couldn't read her face, or see in her eyes how she was feeling. I suppose a part of me was afraid if I wasn't there to remind her of how much I loved her and wanted to support her, she'd disappear on me again. Maybe not physically, but emotionally. And that would be just as devastating.

After the sun had set and a lot of the family had left for the evening, Halah, Ma, Pops, Kalli, and I were sitting on the deck around the fire pit. My aunt and uncle had turned in for the evening.

"Did you have a good birthday, sis?" A smile spread across Halah's face, but her eyes never left the fire.

"Yeah, I did."

"It was good to finally have you home," Ma said. "You don't come home often enough."

I watched as Halah resisted the urge to roll her eyes at our mother. I could see both of their points. Ma missed Halah. Halah wanted to be independent. It was every mother-daughter relationship I'd ever witnessed.

Ma must have picked up on the tension and didn't want to upset Halah any more than she already had. "Kalli, would you like to go inside with me and look at some baby pictures of Riot?"

Kalli's eyes lit up like my mother had offered her a diamond-encrusted tiara. "That would be incredible."

My mother gave a small clap and then stood up and walked toward the house. Kalli stood too, but before she made it too far, I tugged on her hand and pulled her toward me, then tugged again, bringing her face down to mine.

"Don't be gone too long," I said, just before I captured her mouth with mine.

"Okay," she breathed. I was satisfied I'd made her breath falter, so I let her go, watching her disappear into the house with my mother.

"I'm going to make sure the front of the house is all closed down. You never know which windows and doors have come unlocked with all our crazy family members visiting," Pops announced as he stood and headed for the house.

We were alone for just a moment before Halah broke the silence.

"So spill, Riot. Is it serious with her?"

Halah had never been one to beat around the bush, so I wasn't really surprised by her question.

"I don't ever plan on being with anyone else."

Halah was quiet for a moment, but then her eyes met mine over the fire. "Good. I like her."

It had never occurred to me that one of my family members might not like Kalli; there was absolutely nothing to dislike about her as far as I was concerned. So I wasn't expecting the wave of relief that washed over me when my baby sister gave her approval.

"What about you? Why haven't you been home in so long? Ma and Pops worry about you."

She shrugged. "It's a different life out there, Ri. Your boat docks in the most amazing places and when you get some time off you have to choose between going home or, I don't know, spending a week in Italy. I'm never going to be young and carefree again. I was just trying to take advantage of the perks of the job."

"What do you mean you're never going to be young or carefree again? Halah, you're just twenty-five. You've got plenty of time to figure life out."

"I've got thirty more weeks to figure life out."

Her tone was despondent and she was suddenly morose. "What happens in thirty weeks?"

"Never mind, Riot. It's not important."

"Of course it's important. You brought it up, now explain it."

"Really, big brother, it's nothing." She gave me the weakest smile I'd ever seen grace her face, but I could tell she really didn't want to talk about it.

"Okay, well, I'm here if you ever need to talk. When do you have to be back to work?"

"I have a lot of vacation time saved up, so I'm not sure yet."

"Kal and I are going to go down to the pier tomorrow before we head back to LA. Want to come with us?"

Finally, a genuine smile crossed her face when she said, "That sounds like fun."

"I'm gonna head inside and make sure Ma isn't embarrassing me."

"I can guarantee Ma is embarrassing you," she said with a laugh.

"Well, I'm heading in to do damage control then. You coming?"

"Nah, I'm gonna sit out here and stare at the fire for a while still."

"Okay, sis." I stood up and walked toward the door, but turned before I went in. "Halah?"

"Yeah?"

"I can tell you're going through something, but I just want you to know that you can count on me. If you ever need anything…." I trailed off because I wasn't sure how to put into words how much my little sister's welfare meant to me. I wanted her to be happy, and if I could help in any way, I wanted her to let me.

"You're a good big brother," she said softly. "If I need anything, I'll let you know."

I nodded. There wasn't much else to do. I couldn't hold her down like I had when we were kids and force her to tell me by threatening to spit on her. We were adults. She had to deal with her own issues and I had to hope she'd let me in if there was something I could do to help. Being an adult really sucked sometimes. I gave her one last smile and then opened the door to head back into the house.

I found Ma and Kalli sitting at the kitchen table, a giant photo album open between them. Ma was pointing out pictures of me when I was younger, and I could visualize the picture by just her description.

"And this is when Riot won first place in his youth bowling tournament." I groaned. I'd been nine years old, I was wearing tube socks, and I had braces. It was, quite nearly, the worst photo she could have showed her.

Kalli saw me walk in and her eyes turned to me. They were sparkling with amusement.

"You were a bowler?" She could hardly make it through the question without choking on laughter.

"I was nine. Bowling is cool when you're nine."

Smart as always, she didn't say anything in response, just smiled wider and returned her gaze to the album.

"This is when he came in third for the county spelling bee."

"I see you were still a fan of the tube socks during the spelling bee years." The giddiness in Kalli's voice was almost cute enough that I didn't care she was making fun of me.

"Perhaps we should look at some photos of you when you were nine years old and see how fashion forward you were."

Kalli didn't raise her eyes from the photo album when she muttered, "My mom worked two jobs when I was nine and I let myself in the house after school with a key that hung around my neck. There are probably only a few pictures of me when I was nine."

"Babe," I said, mentally punching myself in the face for shoving my foot in my mouth.

"You must have been really brave to stay alone every day after school by yourself," Ma said, coming to my rescue.

Kalli just shrugged. "I did get really good at cooking in the years between my dad leaving and my mom remarrying. I tried to make my mom dinner every night so she wouldn't have to when she came home."

"Well, I'm sure Riot could benefit from some cooking lessons. Getting him to cook anything when he was younger was like pulling teeth. I think he burned things on purpose so I'd stop asking."

"No, Ma, I'm just that bad at it." I was hoping my attempt at humor would make a smile appear on Kal's face.

"I'd be happy to teach him a thing or two," she finally said, her eyes meeting mine, a small, shy smile on her face. I wanted to walk to her, take her chin in my hand and apologize, then kiss her. But I knew she wouldn't appreciate that with my mom right next to her. So I settled for mouthing, "Sorry," at her, and let out a sigh of relief when she winked back at me.

An hour later we were back at the hotel. Kalli had been quiet on the ride there, and even though I wanted to know what was running through her mind, I settled for keeping my hand on her thigh and letting my thumb trail light circles there. I held her hand the entire way up to our room and she was still silent.

"Are you all right?" I finally asked as she walked to her side of the bed and flipped on her lamp. "You've been really quiet."

A weak smile crossed her face as she shrugged off her jacket, laying it over the chair next to the bed. "Just thinking a lot."

I sat down at the foot of the bed as she walked toward me. "Care to tell me what's going on in there?" She stopped just in front of me and leaned down, pressing a small kiss against my lips. It was fast and sweet.

"I think I'm going to change into my pajamas real quick. I'll be right back." I watched as she rummaged through the small closet that held our bags, then disappeared into the bathroom with a bundle of clothes in her arms.

I let out a loud breath, scrubbing my hands up and down my face. I knew Kalli's home life hadn't been great growing up; she'd told me all about her dad leaving, on her birthday no less, and how her mom had to do the job of two parents. If I could have taken back my stupid comment, I would. I felt like a complete jackass for even bringing it up.

I stripped my clothes off and pulled on a pair of flannel lounge pants, then lay down on the bed, waiting for Kalli to come out. I listened as the water ran, imagining her brushing her teeth and doing all the other routine things women did to ready themselves for bed. A few minutes later the door opened.

All I could see was the outline of her body, her hair piled on top of her head, a large t-shirt hanging from one shoulder. She took a step into the bedroom and flipped off the bathroom light, allowing my eyes to adjust and see all of her. My chest tightened when I realized she was wearing one of my t-shirts, one shoulder peeking out of the neck as it draped over her body. My eyes traveled downward, taking her in.

The tightness in my chest eased a little, but the sight of her did all sorts of things to my body. My hands ached to touch her, my eyes roamed her body, wanting to see all of her, and my dick began to swell, filling with need. My eyes made their way down her body and my breath halted when they landed on her calves.

Fuck.

My girl was standing at the foot of the bed in my t-shirt and a pair of tube socks.

"Christ, Kalli," I groaned. A flirty smile played on her lips and I watched, trying to remain calm and not simply devour her, as she climbed onto the bed and began to seductively crawl toward me.

"I brought the tube socks because I was worried my feet would get cold. But now I think they're keeping you warmer than me." Her hands and knees straddled my legs, and damn if my eyes didn't peek down the neck of her shirt, taking in the sway of her naked breasts beneath the fabric.

When she sat up, she was straddling my hips, my erection fitting snugly between her legs. I knew she had to feel it, I was raging with need, but all she did was continue to smile. My hands automatically came to her bare thighs, squeezing them and pulling down, forcing her body to press against my dick more firmly.

"I wanted to talk to you," I growled, my hands itching to roam, to feel all of her.

"No, you want to apologize, but it's unnecessary. My childhood sucked a little. It's not your problem or your fault. I shouldn't have said what I did. I wasn't trying to make you feel bad." Her hands came to rest on my lower stomach, just above the waistband of my lounge pants. Her hands started slowly sliding up my abs and her eyes followed her fingertips. "All I want, for the rest of the night, is for us both to feel good."

Her hands slid all the way up to my shoulders and she bent down to lean against me. Her breasts pressed against my chest and I wanted to rip the shirt from her body and feel her flesh against mine. My hands slid to the back of her thighs and then up to round over her perfect ass, pressing her against my cock with even more pressure. I slid my fingers under the edge of her panties, gripping her ass and feeling her there. She let out a soft gasp and my dick hardened even more.

She sat up, gripping the bottom of her shirt, and slowly pulled it over her head, the smile never leaving her face. My hands found her waist, but then slid up, watching as goose bumps formed along her skin, until my hands covered her perfect breasts. I palmed her, but it wasn't enough, not even close. I knifed up, quickly wrapping one arm around her waist to keep her center right where I wanted it: against my cock. Then I scooted backward on the bed until I came to rest against the headboard.

"I want nothing more than to sink into you right now," I said, one hand coming to grip the back of her neck, pulling her face to just within a hair's breadth of mine. "Every part of me is throbbing, aching to be inside of you, to feel you all around me. But I want you to know, it's not the sex, Kal. I'm not just asking for sex. I'm asking to come home. You're home to me. All of you. I want back in to the place where I belong, the place I want to be forever." I pressed a kiss just above her left breast and felt her breath tremble with my touch. "I want back in here, baby." I continued to lave kisses just where her heart was pounding through her skin.

"You've been there all along," she whispered, her words laced with a combination of pleasure and pain. "Please," she begged. "Make love to me."

That was all the invitation I needed.

I brought my lips to her breast, sucking her nipple into my mouth, taking her deep. She mewled and I knew her nerves were just as frayed as mine. Like me, she was balancing between needing the buildup and release, and wanting the connection. It would be easy enough to bring her to orgasm so quickly her head would spin, but I wanted more than that, more than just coming for the sake of coming. I wanted to make love to her, reconnect with her, for hours. I wanted to make up for all the time we'd already spent apart.

I released her nipple, but cupped her breast, kneading and rolling her nipple between my fingers. My mouth found hers and our lips met, gaping wide, tongues searching for each other. My free hand slid low and pulled open the elastic at the top of her panties, sliding past it, feeling the heat of her as I crept closer.

When my fingers finally found her, I groaned at her wetness. There was something so carnally arousing knowing that her body was responding to mine, that the way I was touching her body was turning her on, soaking her.

I wasted no time. I wanted to feel her wrapped around me. I slowly pushed a finger inside her, easing my way in, loving the softness of her. She moaned and as I swallowed her noises, she pushed her hips forward, grinding down on my hand. That simple movement, her body asking for more, snapped something in me.

I moved quickly and rolled her underneath me, then used my hands to remove her panties, leaving the tube socks where they were, stretched over her long, slender legs. I stood at the edge of the bed, pushed my own pants to the floor, then gripped her ankles and tugged her toward me. Her eyes were wide as she watched me kneel before her, and I held her gaze as I lowered and brought my tongue to run over her center. One long lick and her eyes closed, back arched, and breath panted.

She tasted fucking amazing, just like I remembered. Just like I'd thought about every night since we'd been apart. I wanted to tell her how much I'd missed her, how much I loved every single fucking part of her, but I couldn't stop.

Her fingers slid through my hair, gripping me there, holding me to her. The more she participated—grinding against me, holding my mouth right where she wanted it— the more enthusiastic I became. I sucked and licked, slowly moving my fingers in and out of her, coaxing a slow yet frantic climax from her.

With every exhale, she moaned, gradually increasing in volume, until finally she erupted. Her thighs clamped around my head, her heat gripped my fingers still inside her, and she tugged on my hair, all while crying out incoherently. It was so fucking beautiful, feeling her come, hearing her pleasure, knowing it came from me, that I gave it to her.

After a few moments she relaxed, went limp, panting. I moved over her, slowly crawling up her body, placing light kisses on her damp skin, loving every part of her, until I was back at her mouth. She leaned up and kissed me. It was a slow and lazy kiss, as though she were drunk from her orgasm. Her hands started at my shoulders, then slid down my arms, moving to my waist and coming up my back. Her legs parted, one wrapping around my waist, and she pulled her mouth from mine.

"I haven't been with anyone. Not since you." Her eyes were searching mine, looking for an answer. I knew what she wanted and God, I wanted it too.

"Do you trust me?"

"I trust you and I love you. I want to feel all of you."

Her words were like slow-moving lava, burning and scorching through me. I'd never be the same after this.

Our eyes stayed trained on each other's as her hand reached between us, wrapping around my cock and lining me up with her. I watched her face as I slowly pushed into her, and not even the memory of making love to her could have compared to what I saw before me.

Her mouth parted, her eyes drifted closed, and her head tilted back. Everything about her told me she was feeling everything I was. I pushed into her until I was buried to the hilt, until there was no more space between us, and I pressed my face in her neck.

"It's so good, Riot," she whispered.

"I know," I whispered back. Her head started shaking against mine and I pulled away to look at her.

"No," she said, her voice raspy and shallow. "It's too good. You. Here with me. I don't think I deserve it, but I'm never going to let it go again. You're too good." She let out a small cry but I silenced it with my mouth, my hands cradling her face. I pulled out just to push back in slowly, and her hands gripped me around my waist, her legs coming to wrap around my ass.

"You're mine," I said, my lips brushing against hers with my words. "What we have is perfect and it's just as much yours as it is mine."

I continued to thrust into her, watching as her sadness melted away, only to be replaced with pleasure again. When I was sure she was wrapped up in the way our bodies were responding to each other's, I pushed up to my hands and started thrusting with more force. I couldn't help the grin that came over my face when her eyes disappeared again. I knew she was feeling me in the best possible way.

I moved quicker, thrusting faster, watching as she slowly started to lose herself to sensation again. I gripped her hip, pulling her ass off the bed and driving into her at just the right angle to set her off again.

"Oh, my God," she cried, and I couldn't help the cocky grin that crossed my face. I stilled as I felt her pulse around me, watching as she came back down from her high. She opened her eyes and gave me a lazy grin as her hands wandered up my abs, wrapped around my neck, and pulled my face down to hers. As we kissed, her hands roamed over my slick skin and I knew she was feeling loose and pliant. Sated. "What do you want?" she asked me, her voice drowsy.

"I have everything I want. I just want you."

She smiled wider, her eyes glistening with what I could only describe as satisfaction. "Okay, well, you have me. How do you *want* me?"

I stilled at her words, but I could still feel the wave of heat run through me. I'd spent nearly every night imagining what it would be like to have Kalli back in my bed, wrapped around me. I'd pictured her in every position imaginable. Some were memories and some were hopeful, yet painful, wishes.

I quickly pulled out of her, gripped her hips, and flipped her over. Like the fucking angel she was, she knew exactly where I was headed, and got up on all fours, her gorgeous ass angled up at me.

"Fuck, yes," I growled. My hands came up to run over the round globes of her ass, and she fucking wiggled it at me. "Don't tease me, Kal."

She laughed, then said, "I'm not teasing. I'm offering."

My fingers dug in to her skin as I tried to keep myself in check. Then, with more force than I intended, I pulled her hips toward me, watching as her arms sprawled out on the bed, and I dove into her. The depth available at that angle was maddening, I grunted as I slid all the way in, and loved hearing her lust-filled yelp. She was wet and tight and made for me.

"God fucking damn it, Kal. You're so fucking perfect." Her forehead was pressed against the mattress, her fingers gripping the sheets, knuckles turning white, and I was driving into her as though I wanted to die doing it. My heart was pounding, breaths shallow and not taking in nearly enough air, and all that was fine because I was either going to come so fucking hard I collapsed, or I was going to die doing the one thing I never thought I'd be able to do again. Either way, I was okay with it. I was always hopeful she'd find her way back to me, but it was never a guarantee, never a sure bet. As my cock moved inside her, as she stretched to accommodate all of me, I was just thankful to have my hands on her again.

I felt the slight tingling start at the base of my spine, the warmth creeping over me, and I knew I was close. I didn't want to be finished, but I couldn't stop it once it started. Instead, I reached around her and found her clit, rubbing it with my finger.

"Come with me," I grunted.

"Oh, Jesus," she cried. "I can't, Riot. It's too soon."

"Fucking come with me," I growled.

I worked her body from both angles and within a minute we were both spiraling into bliss. I collapsed after the last wave of my orgasm rolled through me, but managed to fall to her side, not wanting to crush her. When I slipped out of her, I felt the loss as if a piece of me was missing. She wasted no time flipping over and rolling into me, and we caught our breaths together, my arms wrapped around her, her tube-sock-clad legs wound between mine.

We were both sweaty hot messes, but I kept her close, wanting to feel her breaths slow and heart rate even out. I wanted to experience it all with her in my arms.

"That was intense," she finally said, when her body was back to normal.

"That was… not how I intended our reunion to go," I said with a small laugh I couldn't contain.

Her head tilted back and her eyes found mine. "It was perfect."

I pushed the hair, which had come out of her high knot, away from her face, her blue eyes sparkling at me as I said, "You were perfect." She reached up and touched her palm to my cheek.

"I love you," she whispered. All I could do in response was lean down and press my lips to hers. Words failed me. There were no words to describe the gift she'd given me, or how grateful I was to just have her in my arms. So I didn't say anything. I just kissed her.

Chapter Twelve

Unlimited Pass

Kalli

The next morning was a glorious repeat of the morning before, only the slow and sleepy sex wasn't off the table. It was, in fact, very much on. I'd woken up to Riot's fingers slowly moving inside me and everything after that was a hazy, sweaty, awesome blur. That awesomeness was followed by sweet, slow, earth-shattering sex in the shower.

There was a large part of me that wanted to stay in that hotel room forever, reuniting with Riot, showing him exactly how glad I was that we'd started to work through everything, but I knew I'd never survive. Death by sex, although it sounded appealing, was a very real threat and we both needed to get some fresh air.

Halah had agreed to meet us at Pier 39, and as we approached her, hand in hand, I was hit with another wave of envy at her natural beauty. Her long dark hair was billowing in the cold November breeze, and her stylish jacket was tucked in close to her perfectly toned and fit body.

"I swear, your mom and sister are two of the most beautiful women I've ever seen," I said quietly to him as we crossed the street to meet her.

"I guess I'm pretty lucky to have the three prettiest girls, then, huh?" he said, giving my hand a squeeze.

I smiled at his sweet words. "Your dad probably wanted to kill every guy at your high school, huh?"

"Pops ate tums like they were candy when Halah started high school," he said with a laugh. "He also made it very clear that I had a brotherly duty to protect her innocence. I took that job extremely seriously, until Halah informed me over dinner one night that her innocence wasn't mine to protect, that her beauty didn't define her worth, and that she wasn't interested in dating high school boys because they couldn't see all she had to offer."

"Wow," I said, trying to imagine having that much self-awareness at that age.

"Ma pretty much told her since she was young to put more value on intelligence than beauty. That night Pops kind of realized my sister didn't need anyone looking out for her. But I still did anyhow, just not as obviously as I had before."

"I think your mom has to be one of the coolest people I've ever met."

"She has some pretty incredible stories about growing up in Lebanon, then all her travels when she was younger. I'm sure she'd love to tell you all about it."

"I'd really like that," I said, feeling a warmth spread through me thinking about how Mara and I would have time to talk and tell stories in the future because Riot and I *had a future*.

We walked up to Halah, who was leaning against a railing, looking out at the choppy water, and when she heard us approach she turned to us, smiling. I didn't miss the way her eyes dropped to our joined hands, or the way her smile grew wider when she saw them.

"You been waiting long, sis?"

"Not too long, but I'm starving and freezing, so maybe we could find a place to eat."

"I'm starved too," I added, liking her plan.

"We skipped breakfast." Riot's voice was suggestive and boastful. I couldn't help but pull back and slap his arm.

"Don't be rude," I said through laughter.

"Well, I ate before I left, but I'm hungry again. Let's go."

I was glad Halah didn't seem to mind Riot's joke, but couldn't stop the blush from creeping over my face. I let the two of them lead the way, obviously familiar with the popular San Francisco tourist spot. Within a few minutes we were seated in a restaurant that had a magnificent view of the water.

Our waitress had taken our order and brought us water and bread, but my eyes were glued to the bay outside the window.

"Are those sea lions?" I asked, pointing toward a bunch of floating docks.

"Yeah," Riot said. "They came after there was some earthquake somewhere," he said, waving his hand in the air. "Every winter more and more show up."

"There must be hundreds of them," I whispered, my eyes straining to see them individually.

"I'll be right back," Halah said, standing up quickly and making her way through the restaurant. She'd been pretty quiet since we sat down and had only been picking at a piece of bread.

"Do you think she's feeling all right?"

He shrugged. "Hard to tell. She's been acting kind of strange all weekend."

My eyes wandered back to the sea lions. "When we're done eating, can we go look at them? Like, get closer?"

"Sure, baby," he said, kissing my cheek. "I can't believe you've never been here." He took another bite of his bread, then continued. "Marcus would have gotten a kick out of this place."

He said the words with such ease, as though saying his name caused him no pain at all, and that made my breath halt. My chest tightened and my lungs froze. I wanted so badly to be at a place in my mourning where I could mention his name in passing, think about him and smile, but when Riot said his name, the first thing I did was panic.

Marcus *would* have loved this place, would have loved looking at the sea lions and riding the carousel we walked past on our way to the restaurant. They were all things he'd never be able to do. The weight of grief came to rest on my shoulders, holding me down, pressing me farther into that dark spiral I'd been trying to avoid.

"Hey," Riot said, his hands coming to cup my face, forcing me to look at him. "Hey, hey, hey," his words were coming faster, his eyes moving over my face frantically. "What's happening, Kal?"

I took in a deep shuddering breath, but couldn't say anything. I just felt the pain in my lungs, the pinching in my throat, and the tears welling in my eyes.

"Babe, you need to breathe." He'd started to sound panicked. His face became a little blurry, but I managed to take in another breath and tried to blink away the haze. "Good. Now breathe out slowly, Kal."

My heart was pounding, hands were shaking, but I managed to wrap my fingers around his wrists while his hands were still holding my face close to his. It took a few minutes of Riot telling me to breathe and listening to him count to ten before my body seemed to calm down.

Halfway through the ordeal Halah returned to her seat and I heard her concerned voice whisper to Riot about calling someone or getting help, but he assured her I was getting better and just needed to calm down. In the back of my mind I was mortified that she was seeing me that way, but there was nothing I could do to keep the panic away besides breathe through it. So that's what I did.

Finally, when I felt like the vise had loosened in my chest, I let out a deep breath and leaned against him. I was shaky, clammy, and exhausted.

"Is she all right?" Halah asked, obviously worried.

"I'll be okay," I managed, even though my words were rough and low. Riot held me for a minute more before I felt strong enough to sit up on my own. I pulled away from him and reached for my water glass, suddenly thirstier than anything.

"Wow," I finally said, my eyes darting between Riot and Halah. Riot was studying me fiercely, looking as though he was ready to take me away at the drop of a hat to protect me, even though he couldn't protect me from my own mind. Halah just looked worried and curious. "I'm really sorry. That's never happened around other people before."

"It's happened before?" Riot asked, his previously soothing voice now laced with a touch of anger.

"A few times," I answered meekly.

Halah reached over and rubbed her hand over mine. "Do you want to talk about it?"

I gave her a weak smile. "There's not much to talk about. My brother died a few months ago and sometimes it's just hard to deal with." My eyes turned to Riot. "I don't usually spend a lot of time with people who say his name. It must have triggered something."

"What was his name?" she asked before Riot could apologize. I could see in his eyes that was all he wanted to do. But I shifted my gaze back to Halah.

"Marcus," I whispered. Then I cleared my throat and said a little louder, "His name was Marcus."

She gave me her beautiful smile, patted my hand one last time, then leaned back in her chair. "That's an awesome name. How old was he?"

I swallowed and took in a deep breath. "He was seventeen."

"Sounds like he was an incredible brother, and so lucky to have a sister like you." She smiled again. "Speaking of amazing brothers," she said, turning to look at Riot. "Thank you for taking the third degree from everyone last night. They were so focused on your rising stardom, they forgot all about the fact that I'm single and leading the life of a goalless vagabond."

He leaned away from me at her words, but still left his arm draped around me, his large hand gripping my shoulder. I appreciated his touch, needed him to keep me grounded, even if we were all going to pretend I didn't just have a panic attack over lunch. I reached for my glass again and took another sip of my water.

"You're not a goalless vagabond," he replied, exasperated. "They wouldn't be so curious about your life if you called and talked to them once in a while. Honestly, what do you expect them to do besides use their imaginations and create the worst scenarios in their heads?"

"That's not as easy as it sounds. We don't always have cell service."

"So when people board your ship, and when you drop them off, it's in the middle of nowhere? It's not at some major port?" He asked the question with obvious sarcasm, his voice dripping with it.

Halah shrugged. "Being in port is my time to relax. I don't really want to explain my messy love life to my parents if I have time to explore a new country."

"Is your love life messy, Hal?" Riot's eyebrow rose and even I could sense his big-brother hackles going up.

"No," she cried, clearly exasperated as she brought her hands to her face, resting her elbows against the table.

"Do you call your parents as much as you should?" I asked Riot, not even sure where the question came from, really. It just came out. He quickly turned his head to look at me, confusion painted over his face. "I mean," I said, trying to find a way to defend Halah without making Riot feel like I was ganging up on him. "It's different for girls in our twenties. There's a lot more pressure to get married and have babies, to find Mr. Right. But for guys, no one really cares. Like, no one looks at a thirty-year-old single guy and wonders what's wrong with him, but if a girl is single at thirty, she's a spinster."

"Thank you," Halah said, slapping her hand on the table in a show of sisterly solidarity.

"What does that have to do with calling our parents?"

"When Halah calls she probably gets a lot more crap from them about being single than you ever did." I brought a piece of bread to my mouth, took a bite, and then let my eyes bounce between the brother and sister as if I were watching a tennis match.

Riot's eyes moved to his sister and he was silent for a moment. "Is that true? Do they bug you about being single?"

She shrugged. "Sometimes, yeah."

"You know Ma and Pops just want you to be happy. And they worry about you, because you're always in a different country. It bothers them that they don't always know for sure that you're okay."

"I know," she said meekly. "There's just been a lot of stuff going on lately, and I haven't wanted to talk much. And Mom always knows when something's wrong."

"Is something wrong?" he asked, his voice sounding panicky now. I reached my hand over to his thigh and tried to calm him with my touch.

"No," she said, shaking her head. He exhaled loudly, running the back of his hand under his chin, but I kept my eyes on Halah. Something about her tone of voice, the way she let her eyes drift to the tabletop instead of looking at Riot, made me feel as though she wasn't being truthful. Her eyes crept up to meet mine and I knew from the way she looked at me she was begging me to let it go. She didn't want to talk about whatever was bothering her with her brother.

"Listen, there's no rush to get married. Ma and Pops just want to hear from you. They worry. I'll tell them to give it a rest about the boyfriend stuff."

"You don't have to do that, Ri."

"Hal, I got it," he said firmly, and damn if I didn't feel the heat spreading through my core at his firm, protective, older-brother tone. "You promise me you'll call them more often, and I'll make sure they back off the boyfriend talk."

"Okay," she said, giving him a weak smile.

Just then, the waitress brought our lunches and we all fell into polite conversation as we ate.

After lunch, Halah excused herself to the bathroom again, this time looking as though she wasn't feeling well, but I didn't mention it. Instead, I turned to Riot.

"You're pretty sexy when you're trying to protect your little sister."

He smirked at me. "Oh, yeah?"

"No, really. The way you tried to solve her problem for her, come to her rescue, not taking no for an answer — that's class A alpha hotness." I leaned toward him, putting my lips close to his, but just far enough away to speak. "I kind of like you bossy."

He reached one hand up, caressing the side of my face, as he leaned in and pressed a soft kiss against my lips. It was the opposite of bossy, but still made my blood run hot. When he pulled away he was looking in my eyes.

"Maybe I'll use my newfound powers of seduction to get you to open up to me about your panic attack." His words were halfway playful, but I knew he meant them. I'd known he was going to want to talk about it, I was just hoping I would have a little break between nervous breakdown and discussion of said breakdown.

Before I had a chance to respond, Halah returned, clearing her throat.

"Sorry to interrupt," she said with a smile.

"Liar," Riot said, a beautiful grin appearing on his face.

"Shall we go take a look at the sea lions?" she asked.

"Sure thing," he responded. Thus ensued a five-minute argument on whether or not Riot was going to let his sister buy her own meal, and it ended with Riot using his authoritative voice again. I almost slapped him when he winked at me. It was wrong, what just his voice could do to my body, but entirely sexy also.

"I came here for a field trip in the third grade," Halah said as we slowly made our way down the pier to where the sea lions were all floating on docks. "Josh McMillian took my favorite bow out of my hair and threw it in the water."

"Josh McMillian?" Riot asked. "He was such a douche bag. Kid never learned not to pick on girls. In high school I shoved him in a locker about a million times because he was always talking shit about you to his buddies."

"Newsflash, Riot: not all guys were raised to treat women like queens." Halah's voice was firm, yet quiet. My instinct, that gut feeling you get when your best girlfriend is going through something major, kicked in and I wanted nothing more than to grab her, take her for a coffee, and convince her to confide in me.

"I can't believe how many there are," I said, stopping at the railing. There were hundreds of sea lions, all sitting atop their docks, barking at each other.

"There will be more in a few weeks. They come here for the winter, I guess. During the summer they go someplace else." Riot draped his arm over my shoulders as he said the words and I couldn't help but lean into him and snuggle. The wind was biting at me and the November chill on the bay was making it difficult to stay warm. Being pressed up against his body helped.

I stood there, fascinated by the animals, enjoying watching them sleep or fight, which they were all doing a lot of, but not much else. Suddenly, Halah's voice rang out and she sounded panicked.

"I have to go. I'm sorry, you guys. It reeks here and I think I'm going to be sick." She covered her nose and mouth and started jogging down the pier.

I gave Riot a confused look, and he looked equally worried, so we started after her. We followed her all the way to her car and when she reached it she stopped, leaned one hand against the trunk, and bent over, taking in deep breaths and forcing them out again.

"Are you okay?" I asked as we approached. I gently laid a hand on her back, softly moving it back and forth, giving Riot more worried looks.

"Hals, let us drive you home."

"It'll pass," she said weakly. We stood and watched as she took in countless deep breaths and then pushed them all out, slowly and evenly. When she finally stood up and turned to us, her face was covered with a sheen of sweat and she looked slightly green.

"Are you sick?" Riot asked.

Halah ran the back of her hand over her forehead and said quietly, "I'll be okay."

"Let us drive you home," he insisted.

"I'm fine, Riot. I'm just going to go back to the house and go to bed." She took a step toward him and gave him a halfhearted hug, then gave me the same.

"Will you at least text me to let me know you got home all right?" I could tell by the strain in his voice that he was not okay with the current plan of just letting her go.

"Sure," she agreed. She gave us a tiny wave as she drove away.

"I'm worried about her," he said as he watched her car turn down a street and disappear.

I clasped his hand in mine. "She'll be all right." I didn't know how long it would take for Riot to figure out what was wrong with her, but I had my suspicions. I looked up at him, trying to give him a smile. "Can we do one more thing before we head back to LA?"

"Anything," he said sincerely, his fingers coming up to touch my chin lightly.

I led him back to the pier, and we walked slowly toward the one thing I knew Marcus would have loved the most: the carousel. "I just want to ride it once." I felt a little silly asking my grown-up boyfriend to ride a carousel, but I knew if Marcus were there, he'd want to ride it as many times as I would let him. It would be nice, for once, to do something that reminded me of him and to smile while doing it. For months I'd been crying over his loss, but today, I felt as though I should let myself enjoy something he would have. Perhaps that would make me feel closer to him somehow.

"Baby," Riot said softly, tilting my face to look up at him. "We can ride it as many times as you want. Whatever is going to make you happy, that's what we'll do."

"Okay," I whispered, smiling up at him, getting lost in his gorgeous brown eyes.

Riot led me to the attendant, a teenage boy of maybe sixteen. He looked wide-eyed at Riot, obviously recognizing him, and then looked at me. His eyes started at my face, but then I saw them dart to my chest, and I couldn't help but stifle a laugh. This kid was the epitome of every awkward high school boy.

"Hey, man," Riot said, as if he and the kid were the best of friends. "My girlfriend and I want to ride the carousel, but I was hoping we could just stay on until she's ready to get off. Will this cover an unlimited pass?" Riot held out his hand and offered the kid a hundred-dollar bill. His eyes went even wider as he reached for the bill.

"Sure. No problem." The kid unhooked the chain that blocked off the entrance and let us through.

"You didn't have to pay him that much money. One ride is enough."

"We'll see," he said, squeezing my hand.

I stepped up onto the platform and wandered through the evenly spaced horses. I found one with a blue saddle and knew that was the one Marcus would have chosen. I put one foot in the stirrup and Riot's hands came to my waist, acting as if I needed help mounting my horse, but I knew he really just wanted an excuse to put his hands on me. After I was safely atop, he climbed onto the horse right next to me. It took a few minutes for everyone who was riding to find their horse, but after a few minutes the carousel started to turn.

I closed my eyes and listened to the tinkling music, the wind blowing against my face, and the swirling feeling that is the appeal of a carousel. My hands were wrapped around the golden pole in front of me and I leaned my head back, trying to picture the smile that would have been huge and bright across Marcus' face. I tried to imagine the excitement an unlimited pass to a carousel would have given him.

A few minutes into our ride, I felt something touching my leg. My eyes opened and I saw Riot using a finger to scratch at my leg, then he held out his hand to me. I took his hand and leaned my temple against the golden pole, and

I looked into his eyes as we went around and around in circles. His thumb made lazy circles over the back of my hand and as the carousel finally slowed, he mouthed the words "I love you."

I decided he'd been right, and once wasn't enough. We rode the carousel for an hour, always switching horses between rides, and on the last one, I led Riot to one of the bench seats and cuddled into his side. The ride started to move and I pressed my face into his chest, squeezing my arms around his waist.

We swirled round and round, and I watched as children's faces lit up with joy. It was bittersweet. Sadness was overwhelming because I'd never see Marcus' smiling face again, but I shared their joy knowing his spirit was still within me, and I felt his joy like he was riding with me. Riot's lips pressed up against my temple, placing a soft kiss there, and then I heard his voice, felt his breath against my ear.

"He was so lucky to have you as his sister."

At his words, one tear slid down my cheek, and I snuggled into him even more.

Chapter Thirteen

His Signature Move

Kalli

The car ride back to LA was quiet, but in a comfortable way. The radio was on, but it played softly in the background. My hand was holding Riot's and resting in his lap, and I spent most of my time either looking out the window, or resting my eyes, leaning against the headrest.

So much had happened in just one weekend.

Two days full of changes and transitions; my brain was trying to catch up with all the emotions running through my heart.

We were just outside of LA and it was late enough that the traffic wasn't terrible.

"You've been pretty quiet," he said. I opened my eyes and looked over at him.

"Just thinking." I said, giving him a weak smile. I was honestly exhausted. The panic attack over lunch had used enough emotional energy that I could have slept the rest of the day, and then the ride on the carousel had done me in. I hadn't run a marathon or anything, but my body was spent.

"Anything you want to talk about?"

I could tell he wanted to know what was going on in my head. He wanted reassurance that I wasn't panicking and that we were okay.

"I guess I'm just kind of drained from the whole weekend, ya know? A lot happened."

"Yeah," he replied, still not satisfied with my answer. And that was fine. If there was one thing I could do for Riot from then until forever, it was make him feel secure that I wasn't pushing him away or shutting him out. If he needed me to tell him, straight up, that I was still *there* with him, I would, every time.

"Hey," I said softly, waiting until he turned his face to look at me. "I love you."

He didn't respond with words, but he brought my hand up and kissed the back of it.

"I'm worried about Halah," he said ten minutes later.

I squeezed his hand. "She'll be okay."

"She just seemed off, you know? Well, you wouldn't know because you've never met her before. But she just seemed, I don't know, like something was hanging over her head. And then she kept having to go to the bathroom, and then out by her car…" His voice trailed off and I could practically hear the thoughts ticking in his brain. I bit my lower lip, trying to keep my mouth closed.

"Did you think she was acting strange?" he asked finally, after I'd been silent.

I shrugged. "I don't think she felt well today."

"Yeah, but I mean, it was weird, right? She was fine one minute, then sick the next. She was starving, but then she wasn't hungry."

I cringed because I knew it was only a matter of time before he came to the same conclusion I had. Finally, I let out a loud sigh. I wasn't going to just let him flounder around, he needed to be put out of his misery.

"Do you think, possibly, and I'm just throwing this out there, that perhaps…she could be pregnant?"

My question was nearly a physical force. I could almost see the way it hung in the air between us before it landed right on top of his head with a brutal impact.

"Pregnant?" he asked, but more exclaimed. Loudly.

"I don't know," I said, pulling my hand free from his, wanting to give him all the space and hands he needed to deal with his emotions. "I just thought the way the smells got to her, how hungry she was, how she kept saying she would be okay, or that it would pass, like she knew exactly what was wrong and knew nothing could be done about it." I held my hands up and scrunched my shoulders. "It kind of seemed like she was pregnant to me."

"Pregnant?" he repeated, his face blank except for his eyebrows, which were reaching new and uncharted heights.

"I don't know. I mean, I could be way off base."

"Like 'having a baby' pregnant?"

"I don't know of any other kind of pregnant," I said, trying to lighten the mood. He was quiet for a few more moments and then turned to look at me.

"You think my baby sister is going to have a baby?"

Again, I held up my hands and scrunched my shoulders. "Possibly?"

Then his eyebrows dropped to their regular height, and he got a little quieter. "She did mention something to me about having thirty weeks to figure everything out…"

Oh. My. God.

"Riot," I said gently, placing my hand on his thigh. "She's totally pregnant."

"Shit fucking damn it," he cursed, as he slammed his palm against the steering wheel.

"She's probably ten weeks pregnant, which totally explains why she still has morning sickness, why she isn't showing, and her, uh, emotional instability." I thought of her eyes at lunch and how they were begging me to save her from her brother finding out she was, indeed, pregnant, and suddenly I felt like a traitor to the female sisterhood. "Listen, you can't tell her I told you. In fact, you can't tell anyone. She didn't even tell me, I guessed. But I figured it out at lunch and I'm pretty sure she knew I'd guessed and she gave me *the look* that said, 'Please don't tell my brother.' So, please, don't tell her I told you."

"I'm just supposed to tell her I figured it out myself?"

"No! She'll never believe that." He looked at me, eyebrows back up, offended. "I just mean that she'll never believe that a man who's never had a kid or been around a pregnant woman before would put all those clues together."

"Okay, I won't tell her. But I'm calling her every week. And I'm texting her daily. What's she going to do? Have a baby on a cruise ship?"

Now he sounded like he was getting angry. The rest of the drive was me listening to him list all the reasons why Halah couldn't have a baby. I didn't bother telling him that it was not really any of his business whether or not his sister had a baby. It took me a few minutes to realize he was driving to my apartment, but I didn't say anything because I didn't want to anger the beast. He parked my Rover and then scrubbed his hands over his face.

I let him calm down for a moment and then I quietly said, "Your truck isn't here. It's at the lot. Do you want me to drive you there?"

He leaned his head back and then turned it to look at me.

"No, I just want to drink a beer, relax for a bit, and go to bed."

"Here?" I couldn't even try to hide the surprise from my voice.

"Did you expect, after everything that went on between us this weekend, you would ever sleep alone again?"

My heart swelled at his words. I flung my arms over the center console and wrapped them around his neck, pulling myself to him. He hugged me and one of his hands ran down the back of my head, stopping on my neck and squeezing me there. My pulse picked up with his touch. A hand on my neck had always been something I associated with Riot. It was his signature move, and feeling it in that moment only made everything inside of me heat up and liquefy.

"I don't mind if you want to take things slow, Riot. You don't have to stay with me."

"Babe, I was all in months ago. I'm all in now. If you want me to go to my own place, you just have to say it. But I don't really want to be away from you. Not now. Not when we just really found each other again."

His words were said against my neck and even though I couldn't see his face, I could hear his sincerity, his need. And even though a rational person would take a step back and not rush into such a serious relationship so quickly, there wasn't even a tiny part of me that wanted to be apart from him either.

But there was one thing.

"I don't know if I can stay at your apartment." He didn't say anything, just squeezed me tighter. "Marcus slept in that apartment and I just don't think I could be in your living room without seeing him there and remembering…"

"Hey," he said, pulling away. "It's okay. I can't walk past my couch without seeing him there either." He cradled my face with his big hands and I leaned into one of them. "It was really hard at first, to see the spot where he'd slept. But eventually it got easier. I don't expect you to go there. Not ever if you don't want to. I will come to you." He pushed back the hair that had fallen around my face during our embrace, then said, "Can we go inside, have a beer, relax, and then go to bed?"

"Yes," I said happily.

"Riot, *yes*," I cried, as he thrust deep into me. "God, yes."

I was draped over him, his hands were on my ass, and he was absolutely *fucking* me into oblivion.

I had been exhausted—emotionally and physically—and I wasn't even entertaining the idea of taking advantage of Riot Bentley in my bed, but he'd had other plans. Plans that involved me doing absolutely nothing, but still feeling absolutely everything. My heart was racing, my breaths were panting, and I was wet. Soaked from the orgasm he'd given me with his mouth, and now drenched from his perfect cock sliding in and out of me, hitting every single button inside me that only he'd ever been able to find.

"You're so fucking perfect," he growled. I loved it when he growled. I leaned up, putting all my weight on one hand, and crashed my mouth down on his. He swallowed my cries as I came, and when I fell limply against him a few seconds later, he continued to piston in and out of me, rapidly finding his own release.

It had been quick, hot, sweaty sex. It had been perfect. I couldn't have handled anything more involved than that, and he'd kept his promise that he'd do all the work.

He rolled me over so we were both on our sides, still connected, and he pressed a kiss to my lips.

"I totally owe you one round of effortless, amazing, sex," I said after he'd pulled away, breaking our connection.

"Is that, like, a coupon or something I can cash in on whenever I want? Or is that something I have to wait to enjoy until you feel like gifting it to me?" He was smiling and that made me happy. Since we'd gotten back to my place he'd been pretty quiet, sullen even, drinking his beer and watching late night television. I'd expected to head to bed, perhaps cuddle a little, and then fall asleep. But as soon as we hit the bedroom he'd grabbed me, thrown me on the bed, and his mouth seemed to be on a mission.

"You can cash it in whenever you want, as long as I'm capable," I replied, winking at him.

After a brief moment of silence he asked, "Can we talk about something?"

"Sure," I said, then immediately yawned.

He rolled to his back, bringing me with him, and I moved so that my head was nestled right in the crook of his shoulder.

"At lunch today, that was a panic attack, right?"

I stilled at his words. My panic attack was the very last thing I'd thought he was going to bring up. When I didn't answer right away, his hand came up and started moving up and down my arm.

"Yeah. It was."

"And you said you'd had them before?"

I pushed back a little bit and looked up at him. "Did you just fuck me into oblivion so that you could ask me questions about my anxiety?"

"That wasn't my intention, no, but it doesn't sound like a terrible plan now that you mention it."

I kept looking at him, trying to figure out exactly how I felt about what was happening between us, and then I was laughing softly. He was right. I was exhausted, even more now than I had been an hour before, and I was relaxed.

"Most of the people I surrounded myself with after his death kind of figured out that his name was a trigger for me. Talking about him at all was a trigger. So, for a while no one talked about him, including me. Then I moved here and no one knows about him so no one asks about him. I think about him all the time, but I'm used to that. I wasn't prepared to hear someone mention him so casually."

"I'm sorry," he whispered, kissing my temple.

"It's not your fault, and there's really nothing to be sorry for. I should be able to talk about him. I *want* to talk about him, at least, I think I do. But then, if I'm caught off guard, I guess it backfires on me."

We were both quiet for a moment, his hand still running up and down my arm, his lips still resting against my skin.

"He's part of the reason I fell in love with you." Never before had words affected me the way those words had. "I knew I wanted to get to know you, more so after hearing your story and meeting your brother, the way you took care of him, the way you protected him, but I was a goner after that first time I came to your house and had pizza. You think you were so blessed to have him in your life, and you were, but he had someone smiling down on him when he got you as a sister."

I rolled fully into him, burying my face in his chest, trying hard not to break down and sob. I didn't want to cry anymore. I wanted to smile more than I cried. I wanted to laugh more than I frowned. So, with tears in my eyes, I lifted my face and looked up at Riot, saying, "There's not one person on this planet I need more than you. I can get through anything if I know you're beside me."

"Lucky for you I don't ever plan on going anywhere."

Days passed and we fell into a beautifully comfortable routine. Riot stayed at my house at night and in the mornings we drove to work together. We'd meet at the coffee shop during our lunch break and then our evenings were either spent apart for work reasons, or exploring LA together.

Riot texted his sister daily and she stuck to her "just fine" story, but couldn't give him a date for when she was going back to work, which only fueled his fire. She told him she was staying with their parents for the time being. This worried him, but I tried to calm him by reasoning with him that it was better she was with family if she were actually pregnant. He would usually grumble inaudibly and remain grumpy for a little while until I found a way to pull him out of his funk.

Riot was at work late Saturday night shooting a night scene, which left me all alone at my apartment for an evening. Like I believed most girls did when their boyfriends were away, I was pampering myself. I had a masque on my face and I was soaking in my tub, enjoying the relaxing music playing from my phone.

My calm was harshly interrupted by my phone vibrating against the porcelain of my bathtub. I saw Ella's name and quickly answered and turned on the speaker.

"Fella!" I said with a smile.

"Hey, Kal. Haven't heard from you in a while, so I thought I'd give you a call. You sound happy, and also like you're standing at the end of a tunnel."

I laughed. "I'm in the tub and you're on speaker because I've got goop all over my face."

"Sounds awesome," she said wistfully, and then I heard stupidly cute baby noises coming from her end of the phone. "I'm lucky if I can take more than five minutes in the shower before Mattie starts crying. And then she cries, and then I leak, and it's just counterproductive."

I couldn't help but stifle a laugh, but I tried to be sympathetic. "I'm sorry."

"No, it's okay, just a tiny mom complaint. But it's true, you sound happy."

Suddenly it occurred to me that I'd spent the better part of two weeks with Riot and hadn't told her yet.

"Yeah, about that…"

"Spill, woman," she demanded.

"Riot and I are together."

She was silent for a moment and I wasn't sure if it was good silence or bad.

"Okay… and?"

"And things are good." I offered. I knew between her and Megan, Ella was definitely the more even-keeled sister, but she was literally giving me nothing.

"Good, like, you talked and made nice, or good, like, you get to be horizontal with him?"

I laughed, feeling the pinch of the drying masque on my face. "Oh, we've been horizontal. Every chance we get," I said, trying to waggle my eyebrows but getting nowhere. I heard clapping and whooping, and then I heard Ella's mom voice and I knew she was talking to Mattie when she said, "That's right, Auntie Kalli is gonna give you an Uncle Riot, and then Mommy and Aunt Megan get to look at him forever."

Distantly I heard a distinct and strikingly male voice call out, "I heard that."

"You better watch yourself," I warned through laughter.

"Pshh. Porter's an alpha. I'll pay for that later, but I'll enjoy it." Then after a few seconds she said, more seriously, "Is it good, Kal? I mean, I know it's good, but I mean, are the two of you good?"

"It's wonderful," I said, sounding just as sappy as I felt. "He was really great in the beginning, took it really slow, let me make all the decisions, and then we just kind of stopped being apart."

"That's the best," she said, her voice knowing. "So, will he be coming with you for Thanksgiving?"

Oh crap. Thanksgiving. In two weeks.

"We haven't talked about Thanksgiving. His parents live in San Francisco. I don't know if he was planning to go up there or not. I'll have to talk to him."

"Okay, well, you've got a room here at the beach if you want it. We'd really like to see you. And Riot is more than welcome to come along. But I totally understand if you go to San Francisco with him." She paused, then added, "But I have to say, Mattie told me yesterday that she's starting to forget what you look like."

Ah, the baby guilt trip. I didn't really need one; hearing Mattie's gurgles and baby talk through the phone was enough to make my heart hurt.

"That was low, Ella," I laughed. "How are you doing?" I asked after a moment.

"Good. Great, actually. I mean, besides not having slept more than four hours in a row in six months, everything's great. Porter's work is slowing down a little now that winter's just around the corner, but both the shops are picking up so it's kind of perfect."

"And how's Megan?" Even as I asked the question I knew I should call her soon.

"She's good too. Still in the honeymoon phase. Patrick just got a promotion. They're thinking of selling their condo and buying a house. Just, ya know, life."

"Yeah, life." I sighed as I said the words, thrilled on the inside that for the first time in months, life was just life, and it was good.

"How's your fancy job?"

"It's not as fancy as you'd imagine, but it's good. Riot is on the soundstage right next to mine and we've been able to spend lunches together, so that's been nice."

There was a moment of quiet between us, then she said, "I know you're a strong woman, Kal. And I know you could have gone to LA and done just fine on your own.

But I'm really glad you and Riot worked it out. You deserve to be happy."

"Thanks," I said, my face seriously cracking from my smile.

"Okay, well, I'm gonna go put this little one to bed, then take my punishment from Porter."

"Sounds terrible," I said sarcastically.

"Being with him is such a hardship." We both laughed at that. "Let me know about Thanksgiving, okay?"

"Will do, and thanks for calling."

"Anytime."

I heard her end of the call disconnect and let out a sigh. I knew I was lucky to have met Ella and Megan, knew all along we were all brought into each other's lives for a reason. And in that moment, I was so happy knowing I'd always have their friendship.

After my bath and nightly face ritual, I'd gone to bed a little earlier than normal, realizing I was bored without Riot there. One week of his presence and I was already at a loss without him. So I'd curled up in bed with a book I'd been trying to read for months, but fallen asleep after only a few pages.

When I woke, it was because Riot's strong arm, which was draped around me at the waist, was pulling me closer to him and his nose was nuzzling the back of my neck. I smiled, then rolled toward him, pressing my front as close to his as I could get, letting my face find that perfect spot between his jaw and his shoulder that seemed to have been made exactly for me to lay my head to rest in.

"I missed you," I whispered sleepily against his skin, and felt his arms wrap tighter around me.

"Sleep, baby," he whispered back, kissing my hair.

"Mmmkay."

The next time I woke up, it was to the sound of Riot's deep breaths, the rhythmic movement of his chest under my cheek, and the bright sunlight filtering through the blinds in my bedroom. I was warm, still wrapped up in his arms, and more comfortable than should be possible. Besides the one time I'd woken earlier that night, I'd slept deeply and long. I was well rested and wide awake.

I slowly lifted my head and took a moment to stare at his face. There was no denying, by anyone, that Riot was attractive. You didn't get lead parts on network cop dramas if you weren't. He was becoming somewhat of a household name and heartthrob, and only a few episodes had aired. He was tall, dark, and stupidly handsome. But lying in my bed, holding me close, he looked adorable. His face was almost childlike when he slept. With his dangerously sexy eyes closed, his face took on a wholly different, peaceful quality, which was quite nearly innocent looking.

I knew he'd worked late the night before, or even early that morning, and I didn't want to wake him, so I tried to sneak out of his grasp slowly. I'd made it almost out of the circle of his arms before his voice startled me.

"If you leave, I won't be able to sleep," he said with his adorably cute, sleepy voice. My body went lax where I'd been stopped and I leaned over, resting my head against his stomach.

"That seems a little extreme."

"Are you calling me a liar?"

"No, I'm only saying, we've spent just as many nights together in the last week as we had in our whole relationship almost. It's brand-new. You can't be that reliant upon my presence for sleep yet."

Riot knifed up in the bed, grabbed me, and then, suddenly, I was on my back and he was above me.

"I spent so many nights without you because it's what I thought you wanted, what I thought you *needed*. If it had been up to me I never would have left your side, I would have been there every moment to help you through your mourning. But you told me to go. And that's okay. I understand. But I'm not going to lie to you and tell you it was easy for me. It wasn't. Every night I lay in my bed wishing I could hold you, hoping for just a faint waft of your shampoo from the one pillow you used, which I slept with every night. I hoped you were okay. Prayed you were eating enough, that you weren't alone all the time, that someone was there to make you laugh every once in a while just to remind you that it wasn't all darkness everywhere.

"So, yes, the last few nights I've not only gotten used to you sleeping next to me, it's given something back to me that I thought I might have lost forever, and I'm not ready to take it for granted yet. So, unless you've got somewhere pressing to be, please, just lie with me."

"Okay," I said, nodding slightly. He let out a large sigh, rolled off me, then pulled me to his side again. I found my special place made just for me and tentatively snuggled in. A few moments passed, thick with silent tension. I slowly reached up and placed my hand on his chest and when his hand came up to cover mine, I let out my own thankful breath.

"You know it wasn't *you*, right?" He didn't answer my question, but I felt his chest stop moving, so I knew he'd heard me. I continued anyway. "I didn't push *you* away, I was hiding myself from you. From everyone. Everything. It's true that seeing you was difficult, but only because it ate at me that I was with a man when Marcus had his accident. Or, more to the point, that I wasn't with him. Right after his death there was an enormous part of me that was eclipsed by guilt. As the guilt waned, rationality came back, and I understood, mostly, that it wasn't my fault, but I still struggle with that sometimes.

"But aside from that," I continued, "the whole experience sort of fit into what I'd pretty much built my entire adult life around. I'd told myself that I wasn't ever going to be in a committed relationship with a man, that I wasn't meant to have that as a part of my life."

"And now?" he asked, still not looking at me, breaths shallow, hand still clasped around mine.

"Now I know that I was standing still before you, tethered to a good life with Marcus, but never reaching for greatness, never looking for anything *more*." I leaned up on an elbow to look at him, my hand pulling away from his but smoothing over his chest and trailing down his rib cage. "You set me free, Riot. I'm never tied down with you, never stifled or smothered. The only thing I want to be tied to, is you."

"You know I'm bound to you too, right? Being away from you was unbearable, but I knew it was something you needed. I knew that if I forced myself into your life, if I didn't let you figure it out on your own, we'd never stand a chance. But I was never whole without you." His hand came up and cupped my face, his eyes never wavering from mine. "That all being said, it's Sunday morning and I want you in bed with me."

I smiled at that. "Okay." I leaned down and gave him a small kiss, then snuggled back into my place. A few minutes later, when I knew Riot hadn't gone back to sleep, I asked, "Do you want to go to Ella and Porter's beach house for Thanksgiving?"

"Sure," he said immediately.

My brow furrowed. "You don't need to spend Thanksgiving with your family?"

"Can we do Christmas there?"

"Sure..."

"Then it sounds like it's settled."

Chapter Fourteen

Park Place

Kalli

Thanksgiving at the Oregon Coast was, by far, the best way to spend the holiday. Ella and Porter's house was full, but not packed. Megan and Patrick were there, along with Tilly, and Ella's parents. All the parental units were only there for the day, and it was nice to have mom hugs from Tilly and Susan, but it was also great to spend time with Megan, Ella, Patrick, and Porter and not feel like the fifth wheel.

Riot, of course, was loved by all. Tilly nearly fainted when he walked in the house, Susan blushed as she introduced herself to him, but Patrick and Porter just shook his hand, offered him a beer, and then invited him to watch football in the living room with them and Richard.

I tried my best to help with the meal prep, but lucky for me, being the person who lived farthest away and saw her the least often, I got put on Mattie patrol, so I spent a good portion of the day playing with the sweetest and most adorable little girl ever.

"I think her cheeks have grown to twice their previous size since I saw her last," I said, making faces at Mattie as she tried to fist my hair and shove it in her mouth.

"It's not only her cheeks. The chub is everywhere," Ella said, chopping something on the other side of the kitchen.

"You guys are going to give her a complex. She's perfect," Megan added.

"When are you going to have a baby?" I asked with a smile, knowing she would glare at me.

"That's what I would like to know," Susan said from where her head was buried in the refrigerator. It was then that Megan sent me the glare I was waiting for.

"I've told you all this before; Patrick and I are in no hurry to have kids. We have a perfect niece we can spoil whenever we want, then her return to her parents and go home to sleep all night. We're just starting our careers. We've got plenty of time."

"She's right, you know," Ella chimed in, coming to Megan's defense. "Porter and I already had our careers all figured out before we got pregnant. I can't imagine trying to do this at Megan's age. Give her a little while to figure life out."

"Are you and Riot going to get married?" This came from Megan and then she stuck her tongue out at me. I laughed while rolling my eyes.

"Now, that's something I can get behind," Susan said, emerging from behind the door of the fridge, eyebrows reaching for the sky, dreamy smile on her face.

"Yes," Tilly agreed, expertly hand-mashing some potatoes. "Or you could just use him for his body until you get bored."

At that, Ella, Megan, and I exchanged surprised glances until we all busted up laughing at the same time.

It was hours later, and Ella and Porter had walked her parents to their car, Tilly had left a few minutes before, and the rest of us were all sitting in the living room.

"We could watch a movie," Megan suggested.

"I think if we sit on this couch any longer, I'm going to fall asleep, babe," Patrick said, running his hand up and down Megan's thigh. "It was damn good turkey."

"Well, I'd say we could go for a walk on the beach, but Mattie's asleep and besides, it's cold as crap out there," Ella said, locking the door behind her. "I know," she said, rushing to a closet right off the dining room. "We could play a game, and drink!"

Ella obviously needed a reason to drink.

"That sounds fun," I offered. Riot reached his arm behind me, resting it on my shoulders, and I leaned into him. We were both sitting on Porter's large couch, our feet up on his coffee table which he insisted "was made for feet." Everything about their house was gorgeous, comfortable, and handmade if possible, like his coffee table.

"Hey, give me some sugar," Riot whispered in my ear. I turned to look at him, smirking at his request.

"You want some sugar?" I asked. "What are you? Fifty? Who says that?"

He grinned. "I say it. You gonna give it to me or not?" He curled his arm, bringing my face closer to his.

"I'll give it to you when you ask like a normal person." He kept pulling me closer and closer until our mouths were just barely touching, but I was resisting, a smile still playing on my face.

"Fucking kiss me, Kalli," he growled.

"See?" I said, running my hand through his soft hair, and using only the tip of my tongue to trace his bottom lip. "That's all I needed." He then trapped my tongue by capturing my mouth with his. I was well aware of the fact that we weren't alone in the room, but I couldn't stop myself from enjoying him taking the kiss from me. He asked for it, wanted me to give it to him, but in the end he ended up taking it, which was more his style.

"You guys better hurry up with the game. Kalli and Riot are going to have sex on your coffee table soon."

"The table was made for feet, not sex," Porter said, coming back into the room after checking on Mattie.

Riot pulled away, but not far, his breath panting across my face. "That was some good sugar, sugar." I couldn't help but smile.

"Okay, teenagers," Ella called out, obviously referring to us. "The only game we have that six people can play is Monopoly."

"I love Monopoly," Megan cried, and out of the corner of my eye I saw her shoot up off the couch, Patrick following, albeit slower.

I, on the other hand, froze in place, my hand still in Riot's hair, his face just inches from mine. He must have felt it because his hands went from being wrapped around my body to framing my face.

"Just breathe, Kal," he whispered.

I couldn't. My lungs were like blocks of ice in my chest, frozen and unyielding, even for the air they were starting to burn for. My hands were shaking, my throat closing, and my vision was blurring.

"Kal, look at me," he said, a little more urgently.

"Is she okay?" Someone asked from behind me, their voice laced with concern. I tried to focus on Riot, but felt my eyelids fluttering closed.

"Kal, damn it, breathe for me. In deep and out slow, okay?"

I looked in his eyes, the only thing I could focus on, and tried to take in a breath. It dragged in, as if I were pulling in air through water, as though I were drowning on dry land.

"That's good, baby, now out."

I pushed it out, concentrating on his face.

"In, again." He turned and I wanted to yell at him to turn back to me, to not abandon me in the middle of it, and I heard him yelling, "Get me a glass of water."

Finally his face returned to my vision and he said, "Deep, baby. Get in as much as you can. Good," he said as I tried to do as he was asking. "Now push it out slow." Slow wasn't a problem, the air was coming in through water, but I was pushing it out through sand.

He continued to remind me to breathe for a few minutes, which seemed like years, until I could breathe easier, until I didn't feel like I was on the very edge of death, about to topple into its depths. When I was breathing on my own, head resting against the back of the couch, brow sweating, I heard Ella's voice.

"Should we call someone? Take her somewhere?"

"She's okay," I heard Riot answer, then felt his lips on my forehead as he gave me a quick kiss. "She just needs a minute." His hand was at my face then, thumb sweeping over my cheek. "Baby, I need you to open your eyes and take a sip of this water."

I did as he asked, but when my eyes opened they found his and never moved from them.

"Was that a bad one?" he asked, but I could tell he already knew the answer. I nodded.

"Is she having an asthma attack?" Patrick asked, and I could hear the genuine concern in his voice. I wanted to curl into a ball and go to sleep. I wanted to simply disappear.

"Panic attack," Riot answered for me. I was grateful he was taking control, but I wasn't sure how I felt about all my friends knowing my weakness.

"Does this happen often?" That question came from Ella and she sounded like she was near tears.

"I'm not really sure. She has triggers. This is the second one I've seen her have this month."

"Oh, God." That was Ella again, but her voice was muffled. I couldn't see her, but I imagined her hand over her mouth. I wanted to cry.

"Just give us a minute," Riot said to everyone, but then his face was in front of mine again. "I'm gonna pick you up and take you in the bathroom, okay?"

I nodded and felt his arm slip under my knees while the other came to my back. I wrapped my arms around his neck and buried my face in his chest as he carried me through the house and up the stairs to our room. He continued into the bathroom and gently set me down on the counter. I gripped the edge, trying to keep my balance as he let me go. His hands came to my shoulders and he leaned down so I could see him.

"You okay?"

"Yeah," I managed.

He stood up and wrapped his arms around my shoulders, bringing me into him, gently rubbing his hands up and down my back. I wasn't having a hard time breathing anymore, but my throat still felt raw and my heart was still pounding. I let his hands soothe me and we stayed that way in that bathroom for a while.

Eventually he pulled away and found a washcloth. I watched as he ran the faucet, wet the washcloth, came to me and wiped it gently over my forehead and cheeks. I let him take care of me, let him help, mostly because I knew he needed it, but partly because I needed it too. My eyes stayed on his face, but he was concentrating on making sure I was cool and dry.

"You're flushed," he said softly. "Are you sure it's over?"

I shrugged. "I think so. I'm feeling a little better. Just tired now and my throat is dry."

"Do you want to go to bed? I could go get you some more water."

I thought about his question, and bed seemed like a good place to be at that moment. The idea of slipping into our plush, comfortable bed, wrapping myself up in the fluffy comforter and Riot's arms seemed like the smartest step I could make. But then I thought about Ella's voice, how she and Megan sounded so concerned, and I didn't want to disappear. I didn't really want to face them, to talk to them about what I'd just been through, but I cared too much about them to let them come to their own conclusions. I shook my head at him and he nodded, touching his lips to my forehead again.

After a few minutes, when I'd felt more like myself, I took in another deep breath and then pushed it out slowly.

"I think I have to go back out there."

"You don't have to do anything you don't want to," he said, protective Riot making an appearance.

"I know," I said, bringing my hand up to cup his cheek, "but I do want to. I want to go back out there and show them that I'm okay. And I want to try and play Monopoly like a normal person."

"If you start to feel stressed out at all, or like you're going to panic again, I want you to tell me, and we'll come back in here. Promise?"

"I promise."

He held my gaze for a moment longer, but then backed away and helped me hop down from the counter.

When I came back into the kitchen both Ella and Megan stood up straighter and both their men flanked their sides. I felt Riot at my side as well, and then he laced his fingers through mine.

"I'm sorry about that." I took in a deep breath then pushed it out. "Ever since Marcus passed, sometimes when someone says his name, or brings him up, or something that reminds me of him, it makes me panic. It usually happens when I least expect it, and the only thing I can do is ride it out, try to keep breathing through it. I'm really sorry if I scared you, but I'm okay."

"How can we help?" Ella asked immediately.

"Forget it happened?" I replied, giving a weak laugh. She wasn't amused.

"Seriously, Kalli."

I shrugged. "There's really nothing to do. Riot reminds me to breathe, breathes with me, sometimes he counts. But besides that, try not to tiptoe around me. The only way it gets easier is to get through it. So don't treat me any differently."

"Riot said you have triggers," Megan said.

"Yeah," I nodded. "Marcus and I played Monopoly almost every night." I felt Riot's lips on the top of my head, and I'd never needed a kiss more than I needed that one.

"Oh, Kalli," Ella whispered, her hand coming to cover her mouth as Porter turned her into his arms.

"We didn't know," Megan whispered, Patrick wrapping an arm around her shoulders.

"No, I know, and this is what I didn't want," I said, tears starting to form in my eyes, stinging and burning. "I don't want you guys to feel like I'm fragile, because I'm not. I can handle all this, I can handle the panic and the sadness and the emptiness, because I know it's only a fraction of my life. Yes, I miss Marcus, and no, nothing will ever replace him, and sometimes the loss of him overcomes me, but I'm okay."

My friends seemed stunned by my declaration, but I didn't want to be the poor emotional friend. I needed them to look at me like they had before his death, before they saw me crumble.

"So, I need a shot of vodka and I call the thimble."

It took a little while for my friends to relax after I'd basically yelled at them that I was emotionally stable. But the shots Porter and Patrick brought to the table helped immensely. We all gathered around their big kitchen table and began playing Monopoly. I wanted to make it through the game, or at least last as long as everyone else, without having a breakdown. And surprisingly, actually playing the game didn't send me into a spiral of depression or anxiety.

On my first roll of the dice, when I'd landed on the railroad, it was almost as if Marcus had rolled the dice for me, leading me to my old comfortable routine. Whenever I used to play with him I'd buy all the railroads, never trying to buy properties. I recognized that strategy for what it was. It was the same way I'd coped with life: never put down roots, have a soft spot to land wherever I went, but heaven forbid I invest in anyone else, or myself for that matter. So, when I landed on the railroad, I made the decision not to buy it. No one really noticed how big of a decision it was for me, but I knew. It was symbolic of how my life had changed in the last few months, how it was a representation of how my life had changed since Riot came into it.

Later, when I bankrupted everyone with my purchase of Boardwalk and Park Place, as I watched all of my friends and the love of my life slowly lose all their money and curse my name, I realized I'd been playing the game all wrong my whole life.

Chapter Fifteen

Viewpoint

Riot

"See, this is why I love road trips."

I turned my head to see Kalli sitting in the passenger seat of our rental car, sunglasses on, holding a bottle of Diet Coke in one hand and a package of mini chocolate donuts in the other.

Fuck if I didn't love her.

"You love road trips because you can eat crap and not feel guilty about it?" I gave her my sexiest smile.

"Correct! I love road trips because every time you stop to get gas, it's like a wonderland of crap and anything you could possibly think of that you would never regularly buy are the only things available. You're hungry? Eat a bag of dehydrated potato bits covered in flavored dust that contains ingredients so bad for you, even the government has given up on regulating it. Oh, you're not hungry? Doesn't matter. The crap you ate earlier tricks your stomach into thinking you are, so grab those pastries that are so full of preservatives they'd survive a nuclear apocalypse."

"So, what you're telling me is that you want me to pull over at the next exit with a gas station?"

She laughed and I felt it in my whole body. My heart skidded to a stop, then thundered back to life. My fingers tingled with the need to touch her. My dick hardened in my jeans. Even my arms wanted to wrap around her at the sound of her unrestrained laughter. When she was done laughing, she leaned over the console and kissed my cheek.

I wanted to pull over and show her what kind of kiss I needed. But instead I reached for her hand and held it in my lap as I continued down the highway.

When planning our trip to Oregon for Thanksgiving, we decided to fly up, but rent a car and drive back, taking Highway 101 down the coast, planning to stop at every viewpoint we came across. So far we'd managed to get quite a few selfies with the Pacific Ocean behind us. A few times there'd been other people admiring the view who offered to take the photo for us, but most of the time it was only the two of us, and I preferred it that way.

I preferred to have Kalli in front of me, facing away, my arms around her waist, the scent of her shampoo mixing with the scent of the ocean, and everything important to me within my grasp.

When we weren't admiring the beauty of the west coast, or indulging in convenience store fare, Kalli was bound and determined to keep us entertained with a plethora of road trip games. This was day two of games and I'd given up trying to win because she was much better at spotting letters in license plates and road signs, what with all the driving I was doing.

"Okay, I have something better for us to do," she said, her thumb moving on the screen of her phone. "I found this list of 100 Things You Should Know About Your Significant Other." She looked at me with another brilliant smile. "Are you my significant other?"

"You better fucking believe it," I said, bringing her hand to my mouth and kissing her knuckles. I caught her blushing and I wanted so badly to pull over again so I could make her whole body turn that same color.

"Okay," she said, trying to pretend as though my words hadn't affected her. "I'll ask you a question and then after you answer, I'll tell you my answer. They look pretty run-of-the-mill."

"Shoot," I said.

"Favorite color?"

"Orange."

"I've never seen you wear orange." Her tone was accusatory, as though I'd lie about my favorite color.

"So?"

"So how can it be your favorite color if you don't own any clothes that color?"

"I didn't realize I had to advertise my favorite color in my wardrobe."

"My favorite color is purple. Half the shirts I own are purple." I thought about her statement, and she was right; she did wear a lot of purple. The color looked great against her pale skin and straw-colored hair. "If I was judging by *your* wardrobe, I'd think your favorite color was blue."

"I look good in blue," I said, shrugging.

"You do. Although," she said, leaning back so she could take more of me in, "You have the right coloring to do orange. Not many guys can pull orange off. But your skin is tan enough and your hair is dark enough. I'll get you an orange shirt. Don't worry."

"Crisis averted," I said with a smile as I checked my blind spot and switched lanes.

"Dogs or cats?"

"Dogs."

"Agreed. Summer or winter?"

"Uh, summer in the north, winter in the south."

"Agreed," she said, her voice rising an octave, as if our agreement on these trivial questions was proof of the fact we were meant to be.

"City or country?"

"That's not really a great question. Ideally, I'd like to live close to a city, but on the outskirts. But not so far out in the country it's going to take me thirty minutes to get to a grocery store."

"Hmm. Good point. I think I'd like to live in the city until I have kids, but then move to the suburbs."

"Kids?" This was the first she'd ever mentioned having kids of her own. "You think you want to have kids?" I glanced over at her and suddenly she looked nervous, like she'd stumbled into some sort of relationship quicksand. I rubbed my thumb over the back of her hand. "Don't freak out, just answer honestly. You can't give me a wrong answer unless it's a dishonest one."

It took her a moment, but she finally spoke.

"There was a time in my life where I thought kids weren't really an option for me. You know how I was: I never wanted to be with someone long enough to get to a third date, let alone have kids with them. I thought, with Marcus, it would be too disruptive or too difficult. So I kind of accepted that kids wouldn't be a part of my future. But I guess, in the last month or so, kids have become a reality again."

Fuck but I loved her.

"So how many kids do you think you'd like?" I asked gently, not wanting to freak her out by having a serious relationship conversation over Cheetos and Diet Coke.

"Well, I mean, I guess the smart thing would be to start with one and see how it goes from there, right?"

"Like with dogs?" I asked, laughing. Luckily, she laughed too.

"Yeah." Her laughter tapered off and then she asked, "How do you feel about kids?"

"I'd love to have kids with you, Kal."

"That's really sweet, Ri," she said shyly. "But how do you feel about kids in general? How did you feel about them before you met me?"

This time it was I who shrugged. "I hadn't thought too much about it. Kids were just always a part of my future. It was usually a distant, hazy future, but they were there."

"How distant is it now?" Her voice was still painfully shy and I could almost feel the heat radiating from her cheeks.

"The vision is becoming clearer every day."

She paused but then asked, "Have you ever had a near-death experience?"

"Well that escalated quickly." I laughed. "And no, I never have. You?"

"Thankfully, no." I saw her thumb move over her phone out of the corner of my eye, but then I heard her say excitedly, "Viewpoint!"

Sure enough there was another viewpoint one mile up the road. As we pulled off the highway and onto a glorified shoulder with a few parking spaces, I noticed a lot of the lookout points in Oregon and Northern California were abundant with trees, but the farther south we headed, the dryer and more brown everything became. This viewpoint was drastically different from the one we'd first met at back in Seattle so many months ago.

We met at the front of the car and she took the hand I held out for her. We walked toward the railing and she leaned into my side, resting her free hand over my heart. We watched for a few minutes as the waves crashed onto the rocks below. Sometimes my eyes wandered out to the horizon, like they had my whole life, straining to see as far as I possibly could. I don't know what I thought would magically appear at that imaginary line where water met sky, but sometimes I thought if I looked long enough I'd see something spectacular—like the edge of the earth or something.

We were still a few hours outside of LA and the sun was getting lower in the sky, inching toward the water, coloring the horizon the oranges and reds I loved to look at. I could smell the flowery scent of Kalli's shampoo, feel her soft curves pressed along the side of my body, and for as far as I could see was blue water with the shiny reflection of the sunset. I couldn't remember a moment more perfect than that one. It was remarkable.

Gripping Kalli's chin between my thumb and forefinger, I angled her face toward me and then feathered my lips across hers. She melted into the kiss, turning her whole body into mine, moving her hand up my chest to grip my shoulder. I pressed our still linked hands into the small of her back and swept my tongue into her mouth.

Her hair was up in a messy knot atop her head, she was wearing one of my t-shirts and a pair of leggings, she had no makeup on, and her mouth tasted slightly of chocolate donuts and Diet Coke. I loved her. More than anything in the world, I loved her.

"I want a life with you, Kalli. I want this, us, forever." My forehead was pressed against hers, our lips still barely touching, and I could feel the grip she had on my shoulder tightening.

"You've got me." Her voice was a whisper, almost as though it hurt her to say the words. "I'm not going anywhere. I promise."

I moved my free hand up to her nape and gripped her there, using it for leverage as I covered her lips with mine, taking the kiss I so desperately needed at that moment. I needed to feel her, to feel like I had everything from her I could. My tongue took wide, deep, swipes through her mouth, and she met me at every pass, giving me exactly what I was looking for: reassurance. I wasn't in this alone. I could give and give and give, without having to worry that she wouldn't give right back.

She let a moan slip into my mouth and it nearly undid me, and much like the first night we met at a viewpoint, I had to stop kissing her before I took it too far. I had to rein in my basic urges to push her onto the hood of our rental car and claim her right there, and instead I tucked a wayward strand of hair behind her ear and walked her to the passenger side of the car.

Before she climbed in she turned and went up on her tiptoes, pressing her mouth against my ear.

"One day, I'm going to get you to make love to me at a viewpoint." She drew my earlobe into her mouth, biting gently, forcing my eyes to close as a wave of tremors rolled through my body.

"Fuck, Kalli, you can't say shit like that and then expect me to walk away," I said, gripping her waist and pushing her against the frame of the car. My mouth went directly for her neck, sucking on her delicate skin until I heard a gasp, then gently kissing the same spot.

"Maybe I don't want you to stop," she breathed. Her leg then came up and wrapped around my hip and I could feel the heat radiating out from between her legs through the thin fabric of her leggings. I couldn't stop myself from pressing into her, showing her how turned on I was by her. She moaned again as I ground my erection against her, loving the way I could practically feel her melt against me.

"Are you wet?" I pressed against her again. "I bet if I reached into your panties you'd be drenched right now." I said the words between nipping at her neck and sucking on it.

When we'd pulled into the viewpoint we'd been the only car there, but nothing was stopping anyone else from driving up. The thrill of someone coming upon us fucking each other against the car not only shot new, hot blood directly to my cock, but it also made my hackles rise. I didn't want anyone else to see my Kalli while she was experiencing ecstasy—just me. I wanted to be the only one to give it to her and the only one to see her face as I did it.

Public sex was a thrill and sounded good in theory, but I knew I'd never forgive myself if we were ever caught. I hated to do it, but I pulled my mouth from the sensitive skin of her neck and looked her in the eyes as I gripped the back of her neck.

"I'd like nothing more than to take you right here, baby, but I'm not going to let anyone else see what's mine. But when we get home, I'm gonna do all the dirty things running through my mind to you and make you sorry you teased me out here."

She smiled and winked. "I'm not teasing. If you wanted me out here, I'd let you take me."

A growl escaped me and I kissed her again, hard, but then I turned and walked away, adjusting myself as I crossed in front of the car. I climbed in and she had on a grin that was both infuriating and adorable. Her smile said she knew she'd gotten to me, knew I was seconds away from throwing out my reservations and taking her up against the side of a car in the middle of a parking lot on the side of a highway.

"You're going to pay for that later," I said, starting the engine.

"I'm looking forward to it," she said sweetly, still looking at her phone. "Okay, more questions."

I rubbed my hand over my face, still trying to calm down and get rid of the pressure in my pants.

"What's your favorite flower?"

Well, that's one way to make an erection go away.

"My favorite flower?" I repeated, pulling back onto the highway and turning on my lights, as the sunlight was fading quickly.

"Yeah," she replied, laughing.

"Babe, I don't have a favorite flower."

"Really?" She sounded sincere. "You don't like any flower at all?"

I thought about her question a little harder because it seemed like it was weirdly important to her that I liked a particular flower. I searched through my memories, trying to come up with a time when I'd appreciated a flower at all. Suddenly, I had it.

"Okay, well, this is going to sound weird, but Pops' mom lived in a retirement community after my granddad passed away. She had her own little manufactured home, but everyone who lived there was old. Anyway, she spent her days in her rose garden. Every time we visited, she would take Halah and I out in her backyard and show us all the different kinds of roses she had. There must have been twenty different kinds, at least. I was only a kid, and I wanted to be inside playing my Game Boy, but I do remember the way her backyard smelled of roses. And every time I smell that scent, I think of my grandma."

"That's the sweetest thing I've ever heard," Kalli said, her voice high-pitched and sickly sweet.

"Hey, you asked. That's the only opinion I have about flowers at all. Roses smell good."

"It's still cute. You're adorable."

Yep. Erection gone.

"Well, I love peonies," she added.

"Noted. I'll remember that when I inevitably fuck up and need to send you apology flowers."

Kalli let out a sharp laugh. "You don't have to send me flowers ever again, babe. I think you hit your flowers quota for life." She gave another laugh and then thumbed her phone again. I was left completely confused.

"What do you mean? I haven't sent you that many flowers. Just a few times when you wouldn't talk to me after what happened at Lego Land."

"What about all those flowers you sent to my house after Marcus died?"

All the coherent thoughts tumbled out of my head at the same time—it was completely empty. I had no idea how to respond. Someone had obviously sent her flowers and for whatever reason, she assumed they were from me.

"Kalli, I'm sorry, but I didn't send you those. After Marcus died, you told me to go away, to leave you alone, so that's what I did. Looking back, I wish I had sent you some flowers, but it wasn't me." I turned and looked at her and then reached my hand out for hers when I saw the expression on her face. It was a mixture of confusion and fear.

"The neighbor lady who lives across the street said flowers came every week."

Whoa. That was a lot of flowers. Who would send someone flowers once a week? And how could she have no idea who sent them? "Didn't they come with cards or anything?"

"Yeah," she breathed, her voice faint as her hand coming up to cover her mouth with spread fingers. "The lady across the street handed me a stack of cards, but I assumed they were from you and I didn't open them." She looked over at me. "That was before I moved to LA. I was still in so much pain, I didn't want to hurt anymore, so I didn't read them. I knew it would wreck me."

"Babe, I'm sorry, but they weren't from me. I'd tell you if they were."

"Then who sent me flowers once a week for months? Riot, I'm a little creeped out."

I could feel her trembling and I had no words to calm her. Honestly, I agreed it was a little weird, but I wasn't about to let anything happen to Kalli. I didn't care who sent her those flowers, they wouldn't be getting anywhere near her without facing me first.

Chapter Sixteen

Devastation

Kalli

I'd tried not to panic in the car, tried to let the way Riot's thumb was rubbing softly against the back of my hand soothe me. I forced myself to take in deep breaths and let them out slowly. I closed my eyes and listened to the way the tires crackled against the pavement of the highway. All of that only went so far to calm me down. I kept picturing bouquets of flowers sitting on my doorstep with cryptic messages, someone lurking in the darkness between houses, watching my house, waiting for me to come home and receive them.

The more I thought about it, however, the more I convinced myself that whoever was sending the flowers hadn't actually been watching me or my house. Otherwise they would have known I wasn't there and that my neighbor was the one taking the flowers. If the intention was to make me uncomfortable, they hadn't succeeded—until now.

We'd had such a wonderful holiday getaway, aside from my panic attack. But even that brought on a sort of cathartic release in a way. I'd been forced to let my closest friends see what I was dealing with, and in some strange way, it made dealing with it easier. Riot and I were closer than ever, and a three-day drive down the west coast had been absolutely perfect until I brought up flowers. Stupid flowers.

Finally, Riot parked at my apartment, shut the car off, and turned toward me. "You've got the cards from the flowers in there, right?" I nodded. "Okay, I'd like to read them first. I don't want you panicking about it, no matter who they're from."

I thought his concern was sweet, and I loved him even more for wanting to spare me from any more grief, but *not* looking at the cards would drive me crazy.

"How about we look at them together? I don't think I'll be able to sit by and let you take care of it."

"Okay, but if you start to get upset I'm taking them away."

"All right." Relationships were about compromise, right? I knew he was only trying to protect me. I couldn't fault him for that.

He held my hand all the way up to my door then insisted on opening it himself. He followed me back to the bedroom area of my studio apartment and I went straight to my jewelry box. Where else would a girl keep a stack of notes she thought were from the love of her life? My neighbor had placed a rubber band around the stack of cards, and when I pulled it off I noticed my hands were trembling. I sat down on the edge of my bed, Riot taking a seat so close our thighs were touching, and I pulled the top card off the stack.

I flipped it over and ripped open the seal, sliding the tiny card out, holding my breath all the while.

Kalli,

I wish there was some other way to contact you, but all I can find is your address. I hope you're doing well, although I suspect you aren't. I know I have no right to hear from you, but please consider reaching out. I'd love nothing more than to talk to you.

Sincerely,

Kevin

"Who the hell is Kevin?" Riot asked, his voice instantly cold and harsh. It matched what I was feeling on the inside. However, in addition to the cold harshness, I was also feeling immediate anger, raging anger at that. I was enraged. Absolutely aflame with anger. This flame, however, was empty, cold, and dangerous. My fingers tightened around the paper of the card and it started crumpling in my hand. My heart was thundering in my chest and all I could feel was its echo throughout my body. "Kalli? Who is this Kevin guy?"

"Kevin is my father."

As it turned out, the cards were not stacked in any particular order. They also didn't have dates on them. So, after I'd opened them all, read them all, cursed my father's name, then read them again, I only had a general idea of the timeline. The early ones were easy to spot, the first one being the most obvious.

Kalli,

I just heard about your brother and I am so very sorry. I wish things were different and that I could be there for you at this trying time, but I know you're in good hands. I think of you often and wish, every day, I'd made better choices all those years ago.

Sincerely,

Kevin

He knew I was in good hands. Huh. That was interesting. I was in good hands, but those were the hands of people who'd known me less than two years. They weren't family. I'd just lost my last piece of my family. Well, except Nancy. But Nancy had been just as broken as I was.

I was so angry at him. Angrier than I had been in a long while. He had no right to weasel his way into my life, especially not when I was defenseless.

Despite my anger, I was silent as I read the cards. That seemed to be the hardest part for Riot. He sat on the bed, next to me, reading the cards over my shoulder, asking me time and again if I was all right, but I couldn't answer him right away. I didn't know if I was all right. I couldn't fathom anything right then besides devastation.

Kalli,

I know you're going through a lot, but I can't sit by anymore not knowing if you're all right. Please, call me. 619-555-8652.

Sincerely,

Kevin

I read that particular note over and over again, wondering why he'd been able to go for more than twenty years without knowing if I was okay, but all of a sudden he'd been desperate for information. I closed my eyes, tossed the card on the floor, pulled up my knees, and rolled to my side. It wasn't even a full second before Riot's firm warm body was behind mine, cocooning me, his arms wrapping tightly around me.

"He can't ignore me for most of my life and then decide, all of a sudden, to care," I whispered. "It's not fair." A different sort of panic was coming over me. I wasn't anxious, but I could feel the eruption of emotion coming and anticipating it was causing just as much panic.

"I know, baby," he whispered into my ear. But he didn't. His parents had been there from the start. Both of them. He'd never had to wonder why his father didn't love him enough to stick around. Never had to spend nights in bed thinking about the fact that his father felt tied down by him, felt like he wasn't free anymore. Suddenly, it was all too much.

A strangled sob broke free from me, and I cried out. Again, in less than a second, Riot had turned me so I faced him, and his arms brought me close, holding me to him, allowing me to cry into his chest. I didn't need him to understand my pain, I only needed him to be there for me. That's all I'd ever need from him, just his presence. That was also the one thing I was afraid to lose the most. I'd always been afraid I was broken like my father. Afraid that no matter what, I'd never be able to stick around for someone I loved. Afraid I'd fall in love, maybe even have a child, and then realize I wasn't built to love that way.

But I knew, so very deep down on the inside, I'd never leave Riot, and I couldn't imagine ever not being there for our future children. That realization, that level of love I had for Riot, only made the lack of love my father had for me hurt all that much more. Every soft touch of Riot's hand, every tiny display of physical affection, made me wonder why my father hadn't loved me enough.

As best I could, I'd dealt with my father's absence when I was younger. I'd spent countless nights wondering where he was, who he was with, what kind of life he was leading that was better than the one he'd had with my mother and me. Growing up without a father sucked. It scarred me on a level no one would ever understand. But the scar was leftover from a wound that had healed. I had lived, Mom and I had moved on, and we'd managed to build a pretty good life. Kevin coming to me years later and trying to make contact with me, well, that was just the same as opening up old wounds. He'd lost all rights to know how I was doing on my seventh birthday when he'd left and not looked back.

"I don't know what to do with all these feelings," I cried, completely lost in what seemed to be a bottomless pit of anger, fear, sadness, and loss.

"Just cry it out, Kal. Give them to me. I'll take care of it."

If I hadn't already been sobbing, his words would have thrown me over into the abyss. There had been a time in my life where I'd convinced myself I didn't deserve the kind of love Riot gave me. I'd told myself I wasn't worthy of that kind of selfless, all-encompassing love. And perhaps I wasn't. Maybe that was the secret to it all. If I knew I was lucky to have him, maybe I'd never take him for granted. I never wanted him to feel anything like what I was experiencing in that moment. I never wanted him to wonder why I hadn't cared enough about him.

Suddenly, and maybe it was the lack of love from my father staring me in the face, but my love for Riot had never been clearer to me or more tangible. It filled the hole that had been gaping most of my life.

"I love you," I cried into the stubble under his chin, my hands coming to pull his neck closer to me, wanting to smell his scent, feel his heartbeat through the thin skin there. The panic was still there, but now I was panicking that I'd never be able to show him how I loved him, to apologize for pushing him away like I had. "I'm sorry. I'm so sorry."

I was exactly like my dad. I *had* run away. I had left him behind. It had been months, not years, and I hadn't abandoned a child, but I'd let Riot love me, then I'd taken that love away. I was just as bad as Kevin.

"You've got nothing to be sorry for, baby," he said quietly, rocking me back and forth, his hand running down the back of my head, smoothing down my hair.

"I'm just like him."

My face was quickly brought level with his, his eyes searching mine, his hands gripping my face with gentle fierceness.

"You are nothing like him, Kalli," he said in a deep, gravelly voice. "I never want to hear you say something like that again. He's a coward. A man who abandoned his child and the woman who gave him that child. He was selfish and a poor excuse for a man." His eyes grew darker, darting back and forth between mine. "He left because he didn't want to take responsibility for his family. You are *nothing like him*."

I couldn't respond, couldn't find any words to argue with him, even though I was sure he was wrong. He had to be. I was a runner.

"You've spent the last chunk of your life caring for your brother, the most selfless thing I've ever witnessed. And you didn't leave me, Kal. I know that's what you're thinking." He pressed his mouth to my forehead. "People respond to grief in a million different ways and your reaction was perfectly acceptable. You'll never have to apologize to me for that. What your father did was inexcusable."

Without thinking much about it, I pressed my lips to his. My cheeks were wet from tears, my hands trembling from adrenaline, and my chest was heaving from the ragged breaths I was taking in, but all I wanted to feel was his lips pressed against mine. I loved him with everything I was, and I wanted to feel that love.

"Please," I whispered against his lips, pressing my body up against his. He kissed me back, his lips and teeth gently tugging on my mouth, but I could feel his hesitation. "I need you," I said, this time moving my mouth over his cheek and down his jaw. "Make me feel something besides this emptiness."

Those words brought him over the edge with me. Suddenly I was beneath him, one of his hands on my face, the other sliding around my waist. I arched up into him, my hands running through his hair, gripping the strands, holding his mouth to mine.

His hand slid up under the hem of my shirt, grazing over my breast, and I suddenly needed to be bare with him, to have nothing covering me except him. I reached down and tugged off my shirt, throwing it on the floor beside the bed.

I was frantic. I reached for my leggings, starting to pull them down my thighs, when his hands covered mine.

"There's no hurry, baby. I've got you. Let me make you feel good."

And with those words I gave my body over to Riot. I let him lead me, let him set the pace, let him put my mind at ease.

He straddled my thighs, both his hands on my stomach, then slid them up slowly. He gripped the cups of my bra and pulled both down, exposing my breasts. He palmed one of them, but bent low to take the other in his mouth. I arched again, offering him everything. As my back lifted off the bed, his hands snaked around and unlatched my bra, pulling it down my shoulders, then his mouth returned to my breast, sucking and pulling.

He rolled off me, keeping one thigh draped over my leg, his mouth still working my nipple, and his other hand snaked down my front, slipping into the waistband of my leggings. I immediately flexed my hips, trying to give him the access he needed, wanting desperately to feel him. When his fingers slipped into my folds I gasped at the contact. As he dipped into me, he groaned. His sounds made goose bumps pop up all over my skin; the feeling of his voice vibrating against my sensitive nipple was dangerously erotic.

With two fingers deep inside me, gently stroking my front wall, his thumb rubbing gentle circles around my clit, I could hardly contain the fast and powerful orgasm that ripped through me.

"That's it, baby. Give it all over to me," he rasped, his mouth coming back down to lick slow and leisurely circles around my nipple. When I'd finally settled from the hasty and powerful orgasm, he wasted no time sliding down my body and removing the last pieces of clothing I wore, splaying kisses as he went. My body was thrumming, vibrating with need. My hands were gripping his biceps, pulling him up to my mouth so my lips could press against his. He pulled away from me, stood at the foot of the bed and slowly took his clothes off, watching me the entire time as I gripped the sheets, if only to have something to do with my hands.

When he was finally free from his clothes, I watched as he climbed over me. My hands instinctively reached for him, wrapping around his back, while my ankles locked behind his thighs. I could feel his jutting erection resting against my folds, and I wanted to be filled with him. I wanted the emptiness, both physical and emotional, to go away.

"You're mine now," he said, slowly pushing into me, his eyes locked on mine. "I will never let anyone hurt you. You never have to worry about being alone again. I've got you." He said the words as he pushed farther into me than I thought possible. I was gasping from the fullness, breathless, frozen. His mouth crashed down to mine and he kissed me feverishly as he pumped in and out, each time hitting a spot I never knew existed, couldn't have even fathomed the waves of bliss it would bring each time he stroked in, paused, but then pushed in just a fraction more. His arms came to encircle me, his hands gliding around my waist then moving upward, over my shoulder blades and then curving around the top, gripping me on either side of my neck. He pulsed in and out, pulling me down by my shoulders, his mouth laving kisses on the side of my neck between grunts and growls.

Every part of him was wrapped around me and I was fully tangled around him, and I had never felt so right before, so balanced, so complete.

His hips began to pound into me faster, my breaths hitched even more with every stroke, and eventually, with the sound of him groaning as he came, I fell over the cliff with him. We came, but he didn't stop kissing me, didn't stop pushing my hair away from my face, or running his fingertips down my cheek. We eventually fell to our sides, my hands still clinging to his back, his mouth still whispering kisses against me, and we stayed that way until we fell asleep.

Chapter Seventeen

Protect Her

Riot

I woke early the next morning, Kalli still wrapped tightly around me. I loved the feeling of her pressed against me, but I also hated it, knowing the reason behind her tight grasp. We'd finally moved into a better light when it came to her dealing with Marcus' death, and then her father had to fuck everything up with his lame attempt at making amends.

I'd watched Kalli regress the night before. I'd watched as she questioned herself, questioned her own worthiness, questioned whether or not she was even capable of the kind of love we shared. That hurt. But it didn't hurt her enough to push me away. When I saw the doubt in her eyes, all I wanted to do was prove it wrong. I wanted to show her that she was the most loving person I'd ever met, and that she was fully capable of loving someone without this tragic flaw of running away.

Kevin hadn't just run away. No. Kevin Rivers was a fucking cowardly dickwad who would, in about five minutes, understand that Kalli was not to be fucked with. She wasn't a seven-year-old girl anymore. And if she wasn't strong enough to make him see how wonderful she was, how idiotic he'd been to walk away from her so many years ago, well, I wouldn't mind clocking that son of a bitch right in the fucking gut.

I slowly rolled Kalli to her back, kissed her temple, then gently pulled out of her arms. I covered her with the blanket all the way up to her neck because I knew if she got cold, she'd wake up in minutes. I needed more than two minutes for what I was about to do.

I grabbed the card off the floor, grabbed my cell phone, and snuck out onto her front porch. I didn't need Kalli to hear my conversation. I dialed the number, shaking my head at the irony of the San Diego area code, and listened to the phone ring on the other end of the line. It rang five times, and I was afraid it would go to voice mail. That was disappointing. This was a conversation that would be better in person, but would suffice to hear live. A recording of the speech I'd planned for the last two hours as I held the woman I loved, sleeping in my arms, wouldn't be nearly as effective as the live version.

"Hello?" I heard a groggy man's voice ask. Good. He'd been sleeping.

"I'm looking for Kevin Rivers."

"Uh, this is he. Who's this?"

"I know your daughter, Kalli."

"Kalli?" he sounded just as confused as he was tired. Then I heard the instant the panic set in. "Is she all right? What's happened?"

I tried to ignore the genuine concern in his voice, tried to look past the fact that he truly sounded like a panicked parent, and pushed it all aside to get my point across.

"Kalli's fine, and I'd like for her to stay that way. So here's what's going to happen: you're not going to fuck with her mind anymore. You've done enough damage and I won't watch you tear her apart again just to make yourself feel better."

"Who is this?" Now he sounded angry.

"I'm the man who she's finally allowed to help her put the pieces back together. I'm the man that's going to kick your ass if you hurt her again. And I'm the man who will die to protect her. Got any more questions?"

The line was quiet for a moment before Kevin asked, his voice much quieter, "Is she all right?"

"No, she's not all right. But she will be."

"I sent her flowers every week, but finally the florist told me they started getting returned. Something about new residents at the address."

"How'd you get her address?"

"I'd rather talk to her about that. Is she there? Can I speak to her?"

"She's asleep. The only way you'll ever get to talk to her is if she decides to call you. I won't stop her from calling you, but I will be with her if she does. What I called to tell you today is, if she decides to reach out to you, you're not to fuck with her head. Got me?"

"What makes you think I want to hurt her? I only want to talk to her, to have a chance to explain –"

"No, see, that's where you're wrong. I don't give a flying fuck if you want to hurt her or not, the odds are, you will. There is nothing you can say to her about why you left your seven-year-old daughter on her birthday that's not going to *hurt her*. You're going to want to talk to her about her brother. Her brother who died. Her brother whose death she still feels slightly responsible for. There is *no way* to talk to her without hurting her at this point." I took in a deep and ragged breath. I hadn't expected to get so angry. I knew I would get keyed up, knew the adrenaline would pump through me if I got a chance to talk to him, but I didn't expect to see red like I was. "So, what's going to happen if she calls you is, you're going to apologize and you're going to listen to her. You're going to be honest with her, and you're going to give her exactly what she wants from you. Nothing more, nothing less. Understood?"

"My relationship with my daughter is no one's business but mine and hers. I think it would be best if we hung up and Kalli called me back later."

"You don't seem to understand. I'm the one protecting her now. I'm the one who's going to be here to help her back up every time she falls, even if she trips herself. Your relationship with her is unimportant—to me or her. I don't care if she calls you and you fix what you broke, if you convince her you're not a monster and that she should allow you back into her life. What matters to me is Kalli. If she's happy, I'm happy. But if you hurt her by being careless, I will hurt you more."

"So you just called me to harass me?"

"No, I called to tell you that if you can't be a decent human being, if you can't be honest with her, if you can't give her real, truthful answers to her questions, don't pick up if she calls. Do her that one last favor as her father. If you're just going to reel her in and then run away again when shit gets tough, just… don't. She doesn't deserve to be yanked around anymore."

Again, Kevin hesitated before answering, but when he did, I felt like he'd thrown down the proverbial gauntlet.

"I'm going to answer the phone when she calls. And I'm hoping when she does call, she'll be open to hearing what I have to say. I don't intend to 'fuck with her,' as you so eloquently put it. But I do intend to straighten some things out."

"Your call, man. But know I'll be there every step of the way. You say one word to her I don't like and I'll find a way to end it. I promise you that."

There was another pause on the line, then he spoke again, sounding a little more resigned. "I can't say I appreciate the early morning wake-up, but I can't lie. I am glad that Kalli has someone like you looking out for her."

"Yeah, well, it should've been you."

"Everyone makes mistakes."

"No, not everyone leaves their kid on her birthday, disappearing for twenty years."

He let out a loud sigh. "I get what you're saying. I hear you. I'm going to hang up now since I feel like we've both said all there is to say. I'll be looking forward to Kalli's call."

"*If* she calls," I said, pointedly.

Another sigh. "Have a good rest of your day."

I ended the call without responding. Odds were, I wasn't going to have a good day. I was going to spend the day at work, hoping Kalli wasn't having a panic attack on her set. I would be worried that she'd call her father while I wasn't around, while I wasn't there to make sure he couldn't reach through the phone and crush her heart with his bare hands again. She'd lived so long without him, but I knew if he disappointed her again, it would take a miracle to not send her spiraling back down into the black hole I'd already managed to pull her out of.

I tossed my phone on her coffee table as I passed by it on my way back to her. Outside her bedroom door, I paused. I scrubbed my hands down my face, trying to calm myself down. I knew if I went in there with nothing but tension radiating off me, she'd feel it. So I took in a deep breath, pushed it out again, and imagined my sleeping girl on the other side of the door, waiting for me.

Calm washed over me.

I pushed the door open, walked back to the bed, crawled in, and wrapped my arms around her. She didn't wake, but she did stir, pressing her body into mine, finding a comfortable position, then melted back into me. I pressed my face into her hair, which lay splayed across my pillow, and I tried to fall back asleep.

Sleep wouldn't come back to me that morning, but being with my girl who was safe and warm in my arms, well, that was better than an extra few minutes of rest anyway.

"You're done with your night shoots, right?"

Kalli was standing at her counter, spreading cream cheese on a bagel. I'd been watching her all morning, trying to figure out where her head was at. For the most part, she was acting normal, not at all as though she'd gotten letters from her absentee father the day before which had left her reeling and crushed. I figured she was either doing okay, or she was tamping down everything and trying to act okay for my benefit.

"Yeah, babe," I said, stepping up behind her. I pulled her blonde hair over her shoulder and pressed my lips right below her ear, loving the way she shivered against me. "I'll be home tonight." My hands ran down to her waist and then I gripped her hips, pulling her ass right against me.

"If I didn't love everything you were doing to my body right now, I'd call you a jerk." Her voice was breathy and light, obviously turned on. I left one hand on her hip, but smoothed one over her belly, then used my mouth on her neck. She shuddered again, and as much as I wanted to distract her with making her body feel good, I knew it was only a bandage. So I eased my mouth off her skin and brought both my hands to the safer location of her shoulders, giving her a gentle squeeze. "Okay, officially a jerk," she said with a laugh as I retreated.

"We've both got to get to work," I said, regret saturating my voice. I didn't want to let her go. I wanted to keep her in that apartment, inside that bubble, where I knew I could help her if she needed me. If we went to work, well, I wouldn't be around and that bothered me. "Will you make me a promise? Two, actually?"

She turned in my arms, leaving her bagel on the counter where she'd stopped preparing it once I put my hands on her. "Sure. Anything."

God, I loved her.

"I need you to promise me that if you need me today, if you're feeling anxious, that you'll call. I can't promise I'll be able to come immediately, but I'll come. If you call, I'll be there."

Her head tilted and her eyes went softer, then her hand came up to press against my cheek.

"I'll call," she whispered, then stretched up to kiss me lightly on the lips. "And the second promise?"

I took in a deep breath. "Promise me that if you decide to call Kevin, you'll do it when I'm around."

She looked at me for a long moment, her eyes seeming to look for something in mine, as if she were trying to read something in them. But then her other hand came to my other cheek and she said, "I haven't decided whether or not I'm going to call him, but if I do, I promise I'll do it with you." Her thumbs stroked my jaw. "I don't think I could do it without you," she added, her voice quieter.

"You're so strong," I whispered, pulling her closer to me. "But you've been through more than one person should have to endure, and I want to make sure I'm here to hold your hand if you need it." Her hands moved to the back of my neck as her face moved closer to mine again.

"I don't know how I got so lucky to find you, Riot Bentley, but I'm never going to let you go."

She pressed her mouth to mine in a soft kiss, her arms wrapping around my neck and her breasts pressing against my chest. I let her give me that comfort, hoping she was taking the same from me.

The day progressed without much more drama, but I was on high alert. I imagined worst-case scenarios. Someone had given Kevin her address before, that same person could have given him the address to her new place. What if he showed up? I didn't know what was going through her mind, but I wondered how long it would take her to realize her father's phone number had an area code based two hours away. And even if she did figure it out, I couldn't tell which direction that would send her in. I wondered if it would make her want to talk to him more, or do the opposite and make her reject him.

I had no idea. And I felt helpless.

So, I did what I could.

I met her for lunch at our coffee shop. I made sure she was all right, and she seemed to be doing fine. I didn't press her about calling her father and she didn't mention it either. It seemed as though I was the only one torn up about it. So I tried to let it go, tried to pretend that everything wasn't balancing on some tightrope dangling over a large crevasse. If Kalli was cool, I'd be cool too.

That was, until I got a call from Halah over dinner.

Kalli and I were sitting on her couch, eating Chinese takeout, watching her favorite show, and when my phone rang and I saw it was Halah, something in my gut told me it was *the* call.

"Shit," I whispered, swiping my finger across my phone to answer the call. "Hello?"

"Riot?" Halah's voice came through the phone and I could tell she was crying.

"Hal? What's wrong?" I figured I knew what was wrong, but hearing her in tears made my heart rate spike regardless.

She gave a little laugh at my question, but then resumed crying.

"Everything's wrong, Ri." I heard her take in a shaky and stuttered breath, and then she continued. "I'm pregnant."

I'd known it. I'd known she was pregnant ever since Kalli had dropped the bomb on me, but hearing her say the words didn't make it any easier to take. Halah was twenty-five. She wasn't too young to have a baby, but she hadn't really grown up yet. She'd been living on a freaking cruise ship most of her adult life and hadn't really been introduced to the real world. She was about to get a pretty drastic reality check.

I had no idea what to say to her and that had never happened before.

"Ask her if she's okay." Those words were whispered from Kalli and I couldn't have been more grateful. She turned toward me, bringing her legs up on the couch and scooting closer, resting her hand on my thigh. Then she motioned toward the phone, pushing me to ask the question of Hal.

"Are you all right?"

"I mean, technically, yeah. I'm pregnant, though. I'm fine physically, but I don't know what to do…" Her voice trailed off and I imagined all the things running through her mind.

"You've got lots of options," I offered, not sure, again, what to say. All I heard on the other end of the line was sniffling. She was crying a lot and I was hours away. "Are you at home? Is Ma there?" Surely my mother could make her stop crying, or at least hug her or something. My arms itched to wrap around her. Instead, I brought my hand up and rubbed it on the underside of my chin. It had been there just seconds when Kalli captured it with her own hand and threaded her fingers through mine.

"Can you put her on speaker?" Kalli asked.

I nodded and did as she asked. "Hal, you're on speaker and Kalli's here, okay?"

"Okay," she mumbled through a cry.

"Hey, Hal," Kalli said softly. "How far along are you?"

"About fourteen weeks."

"Hmm, that's still pretty early. Have you been to see a doctor yet?"

"I saw a doctor in Florida about a month ago when we docked after a run."

"And the doctor said everything looked fine? The baby's healthy?"

"Yeah," she replied, sounding a little bit calmer with every answer.

"And you're taking vitamins?"

"I'm trying, but I keep throwing them up."

"That's okay. You should start to feel a little better in a few weeks, and the baby will get whatever it needs from you regardless. You're doing fine." Kalli paused, looking at me, but I wasn't about to interrupt the incredible line of questioning she had going on. "Have you told your parents yet?"

Silence.

My mind started spinning a mile a minute. My gut was telling me that Ma and Pops would never turn Halah away. They'd be shocked by her news, perhaps a little disappointed at first, but they'd never kick her out, never make her go away. But her silence had me worried. What if she'd told them and they'd blown up?

"Halah, Riot and I aren't here to judge you, we want to help."

"I'm afraid to tell them."

"Why? Ma and Pops love you."

"I'm afraid they'll be disappointed in me," she said, and started crying again. I didn't know what to say to that.

"They're probably going to be really surprised, Halah. And they might think they're disappointed at first, but they will come around and they'll support you no matter what. I know I've just met your family, but your parents are so loving and caring. There's no way they'll turn you away for this."

Kalli's eyes came up to meet mine and even she looked worried. I could see what looked like indecision in her eyes. She gave my hand a squeeze and then asked a question I hadn't even considered.

"Is the father supporting you with everything?"

The father? For fuck's sake, a guy had gotten my baby sister pregnant. Instantly I was enraged, which was why Kalli's free hand found its way to my chest. My head snapped to look at her, only to see her gently shaking her head at me. Then her hand moved from my chest to my cheek, where she gave me a gentle rub. I groaned, with images of my sister, hugely pregnant, and my fist slamming into some dude's face alternating through my brain.

"I haven't told him." Halah's voice might as well have been a whisper for how quietly she said those words.

"Oh, Halah..." Kalli said, sounding both extremely sorry for Hal, but also not in agreement with her statement. I, on the other hand, was still angry that some dude had gotten my sister pregnant.

"Who is he?" I barked.

"Ri, calm down," she answered, still upset, but the crying was tapering off. "He didn't do anything wrong. We broke up before I found out I was pregnant. He was quitting the boat and I didn't want a long-distance thing. It's not like he knocked me up and then ditched me."

"Who. Is. He?"

"His name is Jordy."

"Jordy?" I scoffed. "What kind of a name is Jordy?"

217 | A n i e   M i c h a e l s

"Riot," Kalli whispered angrily, the space between her eyebrows crinkling as they drew together. "Be quiet. You're not helping." She shook her head at me and truthfully, I instantly felt a little bad about my comment. "Now, Hal, why haven't you told him yet?"

"He took our breakup really hard. I mean, so did I. I love him. But I didn't want a relationship where I never saw him. He was starting an art program at a really good school, and I know if I tell him, he'll drop out and come here."

"Damn straight he will," I yelled, right before Kalli gave me a slap on the arm.

"Seriously, Riot? Your macho big brother routine isn't helping." This came from Halah.

"Don't listen to him."

"I'm not."

"Hey," I cried. "If you didn't want me to act like your big brother, then why did you call?"

"Ugh, Riot, I needed to tell someone. I'm terrified to tell Ma and Pops, Jordy can't know because it'll ruin his life, and sooner or later, everyone's going to find out because I'm going to start *looking* pregnant any day now. Excuse me if I was hoping my big brother could offer me some soothing words or helpful advice. For crying out loud, at least your girlfriend isn't a complete asshole."

"Okay, Hal, calm down," Kalli said with a soothing voice. "I think Riot is just having a hard time processing the fact that his little sister had to have sex with someone in order to get pregnant."

I couldn't help it if I growled a little.

"But seriously, Halah, maybe you should call Jordy and tell him what's going on. It might be easier to tell your parents if you have a plan."

"But I know he'll quit school and come to me,"

I was biting my lip really hard, trying not to explain to her that dropping out of school and coming to her was exactly what he should be doing.

"That's okay. You shouldn't have to be going through this alone, anyway. And it sounds like you guys really love each other. It's not fair to leave him out of the picture. He deserves to have a relationship with his baby."

As the last words left her mouth, I heard them getting softer. And when I turned to look at her, I saw her features soften too. And then she turned and rested her head on my shoulder and I knew she was out. It was my turn to be the reasonable brother who offered only compassionate advice.

"Kalli's right," I agreed. "You need to call him and tell him what's up. Odds are he'll show up and that's okay. It's okay for him to change the course of his life for this, Hals. There are art schools in San Francisco. You are planning on staying in San Fran, right?"

"I can't really imagine having a baby without Ma around," she said softly, and that clinched it for me.

"You need to call Jordy, and he needs to be with you when you tell Ma and Pops. He needs to be there for you. And if you want, I'll drive up when you tell them as well. Kalli and I are here for you. Whatever you need." As I spoke I felt Kalli's hand come to my chest, then move up my shoulder, finally coming to rest on the side of my neck, her thumb gently stroking over my throat.

"Thanks, Ri," she said, and I could tell she was crying again.

"Don't cry," I said softly. "Everything will be okay. You're gonna be a mom." That only made her cry even harder.

After ten more minutes of trying to get my baby sister to dry up, she finally got ahold of her emotions enough to agree to call Jordy and get his ass to San Francisco. I ended the call, tossed my phone on the couch cushion next to me, then laid my hand on Kalli's thigh.

"Well, Halah's pregnant," I said with mock surprise. Luckily, Kalli giggled. She giggled in between sniffles, but she giggled nonetheless. "You all right?"

"Yeah. I guess."

"Lots of stuff happening. Heavy stuff. Stuff that makes you think about things." I ran my hand slowly up and down her leg, trying to coax her into talking to me. I didn't want to push her, and I knew eventually she'd open up and tell me what was going on in her brain, but I also knew that for Kalli, keeping emotions locked inside only did bad things. Things I wanted to avoid if possible.

"What would you say if I told you I wanted to call Kevin?"

God, I loved her.

"I'd say you've got every right to call him."

"Do you think it's stupid and masochistic?"

It was my turn to support her, so I turned toward her on the couch and took her hands in mine, lowered my head, and looked directly into her eyes.

"There is nothing stupid about wanting to talk to your own father. It's natural to be curious and to want some answers. It's not masochistic, but I'm hoping you go into it understanding that you can't let his actions determine your worth. If he ends up being a complete jackass and doesn't see what a great, smart, beautiful, and talented daughter he has, well, that's on him, not you."

"I'm really afraid that if I talk to him and find out he's a terrible person, it'll break something inside me, like the last piece of me that is still intact will crumble altogether. But I'm more afraid of finding out he's great."

"Baby, why would it be bad if he turns out to be great?"

"Because then I'll know I missed out on having a great dad all these years." She said the words and tears tumbled down her cheeks. I'd never really felt my heart break before that moment. Kalli was a grown woman. A successful, grown, sophisticated, independent woman, and the dad who abandoned her years ago could still turn her into a brokenhearted little girl. I wrapped my arms around her, pulled her to me, then lay back on the couch with her body draped over mine.

"It might not be a great experience, meeting him. And I can guarantee, even if you meet him and things do go great, it won't fix everything either. The only thing we know for sure is that you are capable of thriving on your own, and I'll be here to support you no matter what happens."

It took her a moment to gather her thoughts and stop the tears that silently fell down her face.

"I wish I didn't have to talk to him on the phone. I wish I could meet him somewhere, see him face-to-face."

I inwardly groaned. I wanted to protect her as much as I could, and that was easier if they spoke on the phone first. It would be easier to take her phone and hang up on him than to pull her out of a restaurant.

"What about Skype?" I offered. That seemed like a good compromise.

"That will be awkward don't you think?"

"We used to Skype all the time."

"That was different," she said, her shy smile crossing her face. I smiled back because she had a point. The appeal with Skype for Kalli and me was that we could see each other, *all* of each other if needed.

"Point made." I took in a deep breath and then blew it out, knowing my next words would seal the deal. "I don't know if you noticed, but the phone number on that card has a San Diego area code."

Her eyes went wide. "You think he lives in San Diego?"

I pushed a strand of hair behind her ear, then slid my hand up to cup the back of her neck. "I think it's worth a shot to find out."

"So, you think I should call him?"

"If you want to meet him, then yeah, I think you should call him, babe."

"Okay," she whispered, but didn't move off me, keeping her eyes on mine. I put pressure on the back of her neck, bringing her mouth to mine. I kissed her and felt her relax into me, her hands sliding up my chest and up into my hair. When the tip of her tongue traced the seam of my lips, I groaned, opening for her. I loved being in control, loved having hold of her and taking what I wanted, all the while knowing I was going to give her exactly what she needed in the process. But when Kalli initiated, when she took the lead and let me know what she needed, that was sexy as hell too.

So I was following her lead. Kissing her, stroking my hand through her hair, letting my hand roam over her body, but not taking it any further. This particular moment wasn't about sex for her, and I could tell. It was about a connection. Her kiss wasn't telling me she wanted me, it was telling me she was glad I was hers, that she was grateful for us.

"I love you," she whispered against my lips.

"I love you too, baby."

She rested her head on my chest and we let our breathing return to normal, let our heart rates settle.

"You feel like going to San Diego soon?" she asked after a few minutes.

"Babe, he wants to meet you, he comes to LA."

"Right. Okay," she said, pushing out a breath, trying to build up her courage.

"Do you want to wait? You don't have to call him now."

"I feel like I should just get it over with."

I could understand that. "Whenever you're ready."

She pushed off me and reached for her cell phone on the coffee table. Then she dialed the number from memory, which made my chest feel tight. She'd stared at that card enough to memorize his phone number. She took in a deep breath and then hit Send, and then the speaker button.

I took her free hand in mine, and brought it up to my lips, kissing her knuckles, watching her facial expression alternate between worried and scared. It started to ring and I felt her tense, and after three rings, I could hardly feel my fingers anymore because she was squeezing them so hard.

But then there was a click on the line and I heard Kevin's voice say, "Hello?" He sounded hopeful, as if he saw the phone number and was wishing it were hers.

Kalli was frozen, mouth open, prepared to say something, but nothing came out. With wide eyes she turned to me, eyes welling with tears.

"Is this Kevin?" I asked, gently rubbing my thumb over her hand, trying to bring her back.

"This is." His voice turned harder, hearing mine. He obviously didn't want to talk to me.

"This is Riot, Kalli's boyfriend. She's here, listening, and we have a few questions."

"Kalli's there? She can hear me?" All hardness was gone from his voice again, and the hope was back. His voice was soft and warm, and I would have bet money he had tears in his eyes, exactly like Kalli.

"She's here, and yes, she can hear you."

"Kalli…," her father said, obviously overcome by emotion. "God, baby doll, I've wanted to talk to you so many times throughout the years."

And with that, I knew Kalli would be unavailable to talk to Kevin. Her phone dropped to her lap, her hand wrenched itself from mine, and she used both of hers to hide her face. I took the phone, but wrapped my arm around her shoulders, pulling her over to me. I could feel her shake against me, silently crying.

"Kevin, we noticed you have a San Diego area code. Is that where you live?"

"Yes, I'm in San Diego."

"Kalli would like to meet you. So if you could come to LA, where we live, we'd appreciate it. Are you free this weekend?"

"Uh, I'm free whenever. I'll be there whenever she needs me to be."

I had to hold back my acidic response, literally bite my lip to make sure I didn't tell him that she'd needed him for over twenty years and that one eager phone call wasn't going to make up for his absence.

"This Saturday. Noon. There's a coffee shop on the corner near her place. We'll text you the address and meet you there."

"I'll be there, Kalli," he said, obviously hoping she was still listening. He couldn't hear her, but she was still silently crying against me. "I'm so grateful you called."

"We'll see you there, Kevin."

"Okay. I'll be there."

I didn't bother saying good-bye, just ended the call, dropped the phone, then wrapped both my arms around my girl. Once she knew the phone call was over, she started crying in earnest, not holding anything back.

"He used to call me baby doll," she said between sobs. "When I was little. He called me that all the time, when he wasn't yelling."

I was seething. I knew it would be difficult for Kalli to talk to her father, knew it would upset her, but I was sick and tired of watching Kalli cry. I was tired of bad things happening to Kalli, tired of Kalli crying because she was hurting. I didn't want her to hurt anymore. And the worst part was, I couldn't take the pain away. I couldn't fix this for her, even though I desperately wanted to. All I could do was hold her while she cried and that made me feel entirely useless.

"Kal, he's not worth all these tears."

"I know," she said, and I could tell she was trying to contain her emotions. "His voice just caught me off guard, and then he called me that, and I kind of lost it."

"Are you sure you want to see him?"

She shrugged. "I don't know what I want." Her eyes met mine and she looked lost. I brought her forehead to my lips, kissed her gently, and then laid back down, bringing her with me.

"You don't have to do anything you don't want to. Seriously. Saturday comes and you decide you don't want to see him, I'll go down there and tell him to take a hike. You're in control here. You get to make all the decisions. You tell me what you want, what you need, and I'll make it happen."

"Okay," she whispered.

"What do you need, Kal?" I needed her to give me something, I needed to take care of her, to make it better somehow.

"I just need you to hold me."

I sighed against her. "I can do that." So I did.

Chapter Eighteen

With Riot by My Side

Kalli

To say I was nervous would have been a drastic understatement. In fact, nervous, as a word, didn't cover the enormity of what I was feeling that Saturday as I waited inside a coffee shop to potentially see my father twenty years after he'd walked out on me.

The entire week had been nothing short of mind-numbingly slow. I had more than enough time to think about what would happen on Saturday, more than enough time to mentally freak out about it, but by Thursday I was starting to get a grip. By Thursday, I had to. I watched Riot worry about me, worry about his sister, and I saw the toll it was taking on him. Eventually, I just had to tell myself whatever happened, happened. There wasn't anything I could do about it, so I had to push the anxiety to the back of my mind and be present in the moment, present with Riot, okay with Riot, so that he could be okay too.

But all that went out the window on Saturday as I sat in that coffee shop. There was nothing I could say to myself, no nonsense I could slowly repeat in my mind to calm myself down. I just had to ride the wave. And it was easier with Riot by my side.

I couldn't miss him when Kevin finally came into the coffee shop. I hadn't seen him since my seventh birthday, but he looked exactly the same, just older. His hair was still the same blond color mine was, and his face was still the same shape as mine. He walked in and I watched as his blue eyes, which matched mine, swept the coffee shop. When they landed on me, his recognition was instantaneous. He knew me just as immediately as I knew him. So, there was that.

Our eyes locked, and I didn't know what his heart was doing, but mine was thundering so loud in my chest I was sure he could hear it across the noisy coffee shop chatter. We stared at each other for a long moment, neither of us moving, but when he did, it was to say something to someone behind him. Then he started walking toward me, and the person he'd spoken to started to follow, and then, my life changed.

It was as quick as a light switch flipping, or as rapid as the wings of a hummingbird. It happened and I would never be the same.

Following my father was a girl who looked exactly like me.

My throat went dry, my jaw slackened, and my heart, which had previously been hammering away in my chest, simply stopped beating.

Kevin came to our table and the younger version of me stopped right by his side, and both sets of eyes were trained on me as though I was going to give them the secret to eternal life.

"Kalli," he finally said, half smiling and half looking as though he were going to lose his breakfast. "I can't believe I'm looking at you. You're beautiful."

Riot looked between the two of us, and I couldn't manage to say a word, so he piped in with, "Why don't you take a seat." Kevin looked at Riot gratefully, then took the chair directly across from me, while his blonde counterpart took the chair across from Riot.

"I can't believe you're here. The entire drive up I thought for sure we'd get here and you wouldn't show. I couldn't blame you, honestly, but I was sure I'd be stood up." He was talking rapidly, words falling from his mouth almost quicker than I could comprehend them. But as much as he was saying, as many words as he had for me, I had none yet for him.

"Dad," the blonde girl said quietly, her eyes darting to me as she said them, then back to her father—my father. "I'm going to get a coffee. Want anything?"

"I'll take a water," he said gently, then pulled out his wallet and handed her a ten-dollar bill. She took it with a small smile, then stood up and walked to the counter.

"That's Rachel. She'll be nineteen next month. Right after the new year."

"She looks exactly like me," I said, surprised the words had come out of my mouth.

"Well, she looks exactly like me, and so do you." Then he let out a chuckle and it hit me like a tidal wave; I'd heard that particular laugh for the first seven years of my life and hearing it then, I was sure I would have recognized it anywhere. We could have been in a crowded train and had I heard the laugh from the other side of the car, I would have known it was him. I would have felt it deep within me, like I did then. It was a sound that moved through my body, making all the hairs on my arms stand up. "You're both much prettier than I am, but you definitely look like me." He continued speaking like nothing was happening, and perhaps, for him, it wasn't. But I was definitely having a moment.

"We didn't realize you were bringing anyone with you," Riot said. *Thank you, Riot.*

"Well," he said, reaching up and scratching his chin. "I wasn't planning on bringing Rachel. She heard me talking with her mother about our meeting and I couldn't keep her away." His eyes moved to me. "She's always known about you. I have a picture of you in my wallet," he said, leaning over and reaching into his back pocket, pulling it out. "I've always kept it in my wallet and I've always shown it to Rachel, telling her about her big sister. She's always wanted to meet you." He flipped his wallet open and there I was. Five years old. Kindergarten. Blonde pigtails. That same picture had hung in the hallway of every house I'd ever lived in growing up. Although, the picture in his wallet was faded and worn.

It was then that Rachel sat back down in her seat, an eager smile on her face. She looked curious and excited, and truthfully, a little wary. I couldn't help but smile at her, glad I wasn't the only nervous one.

"You're my sister," I said softly, testing the words out. I'd never had a sister. I'd dreamt of a sister, asked my mother for a sister nearly every Christmas I could remember until I realized where babies actually came from.

"Yeah," she said hesitantly. "I'm sorry to ambush your meeting, but, well, I wasn't sure how successful your meeting with Dad was going to be, and if I only ever got one chance to meet you, I was going to take it. So, I stole the keys to Dad's car."

Before I could stop them, my eyebrows were reaching for the ceiling, impressed with her negotiation tactics. "Smart thinking," I said, still smiling. "You're almost nineteen? So, are you in college then?"

She nodded, then pushed a lock of hair behind her ear and even Riot grabbed my thigh under the table because it was like looking in the mirror. "I'm a freshman at UCSD."

"Rachel is majoring in elementary education. She wants to be a schoolteacher."

"I'm majoring in elementary education with a focus on special education. I want to be a special education teacher in an elementary school," she said, rolling her eyes, as if she corrected her father about this point often.

"What?" Kevin asked, raising his hands in the air. "That's what I said."

Rachel rolled her eyes again and looked at me and I found myself doing the same thing. Then I froze, realizing I was no longer nervous, and that made me nervous all over again.

Rachel gave a little laugh and then I saw her eyes naturally move to Riot, back to me, and then with startling speed, back to Riot. Then her eyes went wide. Really wide. And her mouth gaped open to match.

"You're Riot Bentley," she said, completely in awe. My eyebrows drew together and for just one moment I was confused as to how she would know who he was, but then she fangirled all over him and I remembered my boyfriend was kind of famous. "You're on that new awesome cop show, and you're dating Lexi Black. I love her."

My head drew back in surprise at her words.

"I was never dating Lexi. I've been with Kalli for a while now. Ever since we worked together on the Lexi Black music video." His hand squeezed my thigh under the table again, and I loved that he considered himself "with" me, even when we weren't together.

"Wait," Rachel said with more excitement, "you worked on the music video too?" Her bright and wide eyes were now on me.

"I'm a costume designer. I did the costumes for that video. That's how we met."

"Wait a minute…" She took in a deep breath, and I could have sworn she went a little pale. "My long-lost sister is dating Riot Bentley?"

Before I could respond, even though I wasn't really sure how to, she continued.

"I've wanted to meet you forever, don't get me wrong. My whole life I've known about you, Dad talked about you all the time, and I knew as soon as I got the chance I would find you, but to find out that you're actually *dating* Riot Bentley, I mean, this is kind of amazing."

Riot suddenly started to stand. "Perhaps I should just leave you all—"

"No!" Rachel and I said simultaneously.

"You're not leaving me here alone," I said, jerking his arm down, forcing him to sit again. I knew he was only trying to make it easier for me to talk with Rachel and Kevin, but I wasn't prepared to be left alone with them yet. "Please don't go," I whispered, as soon as he was sitting again.

His thumb and forefinger came to gently grip my chin and he smiled at me. "I'll stay. Promise." Then he gave me the tiniest of kisses. Then I heard a swoony sigh from across the table. And I couldn't help but laugh. Riot was totally swoon-worthy. In that moment, I could be nothing but grateful for my newly-discovered sister and her fangirl crush on my boyfriend. Everything was one thousand times less uncomfortable and stressful than I thought it would be, only because she was there to break the tension. I loved her already.

"So, you're an actor?" Kevin's voice had suddenly taken on a remarkably different tone. It was skeptical and protective. He was trying to give Riot the fatherly third degree. My hackles immediately went up. I was feeling a lot less anxious than I had expected, thanks to Rachel, but nothing had really changed. Kevin was still the man who'd abandoned me and, as far as I was concerned, he didn't have a leg to stand on when it came to suddenly acting like my father.

"We're not here to talk about Riot's career," I stated calmly. "I love him and don't care what your opinion of his profession is. If it weren't for him, I wouldn't be here meeting you today. He's here today to support me, not to answer to you. You're the one who should be answering questions."

Kevin held his hands up immediately. "You're right. I apologize, to both of you. I'll answer any question you have with complete honesty."

"Why did you leave?" The question had been on my mind for twenty goddamned years, yet I was still surprised when I spoke the words. I never thought I would get an answer; thought I would go to the grave wondering why my dad didn't think I was good enough to stick around for. The weight of that unanswered question was heavier than anything, and it dragged me down in a way I'd never be able to explain to anyone; it was a heaviness no one could understand but me.

He took in a long deep breath, preparing himself for battle it seemed, but I didn't feel sorry for him. He had to have known I wasn't going to open my arms to him and forget he'd damaged me in an irreparable way.

"When I met your mother, we were really young. Teenagers. And when she became pregnant, it was not the best situation. Neither of us had a decent job, our parents weren't in a position to help, so we had to grow up really fast. I loved her, but I loved her the way a seventeen-year-old boy loves a girl. It was immature and childish. And when you were born, I loved you the best way I could. But I was *young*, Kalli. So young. I knew I wasn't doing enough. I didn't have a good enough education to properly provide for you, I couldn't give you or your mom the kind of life I'd imagined giving my child and the mother of my child, and that put a dark cloud over me. For years I worked to try and build a life, but we could never seem to get out of that state of just barely making it." He ran his hands through his hair and I watched as the strands stuck up, not immediately returning back to the previous kept state. He looked frazzled. He looked worried. He looked guilty.

"I was twenty-four the day I walked out on you and your mother. Twenty-four-years old and I'd spent seven years thinking I wasn't good enough to even give you a decent start in life. That weighed me down, Kalli. I felt trapped. I felt bound. It was stifling. And at some point I just broke. I convinced myself that you were both better off without me, that if your mother didn't have me in the picture, her parents would take pity on her and help her more, do more good for her than I could being in the picture." He shook his head. "I convinced myself of a lot of things that, as I grew older and gained more wisdom from life, I learned were the most disastrous mistakes I'd ever make."

He stopped speaking, his hands flat on the table in front of me, and he looked at me, pleading with his eyes for me to, I didn't know, say something back? Forgive him? Tell him he hadn't scarred me for life? I couldn't respond.

"I'll never be sorrier for anything than I am for abandoning you and your mother. It was selfish, childish, and the biggest mistake of my life."

Well, there it was. Words I never thought I'd hear. Words I never imagined I'd hear coming from my father's mouth. And the kicker was that he sounded completely and entirely genuine. I could tell, just from listening to him tell his story, he was sorry, right down to the depth of his bones, for leaving me behind.

"Every time I saw one of my friends with their father, I wondered why I wasn't good enough. Every time I went to a friend's house and her dad came home from work, hugging her, asking her how her day was, asking her if she'd done her homework, I wondered what I'd done wrong to push you away. Every time I was with a man I wondered when he was going to leave, so I never stayed with one long enough to figure it out. I also spent most of my twenties wondering if I would abandon my own family one day, so guess what? I avoided starting one. You took more from me than a second income. You took more from me than a *good start in life*. When you left me, you took all my security with you. You took all my self-confidence with you. You took away my ability to feel worthy of love and my ability to feel comfortable *loving* someone."

Riot's hand found mine under the table and he squeezed it. I could feel him tensing next to me, likely uncomfortable with my emotional state and not being able to comfort me the way he wanted to. The tears stinging my eyes and the pinching in the back of my throat alerted me that I was close to a meltdown, so I sucked in a shuddered breath and tried to take it deep, then pushed it out slowly, all the while feeling Riot's thumb move lovingly over the back of my hand.

"There's absolutely nothing I can do to fix that, except to say that I'm sorry. I'm sorry. You'll never know how sorry I am, but I will spend the rest of my life trying to make you see how much I regret the choices I made. I can't go back and fix it, Kalli, I would if I could, but I can show you how much I've always loved you. I never stopped loving you. I thought, as lame as it sounds, that both our lives would be better if I left."

I wiped the tears from my face, cursing them, feeling as though they gave a piece of me away that I wasn't ready to let him see. I wanted to seem strong, to appear as if I were made of steel, like his absence hadn't really altered me all that much. But I simply could not keep the pain inside. Hearing my father admit it was a mistake to leave me was every kind of emotional warfare I could imagine. It bypassed every security I'd put in place to keep the pain out. It jumped every wall I'd ever put up around my heart, and it simply hurt.

"I've spent my whole life thinking the one man who was supposed to love me the most never loved me at all." The words were hard to push out past the cries. I'd entered into ugly cry territory, but I was trying to keep it in check due to the fact that we were in public. So I was exceptionally thankful when Riot finally wrapped his arm around my shoulders and pulled my face into his neck, letting me cry into him, stifling the sound of my sobs.

I gripped his t-shirt in my hands, my fingers tightening around the soft cotton, pulling myself as close to him as I could get. In the last year of my life, Riot was the one constant. Even when I'd pushed him away, he was still there, just lying in wait.

"I don't think I can do this anymore," I whispered as quietly as I could against the skin of his neck. I felt his arms wrap around me tighter, holding me even closer.

"You say the word and I'll take you home. I'll carry you out of here and you won't even have to say a word to him," he said quietly near my ear, but there was no way Kevin hadn't heard him. "But, Kal, leaving won't fix what's broken inside you. The only way to mend it is to let him in."

"It hurts," I said with only breath; I had no voice left.

"For now, baby, just for now. It'll feel better after a while, after the wound isn't so raw. And," he said, now caressing the side of my face, dangerously close to my ear, "I'll do my best to make you feel better too."

I pulled away quickly, forgetting for a moment that I was having a life-altering moment with my absentee father, and narrowed my eyes at him.

"Did you just promise to make me *feel better*?"

He winked at me. "Got you to stop crying, didn't I?"

At that I heard both Rachel and Kevin chuckling. I wiped my eyes and turned back to them, halfway expecting to see them cringing at my emotional state, but all I saw was concern.

"I'm sorry."

"No apologies from you, Kalli. I won't lie, it's hurting me right here watching you cry," he said, rubbing the center of his chest, "but I'm not going to ask you to hold back with me. I deserve to know what I've done, the pain I've caused. I know that if you hold back with me now, if you try and shelter me from the damage I've done, this won't work."

"What is *this*?" I asked, still trying to keep myself together.

"It's whatever you want, baby doll. If you want to walk out of here and never talk to me again, I get it. I'll be forever grateful I got to see you and to know you're all right, but I'll understand. If you want to talk on the phone twice I year, I'll take those phone calls and be thankful for them. If you want more than that, I'll give you whatever I've got. I'm here, wide open, just hoping you'll let me in a little bit."

"I'm kind of hoping you'll let me in a lot." This came from Rachel and my eyes darted to her, softening a little. "I've been an only child my whole life, always knowing I had a sister out there, and I'm kind of tired of not knowing you."

Before I could think better of it, I reached across the table and took her hand.

"I could really use a sister." She smiled at me, a real smile, not a worried one, and I couldn't help but smile back.

"Kalli is the best big sister in the world," Riot said from beside me, his voice quiet.

"We were really sorry to hear about your brother," Kevin said.

I pulled my bottom lip between my teeth, but then said, "Thank you."

"Dad told me he wanted to drive up to Seattle to see you when it happened, but I told him it wouldn't be a good time. I convinced him to send you the flowers."

"It wasn't a good time," I agreed softly. I thought about my life the few days after Marcus' death, the few weeks following it, and I wouldn't have been in a good place to receive a surprise visit from my long-lost father. Not at all. That surely would have sent me off the ledge of sanity I had been clinging to. "Wait," I said, suddenly remembering I was missing a huge piece of the puzzle, "how did you know where I lived to send the flowers to me?"

Kevin took a sip of his water, then he put his glass down and laced his fingers together, folding his hands and resting them on the table in front of him.

"About ten years ago I started doing freelance work for a company that has offices all over the west coast. I worked from home mainly, but sometimes travelled in to an office in San Diego, or travelled to other offices if need be. It started as a temp job, something on the side, but a few years in they offered me a full-time position. I accepted and was flown to their Seattle offices to meet with the staff coordinator. Inside the headquarters office was a large framed picture of the Vice President and his family, and it was a memorial to him—your stepfather." He took another drink, cleared his throat, and continued.

"I saw your mother in that picture, and I saw you, and I read the article that was framed alongside it that stated your mother and stepfather had passed, and that they were survived by you and your brother."

"They were on their way to visit me in New York, headed to the airport." He nodded, taking in my words. "I wasn't in that crash. But it left my brother mentally disabled."

"Obviously, the article left me with a lot of questions and a lot of panic. I didn't know what to do, who to call, how to get ahold of you, so I hired a private investigator, and three weeks later, I had your address."

"How long ago was that?" I asked, shocked to think that my father had hunted me down.

"Five years."

"You knew where I was five years ago?" A tiny jab of pain pierced my chest. It was small, but it was there. I'd always figured my father had run away and never looked back. It had never crossed my mind that my father had known where I was at all, let alone known where I was and still hadn't come to find me.

"You have to understand that until I saw that article, I had convinced myself that I didn't deserve to know anything about you, let alone your address or what was going on in your life. I was going to let you live your life, even if it killed me. I told myself you were happy and with your mother, and until I found out that wasn't true, I was going to let you be."

"I don't know what to say."

"You don't have to say anything. I know what you must be thinking, that I didn't care enough to come find you. That's so far from the truth, Kalli. I didn't want to disrupt your life more than it already had been. The PI told me about the settlement you got, that you were already doing a great job of taking care of your brother, and that everything seemed to be all right. And the last thing I wanted to do was cause any more upset. So, I stayed away. But I paid that PI every six months for an update. Nothing intrusive, I only wanted to make sure you were okay."

"You've been checking up on me for five years?" This was beyond anything I could have imagined.

"Checking up sounds bad. I was simply making sure you were all right. That you had what you needed, that you weren't drowning in debt, or foreclosing on your house, fighting an illness. Stuff like that. I didn't want to impose on your life, but I wanted to know you were okay. If that was wrong of me, well, I'm not sure I'd take it back. It's what led me here, back to you."

"So, your PI told you that my brother had died. How did that change anything?"

He didn't answer right away, just looked me right in the eyes for the longest time. Then, he finally said, "I guess I didn't want you to feel like you were alone."

I'd felt alone, in one way or another, most of my life. The only time I hadn't was when Marcus was alive and Riot was in my life. Those few weeks had been gloriously happy and full. But as I drew in a deep breath, feeling the air filling my lungs, pressing my chest outward, I knew there was room enough inside me for more love. I hadn't lost Marcus' love, it was still within me, but I had an empty chamber that had been waiting for my father to fill it.

I could be mad at my father forever. I could tell him I never wanted to see him again, but the hole would still be there, and I would always be partially empty. I was too young when it happened to appreciate my mother's death as a sign that you shouldn't ever take life for granted, but Marcus' passing definitely was starting to settle that notion into my heart. All my life I had wished my father would come back and tell me it had all been a mistake and that he'd loved me all along.

And here he was, doing exactly that.

"And now?" I asked, hoping he would understand what I was asking so I didn't have to say it out loud.

"And now I'm hoping you'll let me be your father again."

"It's been a really long time since I was someone's daughter."

"You've always been my daughter."

I smiled at those words, because regardless of the entirely crappy way he'd left, it was nice to know he'd thought of me, that he'd regretted the decision to leave. If there was one thing I was guilty of, it was pushing people I cared about away. Perhaps we were both done pushing love away.

"Where do we go from here?" My voice was quiet but strong.

"I think we take it slow. I'd like to spend some more time with you, perhaps drive up again in a few weeks." He looked hopeful, as though he were afraid I would turn him away.

"Listen, I'm glad you guys are going to reconnect, and I understand you need to take things slow, but I'm not going to be taking it slow. I need your phone number and we're going to become best friends," Rachel said, pulling her phone out of her purse.

I laughed out loud. "You remind me a lot of my friend Megan." I gave her a warm smile. "I'd love to be your new best friend."

Riot's arm wrapped around my shoulders, bring me closer to his side, and then his lips brushed against my temple.

We spent the next few hours in that coffee shop getting to know my sister and my father.

Chapter Nineteen

She Took Me With Her

Riot

The next couple of weeks were spent watching Kalli
come completely out of her shell. I'd seen her unreserved
in the past, seen glimpses of her true nature when she
wasn't busy protecting and guarding the walls she'd built
around her heart. But ever since she'd reconnected with
her sister and father, it was as if she'd found the key to
unlock the best parts of her. It was amazing to watch, like
a butterfly emerging from its cocoon, spreading its wings in
the sunshine, tentatively testing out its ability to fly.

She really had become best friends with Rachel. After
about three days, I stopped asking who she was texting
when she'd stare at her phone and laugh uncontrollably.
The next weekend after they'd met, Rachel had driven back
up to LA and spent the weekend with Kalli while I worked.
I had to admit, for two women who hadn't spent a day
together in their whole lives, they were eerily similar. They
laughed at the same things, had the same taste in almost
everything, and sometimes even said the same exact thing
at the same time. It was astonishing to watch, but even
more exciting to watch the way the relationship lifted Kalli
up.

Kalli also spoke to Kevin often. Not daily, but enough
times during the week that he was up to date. Sometimes
their conversations were short—just check-ins. Other times
it would be hours of her listening to him tell stories from
when she was younger that she couldn't remember, or her
telling him about her life previous to their reconnection.

I listened to her tell him about the day Marcus died. I was sitting on the couch reading a script, her head was in my lap, and she was telling him about the phone call she'd gotten in the middle of the night. I paused when I realized what she was talking about and slipped one hand down into her hair, gently running my hand down her golden tresses, trying to offer her comfort without being intrusive.

She told him the whole story, the entire thing. Even what came after his death—the months and months of solitude and sadness. Then I listened to her tell him the story of us, and how we'd reconnected. My fingers had been trailing through her hair the entire conversation, but when she started talking about our relationship, and how I'd helped her even if it was by letting her heal on her own, my fingers moved to her shoulder then down her arm. I needed the contact. The words were for her father, but it felt good to hear them nonetheless.

She hung up the phone with him after the emotional conversation, said nothing to me, but twined her fingers through mine, and napped on my lap until I was ready for bed. When I tried to move gently from under her and carry her to bed, she sleepily wrapped her arms around my neck, then pressed her lips to mine, kissing me with ease and patience, as if she knew she had an entire night to use her lips on me.

I placed her tenderly on the bed and she never let me go, pulling me over her as she leaned back onto the pillows.

Slowly, we both removed each other's clothes, and with more tenderness and devotion than ever before, we made love. I watched as Kalli lazily slid onto me, leaning down to take my mouth in a kiss as she rode me with ease, her eyes never leaving mine. My hands wandered her entire body, the silkiness of her skin smoothing under my hands, her curves and angles giving my fingers the most gorgeous playground. I ached to touch her everywhere and knew I was blessed because she allowed me access to all of her.

Sex between Kalli and me had always been incredible, but looking back it became apparent there was always something missing, something she always held back, even if she didn't know she was doing it.

Now, there'd been a shift in her life, as if something jarred her so tremendously that a missing piece had become dislodged and fallen back into place. So when I watched her climb that physical high, looked upon her as she brought us both to our climax, it was the most beautiful sight I'd ever seen. I'd loved the broken Kalli, would have followed her to the end of the earth, but I loved this Kalli more because I didn't have to follow her anywhere—she took me with her.

Later, as we lay wrapped around each other, still naked, very much entangled beneath the blanket, she whispered, "I wish I'd been able to feel this whole when I still had my whole family. Sometimes it's hard to feel this happy knowing they're not here."

I kissed her hairline and said, "Try not to focus on what you've lost, Kal. Try to focus on what you still have."

A few days later when Kalli mentioned off the cuff how it would be nice to spend Christmas with her new family, I wasted no time arranging for just that to happen.

We arrived at my parents' house on the morning of the twenty-fourth, after a lazy morning in bed, complete with lazy morning sex, which spilled over into clean-up shower sex. The drive up to my parents' house was calm and happy, and Kalli held my hand the whole way, asking me silly questions and making me stop at every viewpoint. I acted as though it was a hassle to stop and look at the beautiful sights with her, but in reality I'd always leap at an opportunity to take a breather and appreciate the scenery with the most important person in my life by my side.

Another big development was waiting for us at my parents' in the form of my sister's baby daddy, Jordy. As Kalli had predicted, once he learned of his unborn baby, nothing could stop him from coming to be with Halah, and together they had told my parents. Just as I had predicted, my parents were shocked at first, but quickly settled into the idea of being grandparents, especially when Halah mentioned she wanted to leave her job for good and stay in San Francisco. Nothing could have made my mother happier than hearing that her baby was coming home, and that she was going to *have* a baby.

My parents had graciously opened their home to Jordy, offering the couple a place to stay until they figured out life as a family. Although, I was pretty sure my mother was hoping they'd stay until after the baby was born.

So on Christmas Eve, as I sat around our giant kitchen table with Kalli, my sister, her boyfriend, and my parents, it felt right as rain to be laughing and playing Clue, which was a Christmas Eve tradition we'd not been able to fully enjoy ever since Halah left for her cruise ship life.

When the doorbell rang, I exchanged a knowing glance with my mother, then put my hand on Kalli's back. "Why don't you go get the door, babe."

"You want me to get the door?" she asked, eyes wide and confused.

"Yeah, go," I said, giving her a gentle tap on her ass as she hesitantly stood up and walked through the house. I listened to her footsteps until I knew she was at the front door.

"What the…" I heard her say quietly to herself. "Are you for real right now?"

I had to cover my mouth to keep from laughing, but my smile was as big and full as my heart.

"Surprise!" Rachel shouted, right after I heard the door open. Screaming and jumping ensued, and then I heard Kevin's distinct voice say, "Merry Christmas, baby doll."

The house was quiet for a moment, and even though I wished I could see Kalli embracing her father as I knew she was, I was glad they were having the moment together.

When they all finally came into the kitchen, Kevin's arm slung around Kalli's shoulders, her face was flushed and her cheeks were wet. She left his arms and came straight into mine, caring nothing about everyone else in the room as she pressed her lips against mine.

"I know you're behind this," she said, her lips still pressed to mine, refusing to break our connection.

I kissed her again, but then pulled away and tucked a loose strand of hair behind her ear. "You said you'd like to spend Christmas with your family, so here they are." Her hand ran down my cheek, her eyes, full of love, staring directly at me. I kissed her nose, but then moved her off my lap so I could stand and shake Kevin's hand. He introduced me to the woman at his side, his wife, and told me her name was Sharon. It took all of twenty seconds for Kalli to introduce Rachel to Halah and the three were thick as thieves.

I spent the rest of the night listening to the three girls laugh, watching Kevin as he took in the sight of his two daughters spending a holiday together, tasting Ma's spiced cider, which Halah was terribly upset she couldn't have, and stealing glances at Kalli as she spent a night in a room filled with people who loved her.

When it was time to turn in, we showed Kevin, Sharon, and Rachel to their rooms, then I led Kalli to my childhood bedroom where she spent an hour showing me exactly how grateful she was for my surprise, while I forced her to remain silent as I made her come multiple times with various parts of my body.

The next morning, Kalli woke up like a child, excitedly shaking me awake, telling me it was Christmas morning. I groaned and got out of bed, laughing as she threw her hair into a messy bun and went to wake up her sister.

We found my mom in the kitchen preparing her famous and traditional Christmas morning casserole for breakfast. The table filled with my and Kalli's family, and throughout the entire meal, her hand was on my thigh under the table.

Afterward, we moved to the family room, all finding places to sit around the Christmas tree. I took the overstuffed club chair near the window and Kalli sat on a big pillow on the floor between my knees. Rachel volunteered to be Santa and spent a few minutes passing out presents to everyone, and I smiled every time she brought one to Kalli. She hadn't expected to be spoiled by my parents, but I knew Ma and Pops loved her and wouldn't let her spend Christmas here without a pile of gifts.

Once they were all delivered, the mass opening of presents commenced. I watched as Kalli received concert tickets from Halah, along with a pair of sunglasses that apparently were very much "in" at that moment. The gift from my dad to her was a simple gold charm bracelet, which Halah also received. I saw the way Kalli paused when she realized my dad had given her the same gift he'd given his own daughter, and she smiled shyly as he winked at her.

I got the typical gifts from Ma and Pops—some baseball tickets and necessities; socks and underwear. I rolled my eyes at my mother's gifts, but Kalli laughed in a way that said she thought it was cute my mom still bought me underwear for Christmas.

Kalli finally got to the gift I put under the tree for her and I made her turn around and face me when she opened it. It was a small box and anyone would have guessed it was jewelry. She took the bow off, slid the top off the box, and then pulled out the velvet box that lay inside. She gave me a half grin, but then returned her eyes to the gift as she lifted the lid.

Her eyes went soft when she saw it, and her mouth turned down into the cutest pout, then her eyes snapped up to me.

"Riot, it's beautiful. Thank you." She dropped her hands to her lap but reached up and gave me a short and sweet kiss, attempting to be polite in front of our families, but before she could fall away from me completely, I gripped the back of her neck and held her mouth close to mine, looking her right in the eye.

"That necklace is a combination of two things, Kalli. A heart and an infinity symbol. You've got my heart, and I want you to know you've got it forever." I brought her lips back to mine and gave her a kiss more suitable to my liking. It wasn't inappropriate, but it was definitely more than a peck. I'd take more from her later when I got her alone.

"It's the most beautiful necklace I've ever seen. I'll wear it all the time." I heard her voice go hoarse and I could see in her eyes she was getting emotional. I didn't want that. I wanted this to be a happy day with no crying. Not yet, at least. So I let her go and she turned back around, but then asked me to help her clasp the necklace. I swept a few strands of straw-colored hair to the side which had escaped her bun, then took the ends of the necklace from her and clasped it, letting it fall around her neck once I was finished. She fingered the pendant, then leaned all the way back, her head in my lap, face pointed toward me, and I leaned down to kiss her again.

"I love you," she whispered when I ended the kiss.

"I love you too, baby."

Presents continued and I laughed when my sister got me the matching pair of sunglasses to Kalli's, only more masculine.

"Now you guys can match. It's going to be adorable." Halah was way too excited about our eyewear, but I thanked her sincerely because I knew, as silly as it was, she'd put a lot of thought into our gifts. And the sunglasses were really nice.

Toward the end of the gift portion of the morning, my ma stood up and brought a gift to Kalli that hadn't been under the tree. It was a shallow box, rectangular, and it looked to be a little heavy.

"Kalli, I wanted to give this to you and tell you, from the bottom of my heart, I hope it brings you nothing but happiness. And I hope you understand why I did what I did."

"Ma? What did you do?" I asked, suddenly a little nervous about the box sitting in Kalli's lap.

"It'll be okay," Pops said, gently patting my mother's knee as she took her seat again.

I watched as Kalli unwrapped what seemed to be a photo album, but when she opened the first page, even I was stunned.

Laid out in the pages of that photo album were pictures of Marcus, but it wasn't just the pictures, it was the way the photos were so artfully displayed. These were not photos only put on pages, these were pages specially created to bring out the meaning of the photo.

"Did you make this, Ma?"

She nodded and then quickly wiped her hand under one eye, catching a tear before it fell down her cheek. I looked down again and Kalli was flipping through the pages of the book like she was looking at priceless art. Marcus was smiling up at us, laughing even. He was running through a field, playing video games, even Monopoly. Some of the pictures included Kalli, a few had Nancy and Mr. Bob.

"Where did you get these photos?" Kalli asked, without looking up from the album.

"Well, I hope I didn't overstep any boundaries, but right after your brother passed I asked Riot where I could send a card or condolences. We'd never met you, but Riot had told us about you and he was so upset… anyway, he didn't know your address but gave me Nancy's phone number. Nancy and I spoke a few days after the funeral and she gave me the address and that was that. Then, last month, after we met you, I got the idea and thought maybe she could help. Two days later I had a large envelope full of pictures to make your gift."

"You spoke with Nancy?" Kalli's voice was soft again, and this time she looked at my mother with her question.

Ma nodded.

Kalli's eyes went back to her lap where the album lay. "I don't have any pictures of him with me. I packed them all away because it was too hard to look at them." I placed my hands on Kalli's shoulders, squeezing gently with just enough pressure so she knew I was there for her. "But this is wonderful," she finally said, letting out a large breath with her words. "It's beautiful and I can't believe you went to all this trouble."

Both Kalli and my mom were crying. Kalli stood and started toward Ma, who also stood, and they embraced in the middle of the room, Kalli burrowing her head into Ma's shoulder while Ma rubbed her hands soothingly up and down her back. I saw my sister wipe a tear away, along with Rachel, and even Pops had to clear his throat.

"I love it," I heard Kalli say quietly to my mother.

"Well, we love you."

Even I had to bite my lip at that point to keep my emotions in check.

Finally, Kalli pulled away and Ma went back to her seat.

"Here," Kalli said, pulling a card out from under my chair. "Open this so we all stop crying."

Laughter rang out around the room, and Kalli sat at my feet, her pretty blue eyes still wet, but happy.

"What's this?" I asked, running my finger under the sealed edge of the envelope.

"It's your Christmas gift," she said, rolling her eyes.

I pulled out a bundle of papers, my eyes flitting between the papers in my hand and Kalli bouncing excitedly on her knees. I leafed through them, my eyes catching words here and there. Then suddenly, it dawned on me.

"Did you give me a trip to Bora Bora?"

"Yes!" she squealed, clapping and bouncing on her pillow. "Are you excited? Please tell me you're excited. The dates aren't set because I wasn't sure about your hiatus, but I was thinking about March because it's really nice there in March, but we can go whenever, if you even want to go. I've always wanted to go and it looks so romantic and tropical and I just thought we would have a really great time—"

"This is incredible, Kal," I interrupted her nervous rant. She would have gone on forever if I had let her. "This looks amazing," I said, flipping through the resort brochures and airline information. "It's too much, babe."

Her hands came to my knees as she lifted up from her pillow, her face now almost even with mine.

"It's not too much, it'll never be *too much*. You've given me something I'll never be able to repay you for, so you'll let me take you to Bora Bora." Then she leaned in, wrapping her arms around my neck, taking me in for a hug, but her mouth came to my ear. She whispered quietly so no one else could hear her, "I'll let you pick out all my swimwear."

It's uncomfortable having an erection around the Christmas tree surrounded by your family.

Luckily, Rachel saved the day and said something about shopping for bathing suits and all returned to normal.

Kalli and Kevin exchanged presents and even though they weren't gifts filled with meaning and history, it was a beginning for them, and they both understood that. Kalli seemed to really love the scarf her father gave her, and Kevin was thrilled to have tickets to a Chargers game.

The day had turned out to be nearly perfect. Nearly. But I wasn't done with my gift giving.

Chapter Twenty

Nowhere Else

Kalli

I'd had reasonable Christmas expectations. I'd expected to be happy, to be sad, to miss Marcus on my first Christmas without him, to feel loved spending the day with Riot. But I could have never imagined how wonderful the day actually turned out. Having Kevin, Rachel, and Sharon there was special. I wanted a relationship with them and spending a holiday together seemed like a great way to lay that foundation down. Not to mention how touched I'd been that they'd probably abandoned their own traditions to spend the day with a bunch of strangers. That had meant a lot to me.

It was a little more touching to think of Riot setting the whole thing up for me. He had such a huge heart and I'd never be able to repay him for opening it to me and allowing me in, but I could spend forever trying.

There was nothing I could say about the photo album Mara had made me. It was beyond words. It had been a long time since I'd spent Christmas with my mother, but being with Riot's was special, and she made me feel so incredibly loved.

After we'd cleaned up the mess from presents and finished nibbling on all the delicious food Mara had prepared, Riot and I retreated to his bedroom to finish getting ready for the day. There were some more of Riot's family members coming over for dinner, and he'd wanted a break.

He was lying on his bed, freshly showered, hair still damp, and I was draped over his chest, listening to him breathe as he played with the hair still atop my head in a messy knot.

"How are you feeling?" he asked quietly, fingers stalling.

"I feel good," I answered honestly with a small smile.

"Are you missing him a lot?"

I thought about his question and thankfully I didn't feel the rush of panic that used to come over me when I thought about Marcus. "You know, I miss him, but it's not as bad as I thought it would be." I was silent for a moment, but then continued. "I think your mom's gift helped a lot. It's harder to live life always fixated on the fact that he's gone, but your mom went out of her way to make sure he was here, with me, in a way. I'll never be able to thank her for that."

He pressed a kiss against my forehead.

"I love the necklace you gave me," I said, my fingers finding the pendant. "It's beautiful."

His forefinger came to my chin, pulling my eyes up to look at his. "I meant what I said, Kal. You've got me. Forever. I don't want anyone else but you. I know we've only been back together for a short time, but—"

"Shhh." I silenced him by putting my fingers over his mouth. "You don't have to convince me to be with you. I'm here, and there's nowhere else I want to be. Ever. I want to spend the rest of my life right here," I said, tapping his chest right over his heart, "with you."

"Merry Christmas," he said, just before his lips covered mine and his hand slid to the back of my neck, gripping it the way I loved, holding my lips to his as he slanted his mouth to fit over mine perfectly. His tongue pressed against the seam of my lips and I opened for him eagerly, wanting to taste him, to feel his love for me in that kiss.

He groaned into my mouth and I felt the vibrations shoot directly between my legs, heat pooling there. His free hand roamed down my back, then gripped my waist, pulling me fully on top of him, then wandered down to cup my ass. I wanted his hands everywhere, wanted to rid us both of the fabric between us, wanted to feel him inside me and take me to that place where only the two of us mattered.

His hand slid between my skin and the stretchy fabric of the yoga pants I was wearing, gripping my ass and growling again. For one moment I had a thought about everyone in the house being aware of us, it being Christmas, *my father* being just down the hall, and I almost stopped him. Almost.

Instead, I lifted my hips just high enough to grab at his belt, unbuckling it frantically, popping the buttons on his jeans one by one, and urgently trying to push the denim down his legs. I'd only gotten as far as his hips when I was startled by the sound of his phone ringing.

"Shit," he growled, leaning over to the bedside table and turning the screen of his phone on. "Damn it," he said, with even more anger. I watched as he answered the call although I couldn't see who was calling, but his hand was still on my ass so I figured it couldn't have been too important. "Hello?" His voice was angry and his greeting was short.

I leaned up a little farther, pressing a kiss to the underside of his jaw, a place he rubbed frequently when he was stressed or thinking about something too much. I followed the line of his neck with my lips, passing over his Adam's apple, splaying small kisses all the way down to the base of his neck, loving the way the vibration of his voice tickled my lips.

"Erin, it's Christmas," he said, his voice no more friendly. "They can't seriously be asking me this."

My lips stopped at his words and I lifted my head to look at him as his hand slid off my ass, leaving it cold. His brows were furrowed, his forehead was creased, and he looked pissed.

"I can't believe this," he groaned, rubbing his hand down his face. "This is bullshit, you know this, right?"

I could hear a woman's voice on the other end of the phone, although she didn't seem to be as upset as he was.

"The studio can't just call people in to work on Christmas. It's a shitty thing to do." He listened to the woman, Erin, for a moment, then sighed and closed his eyes. "Yeah, I got it. See you then." He ended the call and then tossed the phone back on his nightstand.

"What's going on?"

"The studio has decided to do a last-minute change in the episode we finished shooting before break, but in order to get it done in time, they have to shoot it tonight."

"But it's Christmas."

"Apparently, they don't care."

"So, you have to go to LA, like, right now?"

His eyes turned to mine and he looked so sad. "Yeah," he whispered, his hand coming up to frame my face. "I'm sorry. I do."

I was sad the day had to end that way, but I felt worse for Riot. Working on Christmas was terrible. "It's okay, baby.

I'll pack up my stuff real quick. I'm sorry you have to ride home with my unshowered self," I said, reaching up to touch my messy hair.

"No, Kalli, you stay. Don't let my job ruin your Christmas."

"You want me to stay?"

"You know I want to be with you, but if you come with me you'll only spend Christmas night alone in your apartment, and I don't want that for you. Stay here where Kevin and Rachel are, where Halah and Ma are. I'll feel better if I know you aren't sitting alone in your apartment."

His words were sweet, but the thought of him driving all alone to LA on Christmas made me sad for him.

"I want to be with you, I don't care if I'm alone tonight or not."

He leaned up and kissed me. It wasn't as full of heat as our last kiss had been, but it was much more tender and sweet.

"You might not care," he said when he pulled away, "but I do. Stay. Please."

I bit my lip as I considered his words. He was pleading with me to stay, and even though it felt wrong on some level, I didn't want to make his day more difficult. "Okay," I relented. He leaned up and kissed me again; this time it was a short, chaste kiss. I rolled off him and watched from the comfort of his childhood bed as he packed his things.

"How will I get home?"

"I'll have my Dad take me to the airport and I'll rent a car. You keep the Rover here and drive home like we originally planned."

"Maybe Kevin can give me a ride? He has to drive through LA to get home anyhow."

Riot called out to me from the bathroom.

"I don't want to put anyone else out because of me, Kal. Just take the Rover, it will make me feel better."

"Okay," I conceded.

He came back into the bedroom, tossing his bag on the floor by his bed, then climbing on the bed, coming over me, his hands resting on either side of my head.

"I'm sorry," he whispered. "I'll make it up to you. I promise."

And that was one of the many reasons I loved Riot Bentley. Even though it was his Christmas that was being disrupted, he was worried about me and how I was feeling. He was the most selfless man I'd ever met and I wanted to never take that for granted. I reached up and placed my hands on either side of his face.

"There's nothing to make up for. I love you and I will see you when I get home."

Something glimmered in his eye, and I could almost swear I saw the corner of his mouth turn up, as if he were trying to force away a smile. Before I could think too much about it, he kissed me. This kiss, however, was meant to be a good-bye, and he took his time.

Thirty minutes later I stood at his parents' front door, watching Riot climb into his father's SUV as they left to get him a rental car. He waved, a forced smile across his face, and I waved back. When the car was out of sight, I let out a sigh. I turned to Rachel, who'd been standing with me, and gave her a sad smile.

"He'll be okay," she said. "Let's go inside. Would you mind if I looked at the album Mara made for you?"

It hadn't occurred to me that anyone else would want to look at pictures of Marcus, but it meant a lot to me that Rachel had asked.

"Sure," I answered, the smile on my face turning from sad to bright. So Rachel and I sat at the kitchen table, flipping pages and looking at photos. She was genuinely curious about him, and listened to me as I endlessly told stories that the pictures conjured up. Before I knew it, I had spent two hours telling Rachel, my sister, all about my brother, and I'd laughed and smiled the whole time.

Kevin had joined us about an hour in, sitting across the table, listening, and laughing along with us. Halah and Mara were in the kitchen, preparing food for the feast Mara had promised, and even though I was missing Riot, it was still one of the best Christmases I could remember.

About two and a half hours after Riot had left, the doorbell chimed.

"Kalli, sweetie, could you get the door for me? I'm a mess."

Mara lifted her hands and she was, indeed, elbow deep in food.

"Of course," I replied. When I opened the door I was met with a giant bouquet of beautiful red roses.

"Are you Kalli Rivers?" the deliveryman asked from behind the enormous arrangement of flowers.

"Um, yes."

"These are for you," he said with a groan, handing the large vase to me. I understood his grunting when I took it; it weighed a ton.

"Are you sure? I'm confused."

"Yes, there's a card in there somewhere."

"Riot called and ordered flowers? Why are you even open on Christmas? I'm really sorry, I don't have any cash for a tip. Let me see what I can do..." I turned away from the door to see if anyone in the house had cash I could borrow.

"Don't worry, Ms. Rivers, the tip has been taken care of. And we usually aren't open today, but Mr. Bentley called two weeks ago to arrange this. Paid a mint for it too. The tip covered Christmas gifts for all four of my kids. I'm happy to deliver these flowers," he said, tipping his trucker hat at me as he turned to walk down the driveway.

"Merry Christmas," I called after him, still really confused. I walked into the kitchen, trying not to trip and fall since I couldn't see where I was going.

"Oh, my word," Mara said breathily.

"Holy crap," Halah cried.

"Whose are they?" Rachel asked.

I let out a breath as I set the vase down on the table, my arms aching from the strain. "Apparently they're from Riot."

"He must feel really bad about having to go to work," Rachel sighed.

"The delivery guy said Riot ordered them two weeks ago." I searched through the flowers, not able to ignore the wonderful scent of the roses as I found the card. I opened it quickly, eager to find out what he'd done, and read the handwritten note.

Kalli,

By now I've left and trust me when I say, leaving you on Christmas was probably harder for me than it was for you. But I did it with good reason. I love you. More than any necklace or long-stemmed roses can say. Throughout this year we've hit a lot of bumps in our road, but we've also stopped to admire a lot of views. No matter what happens, Kalli, remember the beautiful views we've seen together.

Now, there's one more view to add to the list. Please pack your bags and meet me at this address. Come alone, but come knowing I'll be waiting for you.

Love,

Riot

There was an address at the bottom of the card, but the address was all the way back in LA. I looked up to find every person in the house staring back at me.

"Did you guys know about this?" I asked his family, my eyes darting between all three of them.

"No, sweetheart. He didn't mention anything to us," Mara said, looking to Halah and Chad. Both of them shook their heads. "What does the card say?"

"He wants me to meet him somewhere. Back in LA." All of their faces were blank, just as confused as I was.

"Well," Kevin said, "I guess you better get going."

"Yeah, okay," I said, then turned to go pack my stuff, shaking my head the entire way to Riot's bedroom. I reread the card four times before I finally gave in and packed up all my stuff. When I went back into the kitchen it was with my bag packed and a worried look on my face. "I'm sorry to just up and leave. I'm so confused."

Mara came and gave me a big, motherly hug. "Don't worry. Riot has a plan. I'm sure it's good news."

"I feel bad leaving." I looked at Kevin. "I hate leaving you here. You came all this way…" My words drifted off as I thought about everything he'd done to be with me on Christmas. Then he was next to me, his arm around my shoulder in a side-hug.

"It's okay, baby doll. I got to see you open presents on Christmas morning. That's all I really wanted. Plus, we've got years of Christmases ahead of us. Go. Be with him."

At his words I turned fully into his arms and wrapped mine around his waist. My dad and I had a long road of building a stable relationship ahead of us, but his words were genuine and true. I never thought I'd ever spend Christmas morning with my father, so he'd given me a real gift the day he reached out to me.

"Okay," I said, pulling away. Everyone walked me out to my car and Jordy helped Chad figure out how to secure my giant vase of flowers so it wouldn't topple over as I drove. I said good-bye to everyone and that alone took ten minutes. I pulled out, made it to the freeway, and let out a big sigh. I had butterflies fluttering in my stomach, my hands were shaky, and my mind was spinning in a million different directions. Riot was up to something, that was clear.

I let out another sigh, took in a deep breath, and tried to calm myself down. I had a long drive ahead of me. I turned on some music to try and distract myself and that kind of worked, but being alone in my car only gave me time to think about Riot and everything he'd done for me since I'd met him. I focused on those thoughts as I drove to LA.

Chapter Twenty-One

It's Our View

Kalli

Halfway into my solo road trip, I put the address on the card into my GPS to make sure I didn't get lost. LA was still pretty new to me and I definitely didn't know my way around well enough to get there without assistance.

I was surprised when the GPS took me off the highway and brought me onto some roads leading up the back hills of Hollywood. The higher I climbed, and the farther from the city I got, the more beautiful my surroundings became.

The GPS alerted me that my destination was 1,000 feet ahead on the right and my nerves shot through the roof. I slowly drove along the road and finally came to a house nestled on the edge of the tall hill. The sky was getting dimmer as the sun dropped lower in the sky, and I started to appreciate the view.

"What in the world..." I said to no one, but pulled into the empty driveway. The house was huge. Not as huge as all the other houses on that street, but it was still bigger than any house I'd been in. It was white with tall windows and two large columns in the front. I put my Rover in park, shut it off, then tentatively opened my door, expecting Riot to appear. He didn't.

I walked up to the door and I noticed a piece of paper taped to it.

The door is unlocked. Come inside. Follow the trail and meet me at the end.

My nerves were ready to stop my heart. My fingers tingled as I turned the doorknob and pushed the door open slowly.

The beautiful house was empty and made me gasp. It was magnificent and gorgeous. But besides how beautiful the house was, what had been done to it was even more breathtaking. There were red roses *everywhere*. Vases and vases of red roses were strategically placed throughout the foyer and great room past it. Along the floor was a path made from rose petals, lit on either side with candles.

My hand came to cover my mouth and the tears welled, blurring the astonishing vision. Then I heard it. The soft sounds of a piano coming from everywhere. I heard the first word of the song and a sob escaped me. This couldn't be happening. No one could pull this off. No one except Riot.

The song that was being softly piped through the whole house was familiar and I recognized it as the one and only song we'd ever danced to. The song from Tilly's bar, the first night I'd let myself open up to him.

Holding back more sobs I followed the path and found myself at French doors leading to a balcony. I saw Riot through the glass, but his back was to me. He was looking at the view.

When I opened the door he must have heard me because he turned around with a brilliant smile on his face. His smile didn't falter when he saw my tears; I'm sure he expected them. He did, however, hold his arms open to me and I wasted no time going to him.

"You'll be okay, baby."

And he was right. I would be okay. I hadn't been for a while, but I'd pulled myself together over the last few months and tried to get to a normal place. I did most of the hard work, but I was helped by Riot so much. My success was his victory too. His support was invaluable to me. I should be planning surprises for him, leading him on romantic treasure hunts, not the other way around.

"I love you," I said into his chest, trying to keep the tears under control.

"I know," he said as I pulled back to look at his face, his brilliant smile just sparkling all the more. "I love you too."

I looked past him to see the most gorgeous sunset. "Wow," I said on a breath. He turned his head to see what I was looking at, then turned himself and brought his arm around my shoulders, pulling me to his side. I gladly went, wrapping my arms around his waist, resting my head against his chest.

We stood there for a while and watch the sun lower slowly, beautiful oranges and reds painting the sky.

When the sun was barely above the horizon, I looked back up at him. "I can't believe you planned all this so we could watch a sunset together."

He laughed. "You don't like it?"

"No, I love it, I'm just surprised, I guess. All this for a view and a sunset."

"It's not just any view. It's our view." I heard his words and they didn't strike me as unusual for a few moments, but as my mind processed them, I suddenly understood.

"Riot, what did you do?" My voice was wavering again, hands shaking.

"I bought you your very own viewpoint," he said, his lips pressed against my temple.

I knew Riot Bentley was the perfect person for me, knew it to the depths of my being, but I learned right then, standing on the balcony of a house I'd never been to before, watching a sun descend into the ocean, that he might have been the most thoughtful and astounding person alive.

"You bought a house?" I asked, my lips quivering with emotion.

"I bought this house. For you. For us."

"You bought this house?"

He laughed, then turned slightly, bringing his hand up to cup my cheek, which I promptly leaned into. "Yeah, I bought this house. Do you like it? If not, I can sell it again and we can pick one out together, but I couldn't pass up this view," he said, looking directly into my eyes, making them water and sting with happiness.

"I love this house." Tears streamed down both cheeks. He wiped them away and then kissed me.

"You haven't seen it all."

"I don't care. You bought me a viewpoint."

"Yeah." His thumb brushed down my cheek, his eyes blazing into mine. "I have to admit though, my intentions aren't 100 percent selfless. I figured," he said, looking at the land surrounding the house, which was clear as far as the eye could see, "if I was ever going to get to go all the way with you at a viewpoint, it would probably have to be privately owned."

My heart melted at his sweeping romantic gesture, and also pounded at his naughty words. He had always tried to get lucky at viewpoints.

"You think because you bought me a viewpoint you automatically get lucky?" I said, my voice teasing and hopefully sexy.

"Yeah," he replied, moving his hand to the back of my neck. "Was I wrong?"

"Not even a little bit."

His eyes blazed at my words and his mouth parted slightly. I could feel the thumping of his heart underneath my hand at his chest. Then his mouth was on mine. He took everything I had to give, and I gave it to him happily.

Epilogue

Riot

I heard water lapping against the stilts our private cabana was raised up on. The rhythmic sound of the water crashing against the wood had put me to sleep not long ago, but now it was a soothing way to spend a few minutes with my arms still wrapped around Kalli as she slept.

We'd finally made it to Bora Bora, and it had only taken more than a year to get there. Kalli had purchased the tickets with a spring vacation in mind, but we bought the house and got caught up in life and never made it to the tropical paradise. Not to mention that just a few days after our first Christmas together we found out both our television shows were picked up for another season. And then again a few months ago. It was unlikely and rare, but we'd both managed to be hired on to two of the most successful shows in network television in the past two years.

The timing of our careers taking off couldn't have been better; it allowed us to be together without our jobs forcing us apart. I woke up with Kalli every morning, starting our days looking out of the oversized picture window in our master bedroom that gave us a breathtaking view.

Not unlike my view right now.

Blue water, islands, and even bluer skies were all I could see through the cabana doors. That and the newly tanned skin of Kalli's entirely naked body lying next to me in a California king-sized bed. Unless we left the cabana to head to the mainland for a meal or activity, I'd made it clear no clothes were allowed. If we were in the cabana or on the private deck, I preferred her naked. She didn't seem to mind, especially since the rule applied to me as well.

This made for a beautiful toasty-brown color of a tan, with no tan lines from a bathing suit. She was sun kissed everywhere.

I raised my head to look at her face, which was peaceful and soft. Her blonde hair, which she'd let grow even longer, was everywhere—just the way I liked it. I placed my hand on her shoulder, my skin lightly grazing hers, and ran it softly all the way down her rib cage, past her waist, and over the swell of her hips. She stirred slightly, not fully waking, but jostling a bit. My hand continued to roam over her hip, across her thigh, until my fingers were barely sweeping over her sex.

I applied pressure there, wanting her to wake with my hand between her legs, with my fingers sinking into her. Her body cooperated, rolling toward me as her eyes fluttered open. I watched as she blinked, trying to gain her bearings as her legs fell open, granting me the access I was looking for. I spread her lips with my fingers and slowly pushed one in. Her eyes went from hazy and confused to immediately sharp with arousal.

"Good morning, beautiful," I whispered as my finger slowly moved in and out of her. Before she could answer I slipped in a second and watched as her mouth parted with a sigh.

"It's not morning anymore," she responded, her words spaced between sharp and rapid breaths. "It was morning a few hours ago when you woke me up and took me outside to make love while the sun came up."

I had done that. It was my best idea of the day, watching Kalli come as the orangey-pink light of the sunrise washed over her. But my fingers now easily moving inside Kalli's warm and wet sex would run a close second.

She gasped as I moved my fingers to her clit, drawing circles around it, then lightly smoothing over it in a way I knew would drive her mad.

I moved over her fully, pressing a kiss to her lips, then slowly moving downward as my hand still worked her over. I stopped and dipped my tongue in her navel, leaving kisses all around it, then continued lower, moving my whole body to rest between her legs.

By the time I made myself comfortable she was writhing, her body begging me for contact while her mouth was too busy gasping to ask for what she needed.

"Don't worry, baby. I'll take care of you." I lowered my mouth to her and my body, which was already desperately turned on, reacted just to her taste and scent. I loved everything about Kalli, but I was addicted to her pussy. I dove in deep, fucking her with my tongue, loving the way her hips jolted up. I wrapped my arms around her thighs, holding her legs open to give me unobstructed access to her wetness. My tongue moved up to circle her clit and that's when she started climbing into the stratosphere.

"Oh, God, Riot," she crooned loudly, aware that there was no one around to hear us. I'd fully enjoyed her body since we'd been there and the way she was bare to me, holding nothing back. There was nothing that turned me on more than listening to her, hearing her, when I was inside her. Knowing I was making her feel that good, so good that she couldn't contain herself, could bring me from simply aroused to painfully hard in seconds.

"That's my girl," I said, before wrapping my lips around her clit and sucking. Her hips tried to buck up off the bed, but my hands held her down, kept her right against my mouth. I loved watching her get off, loved watching the way her nipples hardened, the way her breasts heaved up and down, faster and faster, with her breaths. I loved watching her try to figure out what to do with her hands; they always started at her head, gripping her hair, but then as the orgasm built they moved lower to her breasts, palming them and pinching her nipples as if that would bring her some relief.

This time, however, as I gazed up at her, she looked down at me. That was rare. Not the eye contact, no, I looked her in the eyes all the time when my cock was inside her and I was face to face with her. Rarely did she ever watch me as I went down on her. It was as if she were afraid watching me work her over with my mouth would make it too intense.

We watched each other, but I kept my mouth on her, loving the way her hips started to move up and down, the way she was trying to fuck my face. I let go of her clit and swiped my tongue over her, listening to her cry out, then pressed my tongue against her, letting her use me to find her release.

"Oh, Riot," she said, her voice shaky and weak. "I'm gonna come…" Her thighs clamped around my head with her words and I watched as the sensations rolled over her body. Her eyes closed, her head lolled back, her hands gripped her breasts, and I felt her pussy clench. It was gorgeous. One of the most beautiful things I'd ever seen; my girl coming apart for me.

After her legs relaxed I wasted no time sliding up her body and plunging into her with one long stroke.

"It's too much," she whispered, her eyes still closed, body still trembling from her orgasm.

"It's just right," I said, pressed into her as far as I could go, as far as her clenching walls would let me.

"No," she said, opening her eyes and looking at me, her hands coming to frame my face. "It's too much, the way I feel about you, the way you make *me* feel, it's too intense." I answered her by pulling out but diving right back in, watching as her eyes rolled back in pleasure at my movement, but then opened again an instant later. She pulled my face down to hers and our lips met in a frantic and deep kiss. Her arms wrapped around my neck, her legs circling my waist, and I used a hand to lift her hips just a little, giving me the deepest angle I could get as I slid in and out of her.

I lost myself in her then, my tongue taking wide sweeps through her mouth, one hand gripping her beautiful golden hair, the other hand loving the way the flesh of her ass gave way to my strong fingers. I was being a little rough with her, as I knew she liked it, and I would never deny that the idea of my fingerprints on her ass later in the day would do nothing but make me hard again.

"I'm gonna need you to come again, Kal. I want you to come while I'm inside you." She didn't respond other than to moan. So I added, "I want to feel you coming, baby. Rub your clit." I backed away from her, pressing her knees wide, giving me a fucking amazing and unobstructed view as she reached down with tentative fingers and started gently stroking her clit. "Fuck, yes," I growled as I watched.

As she started rubbing faster, I started thrusting harder, and soon we were both climbing to the top of the same peak. She came with one hand working her clit as the other gripped my shoulder, her pussy clenching and convulsing around me. That sent me flying, soaring, and I was spilling into her, swearing as I came, sweat dripping off my forehead and landing right between her breasts.

"Jesus," I groaned as her body coaxed every drop from me. When we both started floating back to reality, she reached up and brought my mouth down to hers again, but that kiss was much slower and smoother.

I rolled so we were both on our sides, capturing her face in my hands, loving the way her arms wrapped up my back, holding us together.

Once we'd both calmed, our bodies lax and sated, she pulled away and gave me her sleepy smile.

"What's the point of paying to go somewhere fantastic for vacation if all you're going to do is have sex all day and nap in between?" she asked with a smile. "We could have done this at home."

"Ah," I said, pushing her hair behind her ear, "you're no fun. I like making love to you while I can hear the ocean. And I love what the tropical sun has done to your skin." I punctuated my point be pressing my lips to her shoulder. "Plus, at home, there's no room service."

"Well, you have a point there."

"Are you hungry?" My hand slipped down her back, bringing her body even closer to mine.

"Getting there, but I think we should leave the room. The people who work here are going to start wondering if we're alive or not. We need to make a public appearance so they don't come knocking on our door."

I laughed. "All right, you want to get dinner at the resort restaurant?"

"Sounds good," she said. "I'm just gonna take a quick nap." She said the words with a smile, but then she really did fall asleep. I watched her rest for a while, but eventually, I fell asleep too.

"Babe, let's go," I called through our cabana. Kalli had called and made reservations at the restaurant, but then she'd disappeared into the bathroom and I was starting to question whether or not I needed to go in there and drag her out.

"I'm ready," she said as the door opened. She stepped out and it was as if I'd slammed into a brick wall, or been punched right in the gut. She was so fucking beautiful. She moved around the room, gathering whatever she needed, but I was transfixed by her, simply mesmerized.

Her hair was loose, but she'd curled it so the straw-colored strands were winding around each other. A few locks at each temple were pulled back and pinned on the side with something that sparkled. Her gorgeous skin was only complemented by the white of her dress, her breasts only held in by the straps that tied behind her neck. I could tell she wasn't wearing a bra, as I could see the deep valley between her breasts, and my mouth watered to kiss her there. The white dress cinched right below her breasts and then flowed all the way to the floor in a goddesslike spill of delicate, soft fabric. My hands itched to run along her dress, to see if it felt as soft as it looked.

"You look beautiful," I managed to force out, my words almost inaudible they were so quiet. She gave me the most brilliant smile I'd ever seen and even through the new bronzing of her skin, I could see a blush creep over her cheeks. I cleared my throat and tried again. "Really, Kalli, you look incredible." I walked toward her and held out my hand, pulling her to me when she gave me hers.

"Thank you. I was hoping you'd like this dress," she said shyly, her eyes dropping to the fabric draping so beautifully over her body.

I brought her chin back up with a gentle finger. "It's not the dress," I whispered. "It's you." I leaned in and pressed a chaste kiss against her lips, but then pulled away because I knew if I kept kissing her we'd end up back on the bed. She was a masterpiece and I didn't want to mar her.

I interlaced our fingers, leading her toward the door. We walked slowly down the wooden path that took us from our private cabana to the shore. It was late and the sun was nearly completely set, so the pathways were all lined with tiki torches, casting an orange glow over us.

When we made it to the restaurant we were seated immediately and enjoyed one of the best meals I'd ever had. The food was spectacular, as I expected at the five-star resort we were staying at. But Kalli was everything during that meal. She was funny and sweet, flirting with me over cool, crisp white wine. She was supportive and attentive, listening to me as I worried about work and life, holding my hand from across the table.

At one point I asked her to dance, so we spent a few songs swaying back and forth to a tropical rhythm. I couldn't help but kiss her bare shoulder as I trailed my fingers lightly down the naked skin of her back, watching as her skin pebbled with goose bumps.

"I want to take you back to the room," I whispered into her ear right before I kissed the skin below it.

She pulled away and gave me a nervous smile.

"Okay, but, give me a ten-minute head start, okay?"

I tilted my head, confused by her request. "You want me to wait ten minutes to go back to the room?" Suddenly it dawned on me that she was planning something. "What have you done?" I had so many wonderful images of Kalli's body adorned with sexy lingerie.

"You'll have to wait and see," she said, trying to sound coquettish, but only coming off as ridiculously cute and a little silly.

"Is it sexy?" I asked, raising my eyebrows.

"I'm hoping that when you find out, it will lead to a lot of sex, yes."

"Fuck," I groaned.

"Ten minutes," she repeated, then kissed me quickly right before she turned and walked away. I watched her leave, her dress even stunning from the back, and decided to take a walk on the beach to waste the required ten minutes. I grew impatient during those minutes, wondering what I would find when I went back to the cabana, what kind of surprise she was planning for me.

Finally, when I reached our private walkway, my heart rate sped up, and I could feel the pulse in my neck. I wanted to get to her, to hold her again. I'd been with her for nearly a week uninterrupted, and ten minutes seemed to be too long to be apart any longer.

When I made it to the door, I found a piece of paper taped to the front with Kalli's unmistakable handwriting on it.

The door is unlocked. Come inside. Follow the trail and meet me at the end.

I opened the door slowly to find red roses everywhere. There were so many roses, I couldn't contain the laugh that bubbled up in my throat. It was beautiful, but I couldn't imagine how she'd pulled it off.

A path on the floor was lit with candles with red rose petals scattered all around. I suddenly remembered how I'd done this exact same thing when I brought her to the house for the first time. The pulsing in my neck turned to thundering as my heart accelerated. She was up to something, and it wasn't just lingerie.

I followed the candlelit path, which led me to the balcony. Standing amidst roses and candles, Kalli stood at the railing with a smile I hoped to see every day for the rest of my life. She was beaming at me, simply radiating happiness, and it was all I could do to keep myself from running the rest of the way to her.

"What are you doing?" I whispered when I was finally close enough to her, right before I kissed her quickly.

"Do you like the view?" she asked, her voice wavering the tiniest bit.

"I love the view," I said, placing my hands on either side of her face and kissing her deeper. I pulled away after a few moments and smiled. "You didn't buy this cabana did you? It had to cost a fortune."

She laughed, but then wiped away a tear that had escaped. "No, I didn't buy the cabana, but I was hoping we could come back here every once in a while to celebrate our anniversary."

"Of course, baby." I said, bringing her to me. "But, which day should we count as our anniversary? The day we met on the video shoot, or the day you showed up in my dressing room?"

"How about the day we get married?" I couldn't see her face, but her voice sounded odd, weak and shaky. My first instinct was to laugh softly, so I did. We'd spoken about getting married before, it was obvious, to me at least, that was where our relationship was heading, but we'd been so busy and both our careers had taken off at the same time. Life was running away with us. "Yeah, baby. We'll work on that, I promise."

"Riot," she whispered, her voice so delicate. "I want you to marry me."

"Babe, we'll get married. I promise." I pulled away to tell her how much I loved her, how I didn't want her to worry about our future together because she was all I could see for me in ten, twenty, even fifty years from now. I wanted to tell her how I wanted her to have my babies, soon, how I wanted to start a family with her. I wanted *everything* with her. But when I pulled away to reassure her of all that, I was stopped by the look on her face and the ring she was holding up between us.

"I'm asking you, Riot. I'm asking you to marry me."

My eyes darted between her face and the ring, wondering what I'd missed, how we'd gotten here. In her hand was a men's wedding band. It was black and thick, exactly something I would pick out for myself. Was this really happening?

"You're asking me to marry you? You're proposing?" I took the tiniest step away from her, trying to take it all in. I couldn't help the smile that crossed my face, even if she looked terrified. I didn't understand her nerves; surely she knew I would say yes.

"I want us to get married. I want you to marry me. And the longer I thought about it, the more I thought I should just ask you."

"You want to get married?" I asked, smiling, moving closer to her.

"Yes," she said, her voice suddenly breathy, watching me as I moved into her space so our bodies were touching, her hand with my ring in it still up between us.

"You want this forever?" I tucked a loose tendril of hair behind her ear, then moved my hand to the back of her neck, squeezing it firmly, watching her eyelids flutter as I did.

She nodded slightly, eyes finding mine. "I want you forever."

"Then, you got me." I took the ring from her and slid it onto my finger, laughing slightly at the thought of Kalli proposing to me. She had caught me completely off guard. "Tomorrow, we find a jeweler and we put a ring on your finger," I said, wrapping my arms around her, pulling her as close to me as I could.

"I'd like that," she breathed.

"I'd like to take you back into that candlelit bedroom and make love to my fiancée," I said quietly.

"I'd like that too."

I kissed her, then swept my arm under her knees and carried her back to the bed, looking forward to the rest of my life spent admiring the view of Kalli Bentley.

The End

Acknowledgements

Kalli and Riot's story was a bit of an emotional roller coaster for me. Never Standing Still came with its own hurdles, but I never anticipated the kind of cathartic release I would get when it came time for Kalli to speak with her father. I, truly, never saw that coming; could not have been prepared for the copious amounts of tears shed or the way Kalli's story went a little ways to heal a part of me that will probably always be a little bit broken. So I guess I'd like to thank anyone who read the book and could relate to Kalli in that way. And I'd like to offer you big hugs too.

To Andrea and Kelly, again, you continually blow me away with your generosity in time and effort. It's such a relief to me to know you'll do everything you can, every time, to help me make my books the best they can be.

To Olivia, you've edited a few of my books now and I can't tell you how much I appreciate your thoughtful and immensely helpful wisdom. You did a great job on this book, and it's 100% better for all your work. Thank you. A huge thanks to everyone else at Hot Tree Editing who had a hand (or eyes) on this book. I am forever grateful.

Enticing Journey Book Promotions – you gals rock. Thank you for always supporting me and being so professional.

I have to thank Lindy again, and all the ladies in the Sprinters group, for helping me write this book, every day. I love having such a supportive group of writers around me, who understand that writing X amount of words a day is not easy all the time (...or most of the time...).

Thanks to my family for letting me hide in my room as soon as dinner is over, and for understanding that my work is real work too.

And finally, Giselle, thank you for your time and knowledge you so graciously shared with me. Your years spent in LA and on the Paramount lot came in real handy! Love you!

Other books by Anie Michaels

The Never Series

Never Close Enough

Never Far Away

Never Giving Up

The Never Duet

Never Standing Still

Never Tied Down

The Private Serials

Private Affairs

Private Encounters

Private Getaway

Private Property

Stand Alone Novels

The Space Between Us

The Absence of Olivia

The Presence of Grace – *coming in 2016*

www.ingramcontent.com/pod-product-compliance
Lightning Source LLC
Chambersburg PA
CBHW020242180626
46810CB00006B/2318